BLOOD LINE

A TOM ROLLINS THRILLER

PAUL HEATLEY

INKUBATOR
BOOKS

For Aidan

PROLOGUE

The warlord's name is Aaban Ahmadi. For six months, he's been organizing hit-and-runs on US bases and convoys. He and his men have killed more than twenty American soldiers, caused millions of dollars' worth of damage, and severely derailed advances into Helmand Province.

Two days ago, the CIA received intel as to his whereabouts.

Tom Rollins is one in a team of five. A CIA black ops unit. Best of the best. The chopper drops them off under cover of darkness. They continue the rest of the way on foot. Five clicks across the cool night desert. They take it at a light run, strapped with weaponry and supplies, M4A1s in their hands.

Captain Robert Dale leads the way. To his left, Simon Collins, and on the right is Nathan Sapolsky. Nowhere else they'd rather be, right there beside their vaunted leader.

Tom is bringing up the rear, Ezekiel Greene by his side.

The only man he trusts in this team, the only one he considers a friend.

The house comes into view. Villa-style, seemingly smack-bang right in the middle of the desert. The sand beneath their feet turns to jagged rock.

There are men on guard. The team can't see them at this distance, but they know they're there. The five men huddle together. Captain Dale gives his silent instructions, using hand signals to communicate. They've been briefed; they know what to do.

Tom and Zeke peel off right, Simon and Nathan left, the captain straight down the middle. They duck low, hurry across the terrain, eyes up, watching ahead. Tom goes first, a three-second burst of travel while Zeke stays behind him, covering. Tom stops, takes a knee, raises his rifle. Zeke overtakes him. They're heading for Ahmadi himself. This time of night, it's assumed he'll be in bed. Intel provided the layout of the house, too. His bedroom is at the very back. They've memorized the route and every facet of the estate. Tom and Zeke are going in through the front. Simon and Nate will take the rear. Captain Dale will hold back, observe the outside. He'll join them when it is clear no alarm has been raised.

Within a stone's throw from the building, they duck lower. They monkey run. Keep their heads up, scanning the wall, freezing when they see a patrolling guard. There's one up top, on the roof, and another on the ground. Tom takes out the one on the ground. Waits for him to pass his position, gets him from behind, clasps the guard's face in the joint of his elbow, wrenches back and down to snap his neck. They scale the wall while the guard up top is heading the other way, his back turned. This one is Zeke's. He takes him out with his KA-BAR.

They're inside. They take a moment, just a flash, to get their bearings. Strap their M4A1s to their backs, raise their Colt 1911s and surge on, Tom leading the way. They want things to be quiet. They don't want to have to fight their way out. As well as the guards, there are women and children in the compound. Their target is Ahmadi, Ahmadi alone.

Inside, the way is clear. The lights are off. Tom and Zeke put on their night-vision goggles, keep moving. They stick to the walls and creep along the corridors. Pause at every little sound, listen. Hear no footsteps, only the stirring from within rooms.

Ahmadi's room is in the center of the house. It's the only one guarded. They expected this much. They make a noise, a tap-tapping, get his guard's attention, draw him out, bring him to investigate. Tom and Zeke hide around a corner, wait for the guard to come find them. Eventually, he does. Zeke grabs him, silences him. Tom leaves them to it, heads down the hallway, to the bedroom door. Ear to the wood, he listens for movement. Hears nothing. Opens the door, just a crack, peers in. He's looking into a deeper darkness. Spots the bed at the other end of the room. The vague outline of a sleeping shape picked out with the night vision. Hears the gentle snores.

Tom pulls his knife, creeps forward, scanning the room as his eyes adjust. Ahmadi is alone. Tom gets to the corner of the bed, shines a torch briefly into his face to make a visual ID. It's their man, his face memorized from the one photograph they had that wasn't blurry.

The encroaching movement stirs Ahmadi. His eyes flicker, but he doesn't wake. Tom presses the tip of the knife to his chest, pushes it down into his heart, clamps a hand over his mouth to muffle his cries. Ahmadi's eyes widen; then they close.

At the door, Zeke is keeping guard. Tom nods that it's done. Mission halfway accomplished. Now they just need to get out, return to the extraction point.

Down the corridor, they pause. Listen. The sound is unmistakable. Zeke turns to Tom; they exchange concerned looks.

Gunfire.

It's coming from inside the home. They move fast. They expect the guards have been alerted to their presence, that a firefight has broken out with the other members of their team.

That isn't what they find.

They find Nathan first, filling a room with gunfire before moving on to the next one. Tom grabs him by the arm. Nathan hasn't heard their approach, almost turns his gun upon them. "Jesus Christ, boys," he says, almost laughing. "Don't spook me like that."

"What the hell's going on?" Tom says, eyes darting from Nathan's face to his hot gun and back.

Nathan shrugs. "Orders."

"Orders? What're you talking about? Ahmadi is dead. *Those* were our orders."

Nathan rolls his eyes. "Go see the captain." He shrugs them off like this isn't his concern; then he kicks down the door to the next room and goes in firing. The action is too sudden for Tom to try to stop him. He hears the screams of terrified women inside the room. Children too, he thinks. Tom and Zeke look at each other, then take off running.

Tom has never turned a blind eye to Captain Dale's past indiscretions, nor those of his two sycophantic followers. When they smuggled poppy seeds back to the US, he reported them. When they went trigger-happy on a past mission – as they are tonight – he reported them.

The CIA and the US government, however, have always seemed more than happy to turn a blind eye.

Yeah, sure, we'll look right into it. Don't worry about it.

Tom knew he was being brushed off. They didn't try to hide it. They weren't interested. So long as the dirty jobs were getting done, they didn't care what else happened, what other extracurricular activities Captain Robert Dale and his friends were getting up to.

They find the captain and Simon together, rummaging through a room. Two dead men and a woman lie sprawled upon the bed and the floor. Simon is admiring a brooch. Tom wonders if he has taken it off the dead woman. As he goes to put it in his pocket, Tom grabs it from him, holds it up close to his face. "Is *this* what all this shooting's about?" he says. "You're killing everyone off so you can steal a few damn trinkets?"

Simon grins, pulls his arm and the brooch back out of Tom's grip. "Think you'd better tell him, Captain."

Elsewhere, they can still hear gunfire, Nathan moving from room to room.

Robert steps forward, both hands resting on the gun strapped across his chest. The captain is powerful looking, a deadly mix of speed and strength. Tom has seen him work. Lesser men would be intimidated by him. Would cower in his presence.

Tom steps forward, defiant.

"Orders are we kill them all," Robert says, his face unchanging.

"Orders are we kill *Ahmadi*," Tom says. "Just him. Nothin' about women and children, nothin' about the whole damn household."

Robert raises his eyebrows, just a little. "That's the part we kept from you, Tom. You and your buddy." He flicks his chin past Tom to Zeke.

"What the hell?" Zeke says.

"Didn't wanna have to listen to y'all pissing and moaning about what needs to be done," Simon says, sounding like he's laughing.

"We kill them all, make it look like the work of another warlord," Robert says. "Those were our orders. Couldn't have the two of you compromising that, so we kept you busy elsewhere."

Tom's mind races. They kept this from him. The prime details of the mission. Kept them from him and Zeke, knowing they would object.

And now it's too late. They can't object.

It's already done.

"You son of a bitch," Tom says, taking a step forward.

"Uh-uh," Simon says, stepping in front of him. "Don't you and your boy go doin' somethin' stupid, now."

"Who you callin' *boy*?" Zeke says, and from the sound of his voice, Tom knows he has come forward, too.

Simon doesn't respond, just grins.

Robert watches them all, impassive. Tom notices his finger is close to the trigger.

Behind them, Nathan has filled the doorway. His gun is pointed at them. "Took it exactly how we thought they would, huh?"

Tom takes another step forward. Robert's finger inches closer to the trigger. Simon's smile fades.

"Don't do it, man," Nathan says.

Tom's eyes are locked on Robert's.

This is it. It's happening. In a way, he always knew it would.

Zeke places a hand upon his shoulder. "Easy, man," he says.

Tom takes a deep breath.

"Listen to your boy," Simon says.

"Call me 'boy' one more time, and I'm gonna break your jaw," Zeke says.

Simon acts faux scared.

Robert calls beyond them, finished with this situation, to Nathan, "It done?"

"It's done."

"We gonna stand here all night staring at each other," Robert says, "or are we gonna get the fuck outta here?"

Robert leads the way back to the extraction point. Tom and Zeke are made to walk in the center of the group, Simon and Nathan behind them, watching them. They don't trust them not to try anything stupid. Mostly, they don't trust Tom.

They won't have to worry about Tom for much longer.

He's made up his mind, his resolution growing stronger, firmer, with each step across this night's cold desert.

He's done.

Once they're back in America, the second their plane hits the ground, he's out.

It's over.

1

Anthony and Alejandra are at home when he gets the messages. They're watching TV, sitting together on the sofa, engulfed in its glow, one of his arms around her shoulder and his other hand resting upon her pregnant belly.

His phone buzzes in his pocket. His work phone. He keeps it in his left pocket, his personal in his right, so he always knows which is which. Whenever that left leg vibrates, he tenses up. He grits his teeth. He knows that whatever it is, he's probably not going to like it.

It buzzes again, a second time in quick succession.

Alejandra looks at him, raises an eyebrow. "That you?"

He nods, wordless, pulls the phone out, glances at the screen.

He goes stiff.

His stomach drops.

Alejandra is still looking at him. She sees the changes. "What's wrong?"

He can hear the panic in her voice.

The first message: *we know*

The second: RUN

"*Shit!*" He leaps to his feet, grabbing Alejandra by the hands, pulling her up as gently but as quickly as he can. "We gotta go."

She didn't see the messages, but she understands. This is the situation they feared. This is what they have wordlessly dreaded, but always been prepared for.

Alejandra heads for the front door, grabbing the car keys on the way, while Anthony races to the bedroom, ducks down the side of the bed, grabs the bag he's had packed for this emergency. He's sweating. It's burst upon his skin; it's running down into his eyes. His heart is pounding so hard he can feel it in his chest, can hear it in his ears, drowning out everything else.

Alejandra is outside already, in the car, in the passenger seat. She's put the key in the ignition. Anthony leaves the house door open behind him. They won't be coming back here. He dives into the driver's seat, throws the pre-packed bag into the back. The engine roars into life, and he swings out onto the road, slams his foot down on the accelerator.

"Where we going?" Alejandra says, breathless.

"My dad's," Anthony says. "Only place we *can* go. It's the only place that's safe." He's cursing under his breath, thinking how they should have gone to his dad's a long time ago, right at the start of all this shit. It was out of the way, off-grid – most importantly, it was *safe*. His father could have protected them. His father and all his friends.

Instead, he continued to take this stupid risk. Now it's coming to bite them in the ass. All he can hope is they've gotten out in front of it.

They reach Harrow's town limits. Anthony has one eye on the mirror all the way. There's nothing behind them but darkness and streetlamps. No headlights. No cars. This doesn't make him rest easy, but he'd be far more tense if there was something there. He needs to keep the space behind them empty. He presses his foot down harder.

Alejandra is watching the side mirror. "There's nothing there," she says, like she wants him to slow down. Both hands are resting protectively upon her stomach. She's thirty-eight weeks pregnant. This is a high-stress situation. Anthony hopes it doesn't shake her loose inside, put her into early labor. They can't go to a hospital. They'll have to wait until they reach his father.

"I know, baby," he says. "But we can't slow. We can't stop 'til we get where we're going."

Then, out of the shadows, their world turns upside down.

Another car, out of the darkness, its lights off, waiting for them outside the town. Slams them in the side. Sends them rolling. Anthony hears the crunching of metal, the shattering of glass. Feels shards of it cutting his face and his arms. He hears screams – Alejandra's and his own.

Then the car stops. It's still, resting on its roof. The world is still spinning wildly in his head. Then there's a creaking, a groaning, something being forced open. His door. He looks up, but everything is blurred. Beside him, there's another creaking, another groaning; then he hears Alejandra being dragged from the car, scraping through the broken shards of glass. He hears her cries, her shouts, her protestations. This snaps him back to attention. He reaches out, trying to crawl through the open door, from the wreckage, but he's still strapped in. The belt is loose suddenly, cut. Hands are upon him, strong, they drag him out. They dump him in the middle of the road.

"You fuckin' piece of shit," Anthony hears. Then he feels spit spatter upon his face.

The voice is familiar. He hears a few other voices. They're all familiar.

He can't shake the dizziness. It passed, briefly, when he heard Alejandra cry out, but it has returned. His vision flickers in and out of clarity. Just enough time to see who is here, gathered around them.

The Right Arm Of The Republic. All the elders. Here to deal with him personally.

Michael Wright, Harry Turnbull, Ronald Smith, and Peter 'Terminator' Reid. Peter's brother is not here. Anthony is glad.

Harry kicks him across the face.

"Anthony, Anthony, Anthony." It's Michael's voice. Michael is in charge. Leader and founder of the Right Arm Of The Republic. "You thought we'd never find out, huh?"

Alejandra is struggling. On the road, grit in his mouth, Anthony looks toward her. Peter has her. He holds her by the hair, bats away her hands, bloodied from the crash, while she struggles.

Michael crouches in front of Anthony, obscuring his sight. "Gotta admit, she's real pretty for a beaner. I can see what made you so weak."

Anthony takes a lunge, but he falls short. Realizes his arm is bent at a bad angle, that it dangles uselessly, that as it makes contact with the ground, it screams with pain.

Michael laughs at him. "And she's pregnant, huh? Well, congratulations to you, Mr. Rollins. And here you've been hiding her away from us all this time. What's it been, six months? That sound about right to you, Harry?"

"Far too fuckin' long, whatever it's been."

"That's true," Michael says, nodding. "But here's what

really gets in my craw, more than your pregnant spic girl-friend." He spits. "It's that you're a goddamn *narc*, you piece of shit."

"We oughtta wrap this up," Ronald says, out of sight. "This ain't exactly out of the way. We ain't been quiet, either."

Michael waves him off. "Don't you worry none, my man. We're coming to the end. Ain't much more I wanna say to this scumbag. Plenty I wanna show him, though."

He stands back up, steps aside, so Anthony can see Alejandra and Peter again.

Peter catches his eye, makes sure he's looking. Makes sure he sees the gun in his hand.

He's not holding on to Alejandra anymore. Doesn't have a handful of her hair. She's lying flat on the road, her face bloodied, like she's been struck. She lies, prone. Anthony sees her. Sees Peter. Sees the gun.

Peter raises the gun. It's pointed at her belly. He pulls the trigger.

Anthony screams.

Peter raises the gun higher. He shoots Alejandra through the face.

Anthony screams harder. Screams until his throat burns, until his voice is gone.

Michael gets back in front of him. "Don't worry about it," he says. "You're gonna be joining them both real soon. First, we gotta take a little trip."

"We got the blowtorches ready for you, motherfucker," Harry says.

Anthony doesn't look at them. He stares at Alejandra's motionless body. Sees how the blood runs out of her, into the cracks in the asphalt.

"Pick him up," Michael says, standing.

Peter and Harry come either side of him. They take an arm, hoist him. As soon as he leaves the road, the throbbing in his skull gets stronger, his stomach lurches. He throws up.

"Get him in the van," Michael says. "Let's go crisp our old friend up."

"Ain't no friend of mine," Ronald says, hands balled on hips, spitting.

Anthony is dragged away from Alejandra, across the road, his feet dragging. Then they stop. They freeze. They haven't reached the van yet, the vehicle that ran him and Alejandra off the road. He can see the van off to the side. They're nowhere near it yet.

"Shit," Peter says.

"What we gonna do?" Harry says, addressing Michael.

Anthony doesn't understand.

Then he hears it. The sirens. Police.

And in the distance, off to his right, back the way they came, through his blurred vision he can see the lights, flashing red and blue, coming this way.

Peter drops him. Pulls out the gun he used to kill Alejandra, tucked back into his waistband. "Let's waste him right here."

Michael is looking back down the road. "Ain't got time – let's go."

"The fuck you mean we ain't got time?" Peter sounds pissed.

"What I said, we ain't got time."

"Damn it, I can do it, right here right now."

"'Cause I wanna see him burn!" Michael says, stepping forward.

Ronald is already back at the van, climbing in behind the wheel. Harry grabs Peter by the arm. "We'll get him at the hospital. Then we'll barbecue him like we planned. Now let's *go*."

The sirens are getting louder; the lights are getting brighter.

Peter does as he's told. He goes to the van with the rest. They turn, leave, speed off down the road, away from the chaos.

Anthony lies down, everything spinning. He feels like he's going to be sick again. He tries to turn, to find Alejandra. He can't move. He reaches out for her as the police cars come to a stop, as they get out and run over. Anthony can't reach her. His arms aren't long enough. He can't see her anymore, either, not through the tears.

2

Tom Rollins is a wanted man.

He left his division two months ago. After that mission in Afghanistan, he went AWOL. He's living off-grid now. This is nothing new to him. He's had practice with it. He's good at it.

Currently, he's in Arizona. Been here a week. Doesn't know how much longer he'll be sticking around. He's in a bar, though he didn't come in to drink. He's eating. Sits in a booth at the back, with a sandwich. It's a Friday night, but this is a quiet place. That's why he patronizes it. There are four other men inside, the same four in every night he's been here. None of these regulars sit together. They all sit alone, minding their own business, staring either into their beers or up at the television behind the bar. The bartender absently wipes the counter or a glass, leans against the back and looks up at the television, too.

It plays the news. All it ever plays is the news. The volume is turned up loud so that everyone can hear it. At least one of the old men has a hearing aid.

Tom doesn't pay it much attention. Glances at it every so often while he chews. It's reporting on a Texas senator, Seth Goldberg. The report is from earlier in the day, and Tom wonders how many times the regulars have seen it replayed already.

Senator Seth Goldberg is probably in his forties but looks much younger, handsome like a movie star. He's standing on some steps outside an official-looking building in downtown Dallas. He talks with the reporters about the anti-oil bill he has brought forward, his hope that it will lead to more widespread use of greener, more renewable sources of energy. Tom thinks that if they're reporting on this Texan in Arizona, then the news about his bill likely has a good chance of going national.

The news cuts elsewhere, to a closed room. To a group of men who strongly oppose his bill. Oil men. Barons and tycoons. Lobbyists. They talk about the economy. They talk about the legacy and the heritage of Texas oil. They accuse Senator Seth Goldberg of trying to put many thousands of hardworking Americans out of their jobs.

The screen cuts back to Goldberg. They have his rebuttal fired up, ready to go, this hypothesis already posited to him by one of the many reporters gathered around him on the steps. He says it's not about losing jobs, but creating new ones and, more importantly, ensuring the future of our very planet.

It cuts back to the oil lobbyists, but by now, Tom isn't paying much attention. He's finishing his sandwich, draining his glass of water. He'll finish up here; then he'll go back to his hotel room. He'll take a look at his map, decide where he'll go next. He has no destination in mind. It could come down to as much as covering his eyes and randomly jabbing a finger. Then he'll get a good night's sleep and set off in the morning.

Tom has nowhere to be, nowhere to go. For now, he's just keeping his head low. Moving around. He's sure that eventually a place will present itself to him where he can settle, if not forever, then at least for a long while.

Of course, things being what they are, he'll always be wary. Will always be keeping one eye on the entrance and another on the exit. Checking back over his shoulder. Securing every room, every route. Examining every face that passes him for familiarity, whether it be from his past, or a face that just keeps showing up in his present. He has no doubt that the CIA will be looking for him. Monitoring his accounts. Alerts set up on facial-recognition cameras all across the country. The US government will not be willing to let him go so easily. He's done too much for them. He knows too much. Too many dirty secrets.

He's not going back. He'd had enough a long time ago. The complaints he levied at Dale and his buddies fell on deaf ears. They were brushed aside, ignored, instantly forgotten. Tom couldn't forget. All that he'd seen, that he'd heard. All that he'd been powerless to stop. His only regret now is that he didn't get out sooner.

The door opens to the bar. Tom's eyes go to it instantly, though he's subtle about it. Just a quick glance that takes it all in, assesses the three men who come stumbling in.

They get the attention of the regulars, too. They're young, loud, brash. *Drunk*. Out on the town, enjoying their Saturday, figuring they'll come in here, a place they've never been before. They'll check it out, take in the atmosphere, the locale, the *ambience*. And the prices. They'll get a good look at the prices.

"Hey, guys, we just stepped into a fuckin' mausoleum

or somethin'?" one of them says, striding through, looking around. He leads the way, strutting like a peacock, his head bobbing back and forth. His buddies laugh at what he says. The three of them all look alike. One of them wears a baseball cap. The only difference between the leader and the other guy not in a cap is that his hair's brown and the other's is blond.

They go to the bar, order drinks. The leader keeps looking around the room, at the people present. He double-takes when he sees Tom, zeroes in on him, singling him out as the youngest man present. Tom watches them without looking directly at them, keeps an eye on them. They're troublemakers. They've come in here to *be* loud and brash, knowing no one will tell them to shut up, knowing they can do as they please.

They get their drinks, but the leader leaves his on the counter, nudges his buddies to follow him, to check him out. He crosses the room, walks toward Tom. Tom is unsurprised.

"You look outta place, man," the leader says. "You look a little young to be in here."

Tom runs his tongue around the inside of his mouth, checking the gaps in his teeth for bits of food. Takes his time responding. "Could say the same about you," he says when he's done probing.

"We're just passing through." The leader tilts his chin at Tom's empty plate. "Looks like you got yourself comfortable."

Tom shrugs. "I like it in here. It's quiet. Usually."

"Uh-huh. Maybe you like the smell, huh? That it? It stinks of old man in this place." He twitches his nose, flares his nostrils. Turns to his friend in the cap. "You smell that, don't you?"

"I sure smell *somethin'*," the cap-wearer says. He takes a drink of his beer.

"Smells like body odor and shit," the blond says.

The leader laughs. "That's right," he says. "That's exactly what it is, man. That's *exactly* what that smell is. It's like they're all dead inside." He turns his attention back to Tom. "And that's a stink you like, huh? You just come on in here, take a seat, and wallow in it, really soak it up. That's your kind of thing, right?"

He's trying to goad Tom, to get some kind of reaction out of him. Amusing himself. Tom isn't interested. Doesn't want to be drawn into it. "Sure," he says. "It's exactly that. Can't get enough of it."

The cap-wearer chuckles. "You hear that? He admits it."

It's not enough for the leader, though. "I don't need you to confirm it," he says. "I already know it, man. I already know you're the kinda sick fuck gets off on shit like that. I can see it all over your face."

"Sure," Tom says. "That must be it."

The bartender, who has been watching it all, calls over, "Listen, boys, we don't want any trouble in here."

The blond turns, jabs a finger toward him. "Man, shut the *fuck* up."

"I'm serious, now," the bartender says. "Just leave him be. He ain't doing you any harm."

The cap-wearer turns now. "You didn't hear him the first time? Shut *up*, damn it."

The leader takes a step closer to Tom. "Well?" he says.

Tom sits back, shrugs. "Well what?"

"You ain't got nothin' to say?"

"No."

"No?" The leader is confused, less sure of himself now.

This isn't how he expected things to go. He was expecting belligerence, something he could bounce off, seize upon. Something he can cause trouble with.

"Sounds like you got all the answers."

"You getting smart with me, man?"

Tom shrugs again.

"What the hell's this?" The leader imitates him, looking and sounding like a petulant child. This isn't going how he anticipated. It's getting out of his control, and now he's getting riled up.

Tom doesn't want trouble. Doesn't want to cause a scene, doesn't want to draw any unwanted attention toward himself. As much as he'd like to piss the leader off, he doesn't shrug again. "Just forget about it," he says. "Just walk away. Forget about it."

"You trynna tell me what to do?"

"Just giving you a piece of advice."

"Advice, huh? Now it sounds like you're trying to threaten me. That what you trying to do?"

Tom looks up at him, looks into his eyes for the first time. "If I was, you'd know about it."

The leader can't hold Tom's gaze. He isn't so sure of himself anymore. He clears his throat, knowing he can't look bad in front of his buddies. He shakes it off. Is about to say something else.

Tom can already guess the kind of banalities about to pour out of his mouth. He cuts him off, bored with it now. "I ain't interested," he says, his voice low, but loud enough to be heard by the leader, if no one else. "No one else in here is interested, either. So here's what you're gonna do – you're gonna shut your mouth, finish your drink, and get out. If you don't do that, you're gonna get hurt."

The leader hesitates.

"I will break your bones. Do you understand me?" Tom says. "You and your buddies. I could kill you with my bare hands, but I won't. I'll just use them to hurt you. Am I clear? Do you understand what I'm saying to you? This is your last warning. Get out of my face."

"Man, what's he saying?" the blond says, behind the leader. "I can't hear a fuckin' word."

The cap-wearer drains his beer. "Man, just give the old dude a smack, will ya? This ain't no fun, I'm getting bored of it."

Old? Tom is thirty. He's affronted by this more than anything else.

The leader looks far less sure of himself than he did when he first came into the bar. He can't back down, though. Not now. He takes strength from the encouragement of his friends, knows that they have his back, that they have the strength in numbers. There are three of them, and only one of Tom.

Fired back up, his former alarm forgotten, he steps closer to Tom. Leans down on the table, gets up in his face. Puts a hand upon his shoulder.

Tom reacts without thinking. Before the leader can say whatever idiotic sentiments he has in his head, Tom grabs the hand upon him, wraps his fingers around the thumb, wrenches it back. It cracks, the thumb snapping. Before the leader can register this pain, before he can cry out, with his other hand Tom grabs him by the back of the head, slams his face down into the table. His nose bursts. He crumples to the floor.

The other two take a step back, caught off guard by the sudden taking out of their fearless leader. They don't hesitate long, though. The cap-wearer attacks first, swinging his bottle.

Tom is already out of the booth. He ducks it, comes up in front of the blond at the same time he's raised a leg to kick him away, create some separation. His boot catches the blond in the solar plexus, staggers him, knocks the air from his lungs. While the blond tries to keep his footing, Tom turns, blocks another swing of the cap-wearer's bottle, then kicks him in the side of the knee, blows it out of joint. The cap-wearer goes down on that leg. As his dislocated knee hits the ground, he screams. Tom twists his arm still clutching at the bottle; his wrist crunches; he drops it. It hits the ground with a thud, rolls away. Before that has happened, Tom has punched him in the jaw, knocked him out.

The blond is behind him, coming up fast. Tom can hear his footsteps, his still ragged breathing. He spins, elbow raised and out, the point of it making contact with the bridge of the blond's nose. Blood bursts from it. He falls to his knees, then flat on his face.

The three are down.

Tom is instantly filled with regret.

He's supposed to be keeping a low profile. He shouldn't be engaging in anything like this. It doesn't matter that he tried to ignore them. That he gave them every opportunity to just walk away. They didn't take it, and it came to this. He should have done better. He should have got up and walked away. Walked right out of the bar and back to his hotel.

It's his father's fault, really. The advice he ingrained in both Tom and his brother when they were young. *Never back down. Never walk away from a fight. Even if you know you're gonna get your ass kicked, never walk away. Make sure they* know *they've been in a fight. Make sure they know they're never gonna mess with you again.*

It's so deep in him it's hard to shake.

The bartender has come over. "Damn, son," he says. "You done a number on those assholes." He looks down at them, wide-eyed. "You all right?"

"I'm fine," Tom says, stepping over the blond.

The other men in the bar are all looking at him, awed by his efforts.

"Wait there, son," the bartender says. "You can't just leave. We gotta call the police, tell them what happened here."

"You tell them," Tom says. "I gotta go."

Before the bartender can say anything else, Tom is already at the door, then out onto the street. He crosses the road, rounds a building to get out of sight, then runs back to his hotel.

3

U p in his room, packing his bag, Tom is still
cursing himself. Should know better. Shouldn't
be provoked so easily, especially not by a bunch
of drunken asshole college boys.

It's time to leave town. To pack his bags, get in his car,
and head for the state line, out of Arizona. The bartender
will call the police, just like he said he would. The cops
will want to know about the man who beat up those boys.
They'll get a description, try to track him down. They
manage to track him down, then it's game over. The CIA
will be on this town like a rash, picking him up, taking him
back for their own brand of justice.

Tom travels light. There isn't much to pack. His rucksack contains a few items of clothing, most of which have
never left the bag. There's a Beretta and a KA-BAR kept
near the top, within easy reach. He carries burner phones,
too. It takes him a moment to realize one of them is ringing.

He picks it up, looks at it. It's the one his father has the number for, and only his father. He answers. "I can't talk right now. Give me a couple of hours. I'll call you back."

"Ain't gonna keep a couple of hours," his father says. Jeffrey Rollins speaks quick, to make sure his son can't hang up on him. "You need to come here, right now, as quick as you can."

Tom considers what happened at the bar, figures heading out to see his father in New Mexico isn't such a bad idea. "What's going on?"

"It's your brother."

Tom's spine stiffens. "What about him?"

"He's got himself into some trouble."

"What kinda trouble?"

"I'll tell you when you get here."

Tom grits his teeth. "What about Alejandra? Is she all right?"

"I'll tell you when you get here," Jeffrey repeats, betraying nothing.

"I'm gonna set off right now, but I ain't gonna get there 'til tomorrow."

"Where you at?"

"Arizona."

"All right. Be careful when you arrive – folks are jumpy."

Before Tom can ask why, Jeffrey has hung up.

Tom stares down at the phone in his hand. He thinks about Anthony, but mostly he thinks about Alejandra. Absently, he reaches to his pocket. To the Santa Muerte pendant there. He presses down on it so hard it digs into his thigh, like he's trying to bruise himself, to be certain of its presence.

He has a bad feeling. His stomach is knotting; there is bile at the back of his throat.

But it's no good standing here fretting over it. He won't know anything until he reaches his father. He shoves the phone into his rucksack, zips it up, slings it over his shoulder, and leaves the hotel.

4

The blacked-out van cruises through the roads in the warehouse district. This time of night it's quiet for the most part. They've passed a couple of lit-up forklifts driven in and out under the harsh glow of floodlights attached high to the front of the buildings, but they're nowhere near where the van is going.

There are four men inside. Chuck Benton sits up front, in the passenger seat. Driving is Al. In the back are Jimmy and Pat. Dix hasn't come with them. Dix is back at the safe house, holding down the fort. They never leave it unattended, not if they can help it.

This is Chuck's team. When he was approached with this job, he insisted he pick his own men. A job like this, stakes this big, he needed guys he could trust, people he had past experience with, had performed jobs and missions with before.

The guy didn't care. Said it was his mission, his choice. He could do it how he wanted, so long as by the end of it they'd accomplished everything they were being paid to do.

"It's this one," Al says, "down here, on the left."

He's come by the last few days, in daylight, in a different vehicle. Checked the place out. Al is a good wheelman. It's one of his many talents. He doesn't mess around, doesn't take risks. Scopes the job out ahead of time, checks for multiple escape routes, just in case. Makes a note of anything that could prove problematic, and how to avoid it. Tonight is a simple task, straightforward, but they're not going to take any chances. This is just the first hurdle, and the last thing they want to do is trip up here. They're not amateurs, they're professionals. That's why they can demand the big bucks.

Al pulls the van around the back of the building, pulls it slowly down the road until they're at the rear of the chain-link fence that runs along the back of the warehouse, topped with barbed wire. "Cameras don't point this way," Al says, stopping.

Chuck nods. He looks down the road. It's lined with intermittent streetlights, some of which don't work. They look like they've been smashed. The road, however, is clear. There are only two more warehouses on this side. "That our escape route?"

"One of them."

Chuck grins. He motions to Jimmy and Pat in the back. "Mask up and tool up, boys. Let's keep this quick and quiet."

They pull on their balaclavas, Chuck included. Al does not. Al stays in the van, behind the wheel. If a car passes by, the worst thing for him to be doing is sitting here at the side of the road wearing a mask.

Jimmy and Pat go out the back doors. They carry M16s, though they're mostly for show. Too noisy to use. Chuck strolls around the back of the van, finds Jimmy already halfway through snipping the links in the fence at the rear of the warehouse. Chuck doesn't have an M16. He has a Sig Sauer, holds it down low at his side. Pat pulls on the fence, shines a flashlight for Jimmy to see what he's doing.

Once it's wide enough, Chuck slips through first, leading the way. He steps lightly down the narrow alleyway at the side of the warehouse, his men following behind, equally as quiet. He reaches the corner, peers around. Watches for the night security guard. Knows there's one on duty. Al isn't the only one who did his research.

When the guard doesn't materialize, Chuck figures he must be inside. He turns to Jimmy and Pat, motions for Pat to stay in place, for Jimmy to follow. With hand signals, he details what he wants Jimmy to do.

The main door is to the left of the roller. A camera is pointed at it. Chuck puts a silencer onto the Sig Sauer. It will dull the shot, but it will not lower it to the quiet *thwip* of a Hollywood movie. There is enough noise coming from the other buildings, the distant noise of the men they earlier passed working through the night, to disguise it. He nods at Jimmy. They go to the door, into view of the camera. If the night guard hears their movements, he will check the CCTV. They need to move fast. Chuck shoots out the lock. Jimmy kicks the door open, charges in with the M16 raised.

Chuck follows him in. Jimmy has gone straight to the office, rifle pointed at the night watchman's head. His arms are raised, hands empty. His eyes and mouth are all wide, in the shape of an O.

"He hit any alarms?" Chuck says.

"Didn't get the chance," Jimmy says.

"Deal with him."

"*Sieg Heil*, motherfucker." Jimmy slams the butt of the

rifle across the guard's jaw. He drops to his knees. Jimmy lets him fall.

Chuck goes to the door, gives a thumbs-up to Pat, then returns to Jimmy and the guard. Jimmy has lifted him up into his chair. Chuck pulls cable ties from his pockets, hands them over. "*Sieg Heil?*" he says, laughing.

Jimmy winks at him. "Adding some color to the scene, man. Figured it would complement Pat's new tattoos nicely." Jimmy binds the guard's ankles and wrists with the cable ties, pulls a gag from his pocket and forces it into his mouth.

Outside, Pat has gone back the way they came, returned to the van, to let Al know things have gone as planned, and to pull the van around front.

Using the guard's keys, Chuck and Jimmy get the main gate open. Al, with Pat riding shotgun, pulls the van in, turns it around, reverses it back inside the warehouse through the opening. He's wearing his mask now.

Pat jumps out of the van, runs inside with Chuck and Jimmy to start loading it up with bags of fertilizer. They take as much as they can carry.

They're all dressed the same. All-black sweaters, trousers, boots, masks. They are uniform. With one exception. Pat is in short sleeves. On his right arm is stencilled a swastika. It looks like a tattoo. In reality, Pat does not have any tattoos.

Finished, they close up the van, close the roller doors, kill the lights, lock the door the security guard came out of. The van pulls out, containing Al, Chuck, and Pat. Jimmy closes the gate again, locks it. He takes the keys. They'll dump them out the window somewhere.

All four inside, Al drives off. He doesn't speed; there's no need. It went off without a hitch.

As they get out of the district, back onto the main roads, they take off their masks. Chuck turns around, to Pat. He nods at the swastika. "You show that thing off?"

"Yeah," Pat says. "Paraded it around right under the cameras, made sure they could see it from every angle."

"You sure?"

"Certain."

"Good." Chuck sits back, satisfied. Jimmy passes him the keys they took from the guard. He throws them out the window, toward some bushes; then he calls ahead, lets Dix know they're on their way. That everything went exactly as it should.

5

M ichael Wright looks around the room.
Present, at the round table in his basement
where they conduct their business, are the
elders of the Right Arm Of The Republic. Beside him is his
co-founder, his right-hand man, Harry Turnbull. His oldest
friend.

Directly opposite is Ronald Smith, their elder statesman
of sorts. At fifty years of age, he is the oldest member of
the group, and the most experienced. He's run with many
other cells in his life, long before the inception of the Right
Arm, and has even had a brief run with the Klan. By now,
his bald head is more the result of genetics than of his
taking a razor to it. His body is going soft now, his chest
and his stomach beginning to sag where they were once
firm and strong, but his face remains as hard, as fearsome
as ever. Ronald has been known to silence rooms with
merely a raised brow. He may be getting older, but no one
underestimates him.

To Michael's left is Peter 'Terminator' Reid. One look

at him leaves no doubt as to the reasoning behind his nickname. Peter is their enforcer, and he looks every inch of it.
He wears a vest that shows off his bulging, steroid-
enhanced muscles, as well as his ink. The 88s, the
swastikas, the Norse gods. On his left pectoral, above his
heart and mostly obscured by the strap of his vest, a right-
handed fist proudly holding aloft an American flag,
swastikas where there should be stars – the unofficial
symbol of the Right Arm. Out of the four men, Peter looks
the most worked up. His fists clench and loosen, clench and
loosen, atop the table. His knuckles go bone white each
time.

Michael looks at these men, and he knows each one of
them is loyal. They're loyal to him; they're loyal to each
other; they're loyal to the cause.

And thus he knows that not one of them would have
tipped off Anthony, sent him racing off into the night. He
knows, too, that it was sheer luck they neared the house just
as Anthony and his pregnant spic girlfriend were racing out
of it, making their escape. Knows that if they hadn't
reached the house just as they did, they would never have
been able to take another road, one that didn't directly
follow them out of Harrow but instead met up at the town's
limits, that they wouldn't have been able to intersect them
just in time. That if they hadn't gotten there exactly when
they did, Anthony and the bitch would be long gone, just an
angry memory by this point.

And he knows, too, that none of these men present
would have called the police, either, alerted them to what
was happening on that quiet road right outside town. They
all know it has to have been a further betrayal. No one else
knew they were there. No one had seen them. There were
no other cars, there were no nearby homes. Someone had

called the cops, sent them in that direction, told them there'd be something of interest they'd come across.

"Much as I hate to say it," Harry says, looking around into everyone's face. "There could be a traitor in our ranks. Someone told that son of a bitch to run. Someone sent the cops out looking for him, trying to cut us off."

"Shoulda let me pull the trigger," Peter says, shaking his head. "Shoulda let me just end it right then and there."

"Yeah, but we didn't expect him to up and disappear from the goddamn hospital now, did we?" Harry says. "Especially not in his condition. He sure as hell didn't get up and walk out."

"That's another thing we gotta consider," Ronald says. "Who got him out of the hospital? Where'd they take him?" A contact in the hospital had told them Anthony had been checked out, but he didn't know by whom or where they had taken him. "Is it the same traitor we're talkin' about right here right now, or are there more? Hell, was it someone else entirely, and if so, how did they know what had happened to him, where he was?"

"He was undercover," Michael says, speaking up for the first time in a while, having previously allowed the others to voice their thoughts. "In terms of the hospital, it was probably his buddies in law enforcement got him out of there. They've probably got him in a safe house halfway across the country by now, setting him up with a new identity, trying to make it so we can't find him."

"We'll fuckin' find him," Peter says.

Michael nods. "It'll take some hard work and a lot of digging, but we'll find him all right. We can't just let this slide. Gotta make an example outta the asshole. The law can't go putting no rat in our ranks and thinking they're just gonna get away with it scot-free."

"What'd they even bother putting him in for?" Ronald says. "What were they hoping to find out? You'd think they could find a better way to spend their time than just hassling us."

"You'd think that," Michael says. "But it'd be wrong. That's *exactly* how they wanna spend their time. Just thinking up new ways to aggravate and piss us off."

"They were probably trying to find where the drugs come from," Michael says.

"Maybe there's somethin' we're forgetting to consider," Harry says.

All eyes turn to him. "And what's that?" Ronald says.

"The person who gave us the information on him in the first place." Harry locks eyes with Michael. "The person who told us what he was up to. What part do they play in it all? They have something to do with him getting out?"

"That's an awful complicated way for them to go about doing things," Michael says.

"Yeah, well, with these kinds of assholes, who knows what they're thinking or planning or exactly what they're trying to do."

"We're getting off track here," Ronald says. "We can consider all this other shit at a later date – right now, we need to think about what really matters. Who warned him, and are they in our ranks? 'Cause if so, we gotta flush that motherfucker out and make a real goddamn example. One that won't soon be forgotten."

Michael realizes Peter hasn't said anything for a while. That his fists are no longer compulsively clenching as they earlier were, that he's looking down into the palms of his hands, thoughtful. "Somethin' up?" he says. "Anythin' you wanna share with the rest of us, Terminator?"

Peter shakes his head, clasps his hands. "No," he says. "Just thinking."

"About what?"

"About all of this. A traitor. Just trynna think who it could be."

There's a pause; then Harry is the first to say what they're all thinking. "Your brother was awful close with Anthony." He doesn't say anything more, just lets the statement hang there.

Peter glares at him across the table. "It ain't my brother," he says, but Michael can't help but notice he doesn't sound entirely convincing – neither to them, or to himself.

"You sure about that?" Harry says. "You absolutely certain?"

"Yeah, I am. I know Steve better'n any of you. It ain't somethin' he would do – he wouldn't dare."

"Don't take it personally," Michael says. "Right now, we gotta consider everyone outside this room a suspect. We gotta be wary of everyone. Watch all the boys closely. If any of them are acting weird, anything strange, anything out of place, we bring it here, to the council, straight away. That clear to everyone?"

They all nod, mumble that it is.

"And we spread the word. We get it out, we're still looking for Anthony. We ain't forgot him, and we ain't *gonna* forget him. No matter where he's gone, we're gonna find him eventually."

"We worried about blowback?" Harry says. "It's lookin' like he's got friends."

"From his buddies, maybe. He ain't in any shape to come after us. Tell our boys to stay frosty, keep their eyes open."

"That's a lotta stuff they gotta remember," Ronald says. He's grinning. "Sure they're gonna keep it all in mind?"

"They're soldiers," Michael says. "It's time they act like it. If they can't remember a couple of little orders, then they got no place in the Arm."

The meeting finished, they head upstairs, done. Michael notices Peter remains quiet, still looks like he's thinking. He doesn't press it for now. Leaves it. He'll talk to Harry about it later. Peter may be confident his brother had nothing to do with Anthony's attempted escape, but Michael knows better than to trust anyone unconditionally.

At the top of the stairs, they come out into the kitchen. Linda, Michael's wife, is at the counter, making herself a coffee. She smiles at them as they file through. Michael goes to her, and she kisses his cheek.

"How you doin', Linda?" Harry says.

"Good as ever," Linda says. "Y'all doin' well?"

"That coffee sure smells good," Ronald says.

"Just brewed it up fresh. You wanna cup?"

"Nah, best not," Ronald says, looking like he already regrets his decision not to partake. "I'd best be on my way."

"Same here," Peter says, pulling open the back door. "I'll talk to y'all later." He leaves, closely followed by Ronald. Michael and Harry exchange a look; then Harry gives Linda a brief embrace, says his goodbyes, and makes his own exit.

"What was up with him?" Linda says, drinking.

"Who?" Michael says, though he's sure he already knows.

"The Terminator."

Michael shrugs it off for now, just says, "He's got some stuff on his mind. He's pissed off Anthony got away."

"Mm." Linda nods, like she's just as annoyed. "How was the meeting? Make any progress?"

"Not particularly." He tells her what they talked about, though doesn't go into his potential suspicions regarding Peter's brother.

Linda takes a seat at the kitchen table, still listening. She nods along with what he says, occasionally drinks her coffee. When he finishes, she says, "You'll find the son of a bitch. One way or another. No one can run forever, and he can only hide like a coward for so long."

"Could take us years."

"Could do, but you'll never forget. I know what you're like, all of you. Y'all won't give up. You'll track him to the ends of the earth if you gotta. But let's be honest here, Michael. You killed his woman and his mongrel baby in one fell swoop. You really think he ain't gonna try to come back here? Right now, he's lying low, healing up, but you gotta believe he's gonna return eventually, try some shit."

"That's true."

"So it's unlikely that, in time, you're gonna have to look all that hard."

Michael smiles at her. "We'll just let him come to us."

"Exactly. Just always be ready for him."

"Hell, you know me," he says, leaning down to kiss her. "I'm always ready."

6

Peter doesn't go straight home. He goes to see Steve.

There's a reason Peter is known as Terminator and his brother is known as Skinny. Even before Peter started pumping steroids into himself, he'd always had the better genetics. Taller and broader, he's almost twice the size of Steve. He's more committed to the cause, too. Steve is in the life, sure, but he's never really been a part of it. Peter knows it, and he knows the others know it, too. Steve commits only half-heartedly. If it weren't for Peter keeping him in line, keeping him in the ranks, he'd have tried to get out years ago.

Steve is at home. He always is. Doesn't look too surprised to see his brother when he answers the door. "Hey," he says. "You need somethin'?"

"I was nearby," Peter says. "Just thought I'd stop in, see how you're doin'."

Steve's eyes narrow at this. "Somethin' up?"

"I need a reason?"

"I guess not, but you usually show up with one."

"You gonna invite me in, or leave me standing out here in the cold?"

Steve steps aside, opens the door wider. "It's hardly cold," he says. He walks through the house, heads to the back where his bedroom is. Peter follows. Steve spends most of his time in his room. On his computer. Video games and message boards – this is his life. When Peter reaches the door, sees that Steve has settled back down into his computer chair, he can't help but roll his eyes. Steve resumes his paused computer game, as if his older brother weren't here.

"You can't leave that alone for five minutes?" Peter says.

"I can," Steve says. "If you ask me to."

"I'm asking you."

Steve keeps playing. Blasts a few more space aliens; then he hits pause. He swivels the chair around so he can see Peter, lets his hands dangle down into his lap.

Peter looks him over. Everything about him lives up to his nickname. His arms and legs are like sticks. His stomach is concave. Peter is pretty sure he could wrap one hand all the way around his neck.

"Well?" Steve says.

"Oughtta get you out to the gym with me," Peter says.

"That it?" Steve sounds exasperated. "You came here, get me to pause my game, all so you can tell me somethin' you've told me a million times before."

"That ain't why I came out here," Peter says. He's trying to be casual, though he knows he carries an air of menace with him no matter how he is trying to act. It has been commented on many times by many people – friends,

girlfriends, family. "I'm just making a little conversation
first is all, see how you are."

"As you can see, I'm fine and dandy."

"You look pale and sickly."

"Don't feel it. That's just how you see the world, Pete,
'cause the rest of us don't always look like you."

"You gonna leave the house at all today, or are you just
gonna sit in here and play your little video games?"

Steve shrugs. "Ain't decided yet. I might need to pick
up some groceries, so I might go out to get them later. As
far as anything else goes, no, I ain't got any plans. Besides,
you *need* me here. For my frequent customers. *They* need
me here, too. They're probably gonna start showing up any
minute now – you should stick around, check a couple of
them out. Then you'll see what pale and sickly *really* looks
like."

"I ain't gonna wait around to check out any junkies."

Steve laughs. "That's a sight of weakness you just can't
tolerate."

Peter feels his lip curling. Steve is the only person who
can get away with talking to him like this. Anyone else
would have been warned by now. Anyone pisses him off
too much, they swiftly get a punch in the face. Not too
many people piss him off, and certainly not on purpose.

"Listen, I'm here to talk about Anthony," Peter says,
getting to the point.

The humor goes out of Steve's face. He runs his tongue
around the inside of his mouth, over his teeth, causing his
lips to bulge. "What about him?"

"You were close with him, weren't you? He spent most
of his time here, with you, dealing."

"So? That was the job you and the rest of the council
gave him. It wasn't my decision."

"But you spent a lot of time with him. You probably talked a lot, found stuff in common, had private jokes, all that kinda shit."

Steve shrugs, repeats, "So?"

"You consider him a friend?"

Steve runs his tongue over his teeth again, stares off to the side. Peter is pleased by the expression on his face – it doesn't look happy. It looks pissed off. Betrayed. "I guess I *did*. But now he's just another race traitor."

Peter nods, but tries not to let his satisfaction show too much. "He's still alive."

"I know. I heard."

"You know how he's still alive?"

"Cops showed up before y'all could finish the job."

"Word's spread."

"It's a big story."

"But how'd the cops know where to find us? That's the bigger story. Someone must've called them. Told them where we'd likely be, how to find us."

"Could be. Maybe y'all just got unlucky; it was a random patrol."

Peter shakes his head. "They came straight for us, lights flashing, sirens blasting. They were looking for us. Nothin' unlucky about it."

Steve looks at him, his face impassive.

"Was it you?" Peter says.

Steve's eyes narrow; he gets belligerent. "You fuckin' kidding me right now?"

"I gotta be sure."

"You wanna be sure? Then I'll tell you what you do – you go find that motherfucker, bring him back here, and I'll put a bullet through his head my own damn self." He stares, defiant. Peter notices how his fists have closed.

Peter tries to stare him down, see how well he holds it. Steve doesn't back down. Peter isn't entirely convinced, but he feels better than he did when he first got here.

"All right, then," he says. "I'll take your word for it."

"You bring him to me, you ain't gonna have to take my word," Steve says, still flaring. Looks like he's ready to spit, but they're indoors. "I'll *show* you."

Peter checks the time. "I gotta go," he says.

Steve takes a deep breath through his nose, settles back, calms himself. "Work?"

"That's right." Peter is a doorman. The bar is mostly frequented by supremacists and allies. On occasion a black or a Latino will wander in, not understanding the situation, but they quickly get the lay of the land, drink up and leave.

Moreover, the bar is unofficially owned by the Right Arm. It cleans their money, the money they make from the likes of Steve, and many others dotted around the town of Harrow, selling drugs.

Peter straightens up. He looks at his brother one last time before he leaves, like he can find the truth of his questions in one final glance, like it will be written upon him, or on the walls. Steve has been convincing today, but convincing enough? Peter isn't so sure. Perhaps he's blinded. This man is his brother. If it was one of the others – Michael, or Harry, or Ronald – would they feel the same way? Or would they see straight through him, know whether he was telling the truth or lies?

"I'm out of here," he says.

"Have a good night," Steve says. "I won't walk you out. You know the way."

7

Tom has reached New Mexico, still has a few hours to go before he reaches his father's home. All the way out of Arizona, he's felt sick. Can't shake the feeling that something bad has happened.

If Anthony's gotten himself into trouble, it won't be the first time Tom has had to pull him out of it, clean up his mess. Growing up, their whole lives, Anthony always seemed able to find mischief, to fall in with the wrong crowd, or to simply piss off the wrong people. And every single time, Tom has been there for him. Tom has talked down the angry shop owner Anthony was caught stealing from. He's paid bail, he's paid fines, and he's kicked ass on more than one occasion.

Way more than one occasion.

There are scars on his body that rightfully belong to his brother.

What concerns Tom the most this time around is the presence of Alejandra. She's mostly been a calming influence in Anthony's life, or at least so Tom believed. If he's been falling back into old habits, this worries Tom. With Alejandra so close to him, has she been dragged into it?

She's pregnant, though … surely Anthony wouldn't be so stupid? He wouldn't put himself, or her, at risk when they have a child on the way.

Right?

Tom puts the radio on, trying to distract himself. The news is on. Senator Seth Goldberg talking about his anti-oil bill again; then the airwaves are filled with the voices of his detractors. The DJ takes calls from people, both for and opposed, and Tom can't take it as they spit their vitriol, whichever side of the fence they're on. He turns the radio off, thinks about putting in one of his CDs, decides against it. Decides instead to just drive in silence. The noise wasn't helping anyway, just making things worse.

He remembers the last time he visited Anthony and Alejandra, down in Texas. It had been a while back, maybe half a year, still a while before he'd made the decision to go AWOL. Remembers how the atmosphere in their home had been fraught, how something had seemed off, like their smiles and their laughter were forced. It felt like they were worried about something, something they were keeping hidden from him. He'd asked them, enough times, if everything was all right, but they just kept nodding, kept forcing their smiles, and assured him that yes, everything was fine, never better.

One thing he'd picked up on was the way Anthony kept checking his phone. He tried to be sly about it, to slide it out of his pocket and hide it behind his thigh while he regularly inspected the screen, but Tom noticed. Whoever it was, Anthony didn't respond much. Only once or twice. He kept looking, though. It got to a point, eventually, where it felt like he was eager for Tom to leave, like Anthony all of a sudden had somewhere he needed to be.

He remembers how they saw him off, Alejandra walking him to the door while Anthony held back, checking his phone again. "It's been lovely to see you, Tom," she said. She smiled at him, and it was the first time that day it had felt genuine, but at the same time, he couldn't help but notice how tinged with sadness it appeared.

"It's been good to see you too," he said. He had the Santa Muerte pendant on him, wearing it like a necklace so she could see it. It had been a gift from her. To keep him safe.

Alejandra hesitated then, looked back inside the house, searching for Anthony, checking if he was approaching. She turned back to Tom, opened her mouth, hesitated again, as if she wanted to say something but was afraid to do so.

"What?" Tom said, trying to encourage her. "It's fine, tell me." He looked into the house over her shoulder, saw Anthony was nowhere in sight. "It'll be just between the two of us if you like. I won't tell him anything you don't want me to."

She hesitated further, too long, and then Anthony was beside her. "Sorry about that," he said. "Just a friend, he needs a favor."

Tom nodded along, though he didn't believe a word of it. "Sure."

"Well, it's been good to see you, bro," Anthony said, sending him on his way. "Don't be such a stranger, huh?"

"Well, I can't promise that," Tom said. "But I'll be sure to be here when the baby's born."

Alejandra cupped her stomach, then reached out and embraced him. "Stay safe," she said, into his ear.

For a moment, Tom can feel her breath again, speaking those words in his ear, tickling his lobe. He grits his teeth.

They were in Texas. Why would Anthony now be with their father in New Mexico, and why no mention of Alejandra? Have they split up, is that why Tom has been summoned? He doubts it's anything as banal as this. He can't imagine why he would be drawn into a domestic squabble between his brother and his pregnant girlfriend.

Tom doesn't know what it is, why he's needed, and he won't know until he reaches his father. Until then, his mind will continue to race, to imagine ever new and worrying scenarios that flip his stomach, tighten his throat.

Earlier in his journey, when his thoughts became too much, he pulled over, tried to call his father. There was no answer. Jeffrey's burner phone rang out. He left it to ring out. This made Tom feel worse. He hasn't tried to call again.

He wants to get there sooner, as fast as he can, but he can't speed. Has to maintain a low profile. Can't run the risk of being pulled over, for being caught over something as stupid as a speeding ticket. Especially not now. Especially not when he has such a bad feeling about why his father and his brother might need him.

8

S pecial Agent Ben Fitzgerald sits in the office of Supervisory Special Agent Jake Lofton and bites down on the inside of his cheek. It's an old habit, a nervous habit, goes all the way back to when he was a child. He chews and he chews, the wet flesh there getting all tattered and frayed, the taste of blood filling his mouth. The way he's felt after recent events, he's amazed he hasn't chewed a hole right through.

Jake Lofton wants to talk all about the recent events. "Did you hear what the papers are calling it?"

Ben releases the bloodied cheek from between his teeth long enough to say, "No."

"They're calling it a Night of the Long Knives style purging," Jake says, raising his eyebrows. "I've seen them literally call it that, Part Two. You believe that?"

Ben shrugs one shoulder. "I suppose it's fitting."

The two men are stationed in the Dallas field office, but what happened extends further than just Texas. It hit New Mexico, Oklahoma, Arkansas, and Arizona, too. Twelve men and women killed in one night, each one of them undercover with various neo-Nazi cells. Their details leaked, seemingly from within the FBI itself. No one else could have had this knowledge.

The various cells acted fast, each one independent of the other. If they'd known they were going to make such a big noise in one night, in five different states, it's questionable whether they still would have gone ahead. On Jake's desk and in Ben's lap are the names of the twelve men and women killed. It doesn't say how they died, but Ben knows. Knows that if he looks at this name, they were set on fire. This one was shot through the head. This one had their hands cut off, then their throat slit. One of them was Jewish. She was crucified.

Two names are missing from the list, though. Jake is unaware of them, but Ben knows them. Hasn't been able to stop thinking about them.

Anthony Rollins and Alejandra Flores.

He doesn't know where Anthony is now, but he knows exactly where Alejandra is. What happened to her haunts his dreams.

But he can't talk about it. Not with Jake.

Jake puts his paperwork aside. "Listen," he says, leaning forward. "Our undercovers are getting antsy – they look at this, they know it's a leak, they're asking themselves, *What if it happens again? What if it happens to me?* They want out. Half our people with white supremacist cells have already gotten out, a lot of them unofficially. They aren't waiting around to see if this is going to turn into a national thing."

"Can't say I blame them," Ben says.

"No, neither can I, but it's still leaving us in the lurch. How many did you lose?"

"On the night, or since?"

"Both."

"On the night, two." Texas was hit hardest. Of the twelve (official) deaths, six of them were in Texas. "Since, I've had about four say they're out." Ben does not include Anthony and Alejandra in his numbers, not to Jake. To himself, though, they're there all the time.

"That's bad, but it isn't the highest I've heard. One of our handlers lost all his charges, all his informants, after it happened. None on the night, but that didn't matter. Didn't even matter whether they were with Nazis or not, they got out." Jake presses a finger down onto a paper, the one with all the names on it. The dead names. "We have to find who's responsible for this, Agent Fitzgerald."

Ben nods. He understands.

"It could be someone within the FBI. It could be a hacker. I don't care where they came from, I don't care what their affiliation is, I want them found. And as soon as possible."

Ben gets to his feet. "Got it."

"*Fast*, Ben," Jake reiterates. "This doesn't look good for any of us. We've got to tidy it up."

Ben leaves the office. Outside, other agents pass him in the halls, nod greetings. Ben returns them. He doesn't go straight back to his office. He has somewhere else he needs to go.

9

B en gets his laptop, takes it to Gerry Davies. Gerry is their senior computer analyst. He's in his early thirties, has worked with computers all his life. There's nothing about them he doesn't know. He's in his office, sitting behind his desk and tapping away. He wears a creased shirt, the collar rumpled. There are earphones pumping music into his ears, and he doesn't look up when Ben enters, doesn't look up until he reaches the desk, puts the laptop down on it.

Gerry looks at the laptop first, then up at Ben. He pulls out the earphones. Ben can hear the music blasting. It's a wonder Gerry hasn't gone deaf.

"Got it a little loud, don't you?" he says.

Gerry grins. "I like it loud," he says.

"What're you listening to?" Ben asks, as if he'll have any idea what it is. He's too busy to keep up with music.

"Ministry," Gerry says. "You a fan?"

Ben is surprised to find he *has* heard of them. "I'm unfamiliar with their music."

Gerry taps something on his keyboard, and the earphones fall silent. "But you didn't come here to discuss industrial metal, did you?" He reaches out for the laptop. Ben hands it over. "What seems to be the problem with this?"

Ben doesn't answer right away. He goes back to the door, locks it. Gerry watches him, confused. Ben returns to the desk, but doesn't take a seat. "What I'm going to tell you, what I'm about to ask of you, it doesn't leave this room."

Gerry looks at him, says nothing.

"You got that?"

"Yeah, I got it."

"You know about the recent massacre of our undercovers." Ben takes a seat. He doesn't phrase it as a question. Of course Gerry is aware of it. Everyone is.

"Course I know about it," Gerry says. "Who do you think they've got trying to find the source of the leak? And then who do you think's gotta *plug* that leak?"

"Have you found anything?"

"Not yet, but I will. It's just a matter of time and patience." Gerry looks pleased with himself, the look of a man who knows he's never failed his duties yet, and is confident in his abilities.

"There might be more than one leak to plug."

Gerry cocks his head; his expression falters. "How do you mean?"

Ben taps his laptop. "They took information from this. Information only I had."

Gerry doesn't understand. He leans across the desk, speaks in a low conspiratorial way. "How are you so sure?"

"Because they were details that were only on my

laptop. No one else had them; no one else knew about them."

"Are you talking about off-the-books stuff?"

Ben thinks about Anthony. About Alejandra. He never met her, but he's seen her picture since. Can't get her face out of his mind. "Yes. I had an undercover in one of the cells. There was no record of him anywhere else, no correspondence of him anywhere, except for on this laptop."

Gerry looks at it like it's a bomb. "Shit," he says. "Why wasn't he official?"

"No time. I got some intel; I needed to move fast. An opportunity presented itself, and I took full advantage of it."

Gerry looks at him, raises his eyebrows.

"It's not by the book, but sometimes when we're dealing with these kinds of people, we have to bend the rules a little."

"That's a big bend."

"And I have to live with the consequences."

"Makes me wonder how many other unofficial undercovers may have been killed that night," Gerry says.

"That's crossed my mind too."

"No one else has brought me their laptop."

"Maybe they're too afraid, and for the same reason I'm about to say this to you – this is between *us*. You and I, and no one else. Is that clear?"

Gerry nods.

"Someone hacked my laptop, and they took information pertaining to all of my undercovers, but the one you're looking at is Anthony Rollins. He was the unofficial."

"They kill him?"

"They tried."

Gerry blinks. "He's still alive?"

"Last I heard. But he lost things much more precious than his life."

Gerry frowns, doesn't understand.

Ben isn't going to explain it to him. "Are you clear what I need you to do?"

"Yes," Gerry says. "I'll do everything I can, but I make no promises." He says this, covering his back, but Ben hears that same earlier confidence of a man knowing he can do this.

"I trust you." Ben unlocks the office door, leaves.

Inside, there is a storm raging. It tightens his chest, flips his stomach, makes him feel queasy. He bites down on the inside of his cheek again, tastes the familiar coppery tang of blood.

"Hey, Ben."

He looks up. Agent Carly Hogan is coming down the hall toward him. She's smiling. Ben forces one back. "Hello."

"I heard you got stuck with the Night of the Long Knives Part Two investigation."

Ben winces. "I don't think Jake would appreciate it being referred to as such."

"Well, Jake ain't here." She winks. She wears a black pantsuit; her blonde hair is tied back, clipped tight at the back of her head. It's a plain uniform, but she pulls it off well. She pulls everything off well – her uniform, a towel, his oversized shirts when she stays over, nothing at all. "How's it going so far?"

"I just got started."

"So nothing at the minute."

He doesn't tell her about the laptop. He won't talk about it with anyone but Gerry. "Nothing at all."

Carly looks at her watch. "I'm on my way to lunch," she says. "You wanna join? You can bounce ideas off me."

"That sounds good."

"Then walk with me." She begins striding off on her long legs. Ben keeps pace. "Don't stand too close," she says. "I might feel the urge to reach out and pinch your butt, and we don't want anyone getting jealous now, do we?"

Despite himself, Ben can't help but laugh.

10

T he commune is hidden through woodland. This isn't where Jeffrey Rollins has always lived. Before this, when Tom and Anthony were growing up, his home had been in an area more desert than green. He'd raised his boys alone, after the death of his wife, their mother, Mary. Cervical cancer took her. It hit Jeffrey and his boys hard, but he persevered. Did the best he could.

Tom and Anthony continued to go to school, but on evenings and weekends, Jeffrey would teach them other skills – how to hunt, fish, track, camp. How to load and fire guns. How to properly hold a knife, how to cut with it, and how to stab. They hoarded tinned food, lived off it, only rarely venturing to the grocery store to purchase things they couldn't hunt for themselves or get for free in the wild.

Survivalist skills.

Doomsday prepping.

Jeffrey didn't leave that home until after his boys had moved out, and he met Sylvia. They got in touch through a like-minded message board. They married a couple of years later, and Jeffrey left his fortified home and moved into the commune where she lived.

Now Tom makes his way to it down a dirt road. He takes his time, the car bouncing up and down and side to side, throwing him around a little. His hands are tight on the steering wheel. As he approaches, the sickly feeling he's carried all the way from Arizona is beginning to fade a little, with the knowledge that soon, very soon, he will have the answers to all his questions.

The road is wide enough for only one car at a time. If anything comes from the other direction, he's not sure what they're supposed to do. In the woods, out of the corner of his eye, he spots movement. He slows the car more, but not enough to be suspicious. Watches without turning toward it directly. There's a man there, behind a tree, behind some bushes, almost invisible in his camouflage. The man is armed. He watches Tom pass by. He raises an arm, a walkie-talkie, speaks into it. Warns the commune that someone is headed their way.

Tom remembers what his father said about people being jumpy. In all his worry over Anthony and Alejandra, he forgot about this statement, has spent no time wondering why they might be so.

At the end of the dirt road, the commune comes into sight. Before he can pull out from the trees, three men emerge from the bushes, waving him down. They're armed, dressed similarly to the man hidden in the trees. Their automatic weapons are raised. They motion for him to get out of the car.

Tom keeps his hands in view. He gets out of the car, raises his arms. "Calm down, boys," he says. "I was invited here."

The man in the middle steps forward, gun still raised, pointed at Tom's chest. "Who are you?" he says, jabbing with the rifle to punctuate his words. He's short, heavy in the middle, has a thick red beard, and his hair is likely the same, though it's concealed by a camouflage cap. "And what're you doin' out here?"

"You didn't hear me the first time?" Tom says. "I was invited. My dad called me. Jeffrey Rollins. Since when did this kind of welcome become standard practice with y'all? This is the first time I've been held at gunpoint when I've come to visit."

The two men behind the one asking all the questions don't point their guns at Tom, but they hold them close, their fingers on the triggers. One of them is white; the other is black. The black one clears his throat, says, "Jeffrey did say his oldest son was on the way."

The other agrees. "Said we oughtta just wave him straight on through."

The leader shouts back at them over his shoulder without ever taking his eyes off Tom. "Either of y'all ever seen Jeff's oldest kid? 'Cause I ain't. What's there to say this is even him?"

Tom looks the leader over. He's being purposefully belligerent. Tom knows the type. He has a little bit of power – in this instance, being in charge of the entrance to the commune – and he's loath to relinquish it, wants to shake his dick around a bit first. Tom smiles, is polite, respectful. "I'll wait right here while you go and get him," he says. "That shouldn't take too long."

The leader continues to be difficult. "We oughtta look the car over," he says. "Check it. See if he's got anything hidden." He steps closer to Tom, raises the gun so it's pointing in his face now. "You got anything in there you don't want us seeing?"

Tom looks down into the barrel of the gun, then back at him. He can feel his patience evaporating. He has driven a long way to get here. His back is aching, and he's worried about Anthony and Alejandra. "If you don't lower this gun and calm yourself down, I'm gonna take it from you and stick it up your ass." He stares into the man's eyes. "This is the only time I'm gonna warn you. I'm done being polite."

The leader's eyes blaze. "Who the hell'd you think you are, talkin' to me like that?"

Tom doesn't answer him. He's had his one warning. Tom disarms him, shoves the rifle out of his face while snatching it out of the man's hands, spins him around and clamps an arm around his neck, pulls him close to use him as a shield. "You two," he says to the men staring, dumbfounded, amazed at how fast he moved. "Go and get my dad. Me and your buddy will be waiting right here."

Conscious of the guard he saw further back in the woods, Tom presses himself up against the car to protect his back, still holding onto the leader. He places the rifle he took from him down into the footwell, then gives him a little choke, just to hear him make a noise. Tom grins, puts his mouth close to his ear and says, "Warned you, didn't I? You caught me on a good day – you keep struggling, and I'll follow through on that promise to stick your gun where the sun don't shine."

The leader goes very still.

Jeffrey arrives shortly after with the other guards. He grins at the predicament he finds his son in, shakes his head. "Put that asshole down and get over here," he says. "Come give your old man a hug."

11

Tom drives along to his father's home, Jeffrey in the passenger seat beside him. Jeffrey and Sylvia's place is deep in, toward the rear of the commune's layout. Tom observes the houses as they go. It's grown since he was here last. A lot of the homes look like they've been thrown together, hastily erected. Gives the place an almost shanty-town quality.

There's another new addition. Encircling the commune, closing it in, is a chain-link fence, barbed wire atop it. Tom points it out to his father, who chuckles. "That ain't the half of it," he says. "There are claymores around the perimeter. No one's getting in here who shouldn't."

"There a reason for all this?" Tom says, slowing as some children run across in front of him. "I ain't seen it like this before."

Jeffrey nods. "There's a lot of folk here get jumpy. They wanna keep this place quiet, on the down low. They don't want anyone to know they're here 'cause they ain't supposed to be here."

"Yeah? Where they supposed to be?"

"Behind bars, a lot of the time. We got bail jumpers and fugitives hiding out here, and I suppose that gives them a right to be jumpy."

"Guys like the one on the gate?"

"He's always been an asshole."

Tom changes the subject. "What's happened to Anthony?"

"Got himself in some trouble."

"Shit. It bad?"

"Yeah." Jeffrey's voice is solemn. Tom doesn't like the sound of it.

"*How* bad?"

Jeffrey doesn't answer. He grits his teeth.

12

Anthony is in the back room of the house. He lies on the bed, his head wrapped in bandages, a cast on his left arm. Sylvia is with him, sitting on a chair by the side of the bed, tending to him. She presses a moist towel to his face, rests it on his forehead. Anthony is unconscious. He whimpers in his sleep.

"Jesus," Tom says, looking down at his brother.

Sylvia stands when she realizes they have entered the room. She leaves her post, comes over and embraces Tom. "It's good to see you," she says. "How've you been?"

"Better than Anthony," Tom says, unable to take his eyes from him.

"He'll pull through," she says. "He's got a fever right now, but it'll break."

"He looks like he ought to be in a hospital."

"He *should*," Jeffrey says.

Tom turns back to him. "Then why ain't he?"

Jeffrey and Sylvia exchange a look.

"You ain't told him yet?" Sylvia says.

"It's a short drive from the entrance to here," Jeffrey says. "Ain't like I had the time."

Sylvia returns to the chair, the bed, her moist cloth. Jeffrey beckons Tom to join him outside the room, where they can talk.

"He's got a broken arm and a fractured skull," he says, by way of beginning. "The skull's got him knocked out, like he can't focus. Says he can barely see, when he ain't sleeping."

"Then why ain't he in the hospital?" Tom says.

"I'm getting to it," Jeffrey says. He motions for Tom to take a chair, but Tom doesn't want to sit. He was sitting a long damn time to get here. He remains standing.

"Suit yourself," Jeffrey says, then lowers himself into a wooden chair. The house is made of wood, with corrugated steel on the roof. All the furniture in the house is made of wood, too.

"One morning I wake up, and there's a box on my doorstep," Jeffrey says. Tom folds his arms, listens. "I open the box, and you know what I find inside? A phone. I pick it up, and before I can even tell Sylvia what it is, it starts ringing. So I answer, and there's this voice on the other end, a voice I don't recognize, telling me that Anthony is in danger, that he's in hospital, that he's a sitting duck. I try to interrupt, try to ask questions, but the voice just keeps going, like it's sticking to a schedule. It tells me which hospital he's in – all the way in Texas – and then it tells me, *If they find him, they'll kill him.*"

"You don't know who it was?"

"Not a damn clue. Anyway, I try to call Anthony. I don't get any answer. I don't hang around. I haul ass down to Texas, to the hospital the voice told me. Sure enough, Anthony is there. Told me he'd been in a car crash. A bad one. I check him out, bring him back here with me. While I was gone, Sylvia told the commune about the phone, how it got here. How someone must've snuck in during the night, past the guards, and left the box there for me to find. The folks around here, they weren't happy about that, that someone got in undetected. They ramped up security. By the time I got back, the commune had become what you see now. We're still on high alert."

"Who's Anthony at risk from?"

"I don't know."

"Your caller didn't say?"

"No."

"What about Anthony?"

"He's only said one thing since I got him here."

"What's that?"

"*Where's Alejandra?* Same thing you asked me on the phone, ain't it?"

Tom feels everything begin to spin. His feet sink into the ground, a hole opening up beneath him. He grits his teeth. "And? Where is she?"

Jeffrey holds out his hands. "I don't know who Alejandra *is*."

"What're you talking about?"

"Well? What is she? A friend? A girlfriend? A fiancée? A *wife*? The two of you go off and do your own thing, and I hear from you every couple of years if I'm lucky. If *you* were with someone, would you have gone out of your way to tell me? No, you wouldn't. You think Anthony's any different?"

"Alejandra is his girlfriend," Tom says, speaking slowly. "And she's pregnant. We need to know that she's safe."

Jeffrey is silenced by this. He thinks on it for a while, until the only thing he's able to say is, "Well, shit."

"Yeah," Tom says. "*Shit.*"

"He never brought her around here," Jeffrey says. "I never met her."

Tom chews on his lip, worried. More worried now than he was when in the car driving here. "We need to ask him," he says. "We need to wake Anthony up and ask him."

Sylvia enters the room at this point, closing the door behind her. "You'll have a hell of a lot of trouble doing that," she says. "He's pumped full of painkillers, gonna be out a few hours yet."

Tom clenches his fists down by his sides, impatient, but there's nothing he can do about this. He exchanges a look with his father. Jeffrey doesn't say anything about Alejandra to her, doesn't tell her it looks like they're going to be grandparents and this is the first they're hearing of it.

"You want something to eat while you wait?" Sylvia says.

"No, thank you," Tom says. He goes to one of the wooden chairs, takes a seat finally. "I'm just gonna wait for Anthony to wake."

"You sure?" she says. "Must've been a while since you ate last. How long were you driving for?"

Tom wants some more time alone with his father. Sylvia will be in the kitchen, away from them. "Sure," he says. "If it's no bother."

"No bother at all," she says, smiling, leaving the room once again.

Tom turns to Jeffrey. "The phone you were contacted on – you still got it?"

"I do."

"Go get it for me, will you?"

"It's just a burner," Jeffrey says. "You ain't gonna be able to get anything from it. I already looked. Doesn't have any numbers in it, not even the one that called me – it was screened."

"Bring it anyway," Tom says.

"All right, then," Jeffrey says, getting to his feet. "But brace yourself for disappointment. There's nothin' to be found on it."

He leaves the room, and for the first time since he arrived at the commune, Tom is alone again. His thoughts return, his worries, his concerns. Now, with Alejandra nowhere in sight, and Anthony asking for her, they are amplified. They are worse than they ever were.

He needs Anthony to wake up.

13

B en can't sleep.
It's late, but instead of lying in bed staring at the ceiling, he's downstairs, in the dark, staring at the walls.

He's also on the phone.

Gerry called him, interrupting his thoughtful reverie, to tell him he's been working late on the laptop.

"You're still at the office?" Ben says.

"No," Gerry says. "I'm at home. I took it with me, to get at it with some of my more ... shall we say, *specialist* hard- and software?"

"And?" Ben says, clutching the phone tight.

"Nothing."

Ben isn't sure he's heard him right. "What was that?"

"Nothing," Gerry says. "I've been at this thing for hours, man, and there's no sign who – if anyone – has hacked it. Looks like the only person who's ever accessed it is you."

Ben isn't happy with this. "You sure about that?"

"There's nothing on here that shouldn't be. No spyware, no malware, nothing like that. It's clean, to be perfectly honest with you."

"I highly doubt a bunch of backwoods hillbilly Nazis have the technology or the smarts sophisticated enough to leave zero trace," Ben says. "There has to be a trail. There has to be *something*."

"I've been thorough, man."

Ben is silent for a moment, thinking. "That's not good enough," he says. "There can't be nothing."

"Maybe it had nothing to do with you, Ben," Gerry says. "Maybe they found out their information another way."

"That's impossible. I already told you how."

"But how can you be so sure maybe Anthony wasn't talking to somebody else? Another agent?"

"I don't know that, but I don't think he's the kind of guy with loose lips. He wasn't gonna take that kind of risk, not with his own safety, or –" He stops himself, thinking of Alejandra. "What I *do* know is that his details were on my laptop. Everything was on there, and my best guess, my *only* guess, is they got hold of it. I want to know how, and I want to know *who*."

"I've done all I can, Ben."

"Then do more."

"I don't see how that's possible. I've come at it with everything I've got."

"Then find a way. Find more ways. Get at it again tomorrow. There has to be something you missed."

Gerry doesn't say anything.

"Are you there?"

"Yeah, I'm here," he says, his voice quiet.

"Did you hear what I said?"

"I heard you."

"Good." Ben tries to soften his tone. "This is important, Gerry."

"I understand that."

Ben sighs. "I'll see you in the morning." He hangs up the phone.

He doesn't move from the couch. Remains where he's sitting, presses the phone into his forehead, his hands clasped in front of his face.

He thinks of Anthony. Of Alejandra. He blames himself. It's his fault. There's no one else to blame. He has to atone for this. To make right what he has caused. He just doesn't know how to start. Can't find the beginning. It was all hinging on his laptop, on the truths held therein.

And now Gerry is telling him it holds no truths.

This isn't acceptable. Ben needs answers.

There are footsteps on the stairs. He looks up. Carly comes down. She wears one of his shirts. Her usually perfect hair is spread out and matted where she has been sleeping on it. "Ben?" she says. Her voice croaks, thick with sleep.

"Hey."

"What're you doing still up?" she says. "Why are you sitting in the dark?"

"It's nothing," he says. "I just couldn't sleep is all. Go on back to bed, Carly. I'll be up in a minute."

She comes to the bottom of the stairs, looks at him. "You want me to sit with you? I don't mind."

He smiles at her, shakes his head, though he's not sure she can see this gesture. "That's all right. But thanks."

Carly goes back up the stairs, returns to his room. He doesn't watch her go. His eyes return to the wall. He can't sleep. He doesn't deserve sleep. Doesn't deserve anything good. Earlier, after dinner, when Carly tried to initiate sex, he couldn't. Physically and mentally could not participate. He apologized. She kissed him on the cheek and said it was fine.

So as not to make her worry further, he goes upstairs to the bedroom. She's already fast asleep by the time he gets there. He slides into the bed next to her, lies flat on his back, and stares at the ceiling.

14

Tom stands out on his father's porch. It's dark out. Jeffrey and Sylvia are inside, sleeping. Tom looks beyond the hastily erected chain-link fence to the trees. There's a breeze. The branches sway in it. There are men in the trees, too. From the commune. To an uneducated eye, they would be invisible in their camo and their face paint, but Tom can pick them out. He counts three, spread out in the area he can see. They've seen him, too. Tom waved, and they retreated deeper into the trees, where they thought they would be out of sight.

There are sentries patrolling the grounds beyond the fence, too. They clutch their guns and look stern, taking their jobs very seriously. Tom has recognized one of them as the man he earlier choked at the gate to the commune. He saw Tom on his first loop around, quickly looked away, hurried past. Every subsequent time he's come around, he's wearing his best war face, almost snarling, staring straight ahead. Tom can't help grinning to himself.

He'd asked his father, earlier, if they'd thought about just upping and moving the commune.

Jeffrey rolled his eyes. "You'd think so," he said. "But no, they wanna stay here, stand their ground, show they ain't afraid to fight, no matter who knows they're here. You know what these guys are like. They wanna play soldier."

Tom turns away from the trees, distracted by the men there. He looks away, to the side, to the woodland further off, where his eyes can't strain to pick out the men, if any, who are there.

He thinks about Alejandra.

The first time he met her.

He was still in the army back then. Back from his first tour of Afghanistan. He hadn't yet been recruited into the CIA, hadn't been disillusioned by the things he saw whilst running black ops missions around the world, though usually in the Middle East.

By that time, too, his father had married Sylvia, moved here. Tom had no fixed address. Overseas most of the time, and unmarried, single, no kids, he saw no need for maintaining a home. He stayed with either his father or his brother, or checked into motels or hotels. On this occasion, he was staying with Anthony, down in Harrow, Texas.

One night, while Anthony was doing whatever it was he was doing (Tom knew it was better not to ask), Tom went to a bar. He found a quiet place playing country music as he walked in. Johnny Cash first, then Merle Haggard. Tom's taste in music was broad. He'd have preferred Springsteen, but he didn't mind some country. He took a stool and was promptly served by the pretty young waitress behind the bar.

"What can I get for you?" she said.

What caught Tom's attention first were her eyes. Big, round, brown, like something out of a cartoon. They stunned him for a moment, took his breath away, almost took him too long to answer. "Just a soda," he said.

She cocked an eyebrow. "That all?"

"All I'm in the mood for." He smiled.

She shrugged, got him his drink.

Tom watched her. Couldn't take his eyes away. Her black hair was tied back, showed every angle of her face. Her cheekbones, her delicate jawline. She poured the soda into a glass with ice, slid it across to him. "You take it easy," she said. "Go slow with those things. I don't wanna have to call for the doorman." She spoke with an accent.

"I'll do my best," Tom said. "Say, where you from?"

"What do you mean?"

"Your voice, I notice you've got an accent."

She stiffened.

"I'm gonna guess Mexican, right?"

"What's it to you?" Her big round eyes blazed; she was suddenly defensive.

Tom stayed cool, undeterred, could guess at her reaction. Looking like she did, sounding how she did, she probably got this kind of question a lot, and likely not from people speaking with genuine interest and curiosity like himself. "Just asking," he said. "It sounds familiar is all."

She remained standoffish, but he thought he saw her soften somewhat. "You go to Mexico a lot?"

"I get around," he said.

"Guaymas?"

"Can't say I've been to that part."

"That's where I'm from," she said, softening more, but not completely, a conversational tone in her voice.

"So what brings you up here?" he said.

She remained wary. "Why do you ask?"

"I told you, I'm just asking. I'm curious. I'm making conversation. I'm on leave, I come to a bar, I see a pretty girl serving, and I figure I'll talk to her."

"Leave?" She spoke fast, disguising her blush. "Are you in the army?"

"Yeah," he said.

"How is it?"

He shrugged. "It is what it is," he said, not wanting to share stories of shooting, and being shot at, and worse.

"I've been in America a year," she said, finally.

"A year, huh? Well, that explains how you speak such good English."

"I practiced before I came, and I've practiced since."

"What brought you up here?"

"I have an aunt lives here."

"You still got family back in Guaymas?"

She hesitated, then shook her head. "No," she said. There was a sadness about her suddenly.

Tom picked up on it. "I'm sorry," he said. "I didn't mean to pry."

"My parents died," she said. "That's why I came here. I had nowhere else to go."

"I'm so sorry."

"It was nobody's fault," she said. "It was an accident. A stupid accident."

"What happened? You don't have to say if you don't want to."

She shook her head, like it was fine; she could tell the tale. "A car crash. They had come here, to visit my aunt, my father's sister. They were on their way home, they'd been driving for a very long time, and my father, he ... he fell asleep at the wheel."

"I'm sorry," Tom said again.

She waved her hands like she felt foolish. "Why am I telling you this?" She laughed. "I just met you. We've been talking for, what, five minutes, maybe?"

Tom smiled at her. "I'd like to talk for more."

"I have to work. People will get annoyed if I'm giving one customer all the attention instead of filling their drinks."

"All right, then. What time do you finish?"

She chewed her lip. "I don't even know your name."

"It's Tom," he said. "Tom Rollins. You?"

It took her a moment. She looked along the counter, saw a man approach, empty glass in hand, looking for a refresh. "Alejandra Flores," she said. "People call me Ally."

"I think I'll call you Alejandra," Tom said. "Because Alejandra Flores is the most beautiful name I've ever heard."

She hurried off to serve the approaching customer before she had a chance to blush again.

Tom hung around until midnight, until the bar closed and Alejandra was finished work. He stood with her outside while she locked up. "There isn't much to do, I'm afraid," she said. "Most places are closed by now."

"Then I'll walk you home," Tom said. "Or close enough to it if you don't want me to know where you live."

"My aunt warned me I shouldn't walk with strange men I only just met."

"I can understand that."

"Maybe I'm being stupid."

"If you think this is a bad idea, then just say so. I'll walk away right now, no hard feelings. I'd rather you felt comfortable with me than full of worry every single step of the way."

She looked at him for a long time. She looked straight into his eyes. Finally, she shook her head, said, "No, it's okay, come on. Let's walk."

She led the way, and Tom matched her stride. She didn't head straight home. They walked for what felt like miles around the town of Harrow, just talking, smiling, laughing.

By the end of the night, as Tom left her at the end of the walkway leading to her front door, her aunt twitching the curtains, watching them, Tom knew he was in love.

Now, in the present, he doesn't even know where she is. Doesn't know if she's all right. There is a pain in his heart, a stabbing sensation.

He knows.

He knows that something bad has happened.

Standing, he goes back inside the house, stepping lightly, his footsteps silent. Goes through to Anthony's room. He's still sleeping. Tom takes a seat in the chair by the side of the bed, watches him. Anthony's breathing is ragged. He moans, turns to and fro.

Tom spent the rest of his leave with Alejandra. He'd visit her at the bar. He'd walk with her. He'd learn of her life, of what made her happy, of what she liked and disliked, what she loved. Of how she missed Mexico, Guaymas, how she wanted to go back, how she couldn't imagine living the rest of her life without seeing her home again.

"This is where I live now," she said. "But it's not really my home. It can't be."

His final night, before he was due to ship out again in the morning, he walked her home, and he kissed her on her aunt's porch. It was the sweetest kiss he'd ever had. Even now, he can feel the brush of her lips against his own, the way her tongue probed gently at his.

By the time he returned from his second tour, she was dating Anthony.

15

Senator Seth Goldberg gets out of the shower, dries and combs his hair, gets dressed and goes downstairs. It is Saturday morning. His wife, Abigail, and his daughters are in the kitchen. Abigail sits at the table, reading a book. She looks up as he enters, smiles, marks her place, puts her book to one side. The girls are in the corner of the room, looking out the French doors at the sunny day.

"Girls," Abigail says, "breakfast."

Danielle is six; Deborah is eight. They leave the window, come to their father, say good morning to him, hug him, kiss his cheeks. They all sit together at the table. Seth wears a black suit. Abigail wears a sky blue dress, Seth's favorite. She looks very pretty in it, like she's a young woman again, in college, when they first met. The girls are in matching peach-colored dresses. "You both look very beautiful this morning," Seth says, leaning down close to first Deborah and then Danielle. Danielle giggles.

"What about Mom?" Deborah says. "Doesn't she look beautiful?"

"Always," Seth says, smiling at Abigail over the top of the table. "She's always the most beautiful woman in all the world."

Deborah turns to Abigail now. "Do you think Daddy is beautiful?" she says.

Abigail laughs. "Of course!" she says. "But I think he's more handsome than beautiful."

Deborah looks like she isn't sure what to make of this. She turns back to Seth, contemplates for a moment, then says, "*I* think you're beautiful, Daddy."

Not to be left out, Danielle is quick to say, "I do too, Daddy."

Seth looks at his wife. "There we have it," he says to her. "You've been outvoted. Turns out I am a *very* beautiful man."

"Then I must be a *very* lucky lady," Abigail says.

They eat bread for breakfast. The girls lean forward over their plates, are especially careful not to get crumbs on their clean clothes. Deborah is more successful than her little sister. When they are done, Danielle has crumbs around her mouth, a few in her hair. Seth takes a napkin from the pile they keep in the center of the table for just such an occurrence, and he wipes her face down, picks the debris from her hair.

"Are we ready to go?" Abigail says.

"If we have to," Deborah says.

"Yes," Seth says, smiling. "We do have to. You'll like it one day."

Deborah blows air out of her pursed lips. She doubts this.

They leave the house. There are agents outside,

guarding them. Seth notices, as he and Abigail strap their children into their seats, how the bodyguards speak into their wrists, alerting others to his whereabouts, preparing for his departure.

There have been death threats since the introduction of Seth's clean energy bill. As it makes its way through Congress, these threats have intensified. Seth wouldn't mind so much, he could shrug them off, knowing they come with the territory. He knew when he started this thing that he was going to upset a lot of people. What perturbs him, however, are the threats against his family. Against his *daughters*. The things they say they're going to do to his wife and a pair of little girls. The threats that mean his children must now be accompanied by Secret Service agents when they go to school. The threats that mean his wife can never be left alone in the house. That mean they are trailed at all times.

This is what he has trouble with.

But, as Abigail has told him, "Stay the course. You knew this was going to be difficult. You can't give up now."

"But you and the girls –"

"Are all very proud of you. This thing that you're trying to do is bigger than us, than all of us. Keep going."

Parked across the street are reporters. They observe every move of Seth and his family, report on the taking out of trash as if it's a major world development. The reporters don't come any closer, though. They've been warned, sternly. They will, however, follow him to synagogue.

One agent car leads the way; the other follows, the Goldbergs sandwiched in the middle. They arrive early for Shabbat morning service. There is a gathering outside the synagogue already, people exchanging greetings before they go in for worship.

"This crowd gets bigger every week," Abigail says.

Seth concentrates on parking the car, doesn't answer.

He knows what she's implying. As his bill gains more momentum, more and more people turn up to the synagogue, all of them eager for a glimpse or a word. On the plus side, they've all been supportive.

They approach on foot, agents at their flank and sides. Abigail holds the hands of both children, as she knows Seth will need to keep his free. Sure enough, as they get close enough, there is a lot of shaking of hands, patting of backs. People express their support for him, how proud they are of him for taking a stand against big business. The Secret Service agents stand close by, watching the people, keeping some at bay, all the while trying to usher Seth and his family inside.

This is the routine every Saturday morning. This is where they come. This is where they worship. This is where they can be found.

Senator Seth Goldberg and his family.

This synagogue.

Every week.

Every Saturday morning.

16

I t's dawn. Anthony is awake. Tom hasn't slept.

Tom brings him some water and painkillers. It is more obvious now, as he moves around, how badly damaged his face is, as well as his skull and his arm. It is badly cut and bruised. These wounds were not so clear when he was sleeping, as if every little cut had settled into his features, become part of them. Now, when he moves, they crack, they bleed.

"Where's Alejandra?" Tom says.

Anthony shoots him a look, eyes blazing.

Tom grits his teeth, knowing he shouldn't have opened with this. "How you doing?" he says, sitting down.

Anthony pops the pills into his mouth with his good hand, the glass of water balancing on the mattress and leaning against his belly, then takes a drink. He doesn't drink much. He pulls his face like he feels sick, like he might throw up. "How's it look?" he says.

"Bad."

"Then you have your answer."

Anthony lies back, flat, lets out a long breath. He sounds tired despite his constant flitting in and out of consciousness. He tries to move his left arm in its cast, winces at it like it's a great weight, gives up.

Tom gives him a moment. He notices how Anthony is not looking at him, almost like he won't. "What happened?" he says.

Anthony doesn't answer. He shifts around on the bed, unable to get comfortable. "Jesus, everything hurts," he says. "And I feel like I'm gonna throw up all the damn time." There is a bucket at the side of the bed. There is a little bit of spit and bile at the bottom of it.

"You've got a fractured skull," Tom says.

"You think I don't know that?" Anthony still isn't looking at him. His face is turned toward the ceiling; his eyes have closed.

"What were you involved in, Anthony?" Tom says.

Anthony doesn't answer.

"Who did this to you?"

He doesn't answer.

Tom waits. He's patient. He's waited this long just for him to wake up.

Anthony lies very still. Tom wonders if he's feigning sleep. He's not very good at it. The way his face and his body twitch, it's clear he wants to move, that he's not comfortable, that he's in pain.

"Look at me, Anthony," Tom says.

Anthony opens one eye hooded by a bandage.

"What happened?"

"That's my business," Anthony says.

"Then color me curious," Tom says.

"I'm not gonna color you anything."

"Were you dealing again?"

There is a slight hesitation; then Anthony says, "No."

Tom doesn't believe him. "Bullshit. Is that who did this to you? You owe money? You were robbed? What is it?"

"That what you think of me, huh?" Anthony says.

"It's what I know," Tom says. "From past experience."

"*Past* experience. You got it all wrong. You don't know a damn thing going on here. You don't know a damn thing about me."

"So tell me."

"*No*. I don't want you to fight my battle for me, Tom. Not this time. All my life, you've fought my battles. Every single issue I've gotten myself into, you've pulled me out. Not this time. This time's mine. I have to deal with this myself."

"At least tell me what the battle *is*."

Anthony says nothing.

"You're in no condition, Anthony. You won't be for a while. By the time you're ready to go after them, whoever they are, they're gonna be ready for *you*. What's to say they haven't already gone to ground, disappeared – you tell me now, I might still have a chance to find them."

"They won't run away. It's not their style. They'll stay right where they are, too proud to go anywhere else."

"So tell me who they are before I go and find out for myself."

"This is *my* battle. I ain't telling you again."

"I can go to Harrow, Anthony. I can ask around. You might even have made the news. It'll give me clues, leads. I'll tear the town apart if I have to. It's easier if you just tell me."

"I'm not interested in you doing it the hard way *or* the easy way. I don't want you to do it at all." Anthony is adamant. "This is *mine*. Can't you understand it? Damn it, get it through your fucking skull – I don't want your help!" Anthony is working himself up; he's shouting.

Tom hears Jeffrey and Sylvia in the next room, standing, coming closer to the door, listening in case they need to interject.

Tom is getting annoyed now, too. "Where is Alejandra?" he says. "I can get her. I can keep her safe from whatever mess you've gotten yourself into. You know I can. Tell me where she is."

All the fight goes out of Anthony. He deflates. He falls back. His eyes fill with tears.

Tom feels sick. He grits his teeth. "Where is Alejandra?" There is no response. "*Where is Alejandra?*" He's shouting now, wants to grab his brother by the shoulders, to *make* him tell him.

Anthony looks at Tom. The tears roll down his cheeks now. When he speaks, it isn't with aggression. He doesn't raise his voice. If anything, he sounds surprised Tom doesn't already know. "She's dead."

Tom reels. He falls back in the chair. Flashes of memory run through his head. Her face. Her laughter. When they kissed. Her smile. She's looking at him, and she's smiling.

His hand goes to his pocket, searches out the Santa Muerte pendant. He squeezes it so tight, it feels like it breaks the skin of his palm.

Anthony says something, but Tom doesn't hear what it is. His mind is still racing. It is still filled with thoughts of Alejandra, with his feelings for her. His chest is tight.

But now he knows, now he is certain, he cannot allow Anthony to deal with this himself. Whatever has happened, it involves him now, and he is not willing to wait for his brother to heal.

Tom stops.

All this thinking isn't getting him anywhere. He can mourn later. Now, he needs to be practical.

He takes a breath.

Stares at the wall, through the wall, into the distance. Focuses himself.

He looks at Anthony, studies him. Cool and detached, all business. "This is the last time I'm going to ask you," he says. "Tell me what happened."

"This is my fight," Anthony says.

Tom exhales through his nose. "You said earlier you weren't dealing, but you were lying," Tom says, going through what he has surmised thus far. "But I don't think you were doing so voluntarily. When you were with Alejandra, I believed that you'd left all that behind you. And once she was pregnant, I didn't think that was a life-style you'd ever consider going back to. Unless you didn't have a choice."

He watches his brother's face closely. Anthony tries not to give anything away, but there are uncontrollable tics and twitches under the skin that Tom watches for. "Stop trying to interrogate me, Tom," he says. "It ain't gonna work. I ain't gonna tell you a thing you wanna know."

"How did Alejandra die? In the crash?"

A tic, by the right eye. A flash of unwanted memory.

Tom considers this. "Or was it something else? Was someone else there?"

Tic.

"Who was it?"

No answer.

"Did they kill Alejandra?"

Anthony's eyes can't hide it this time. More unwanted memories. They blaze.

"They were there," Tom says. "At the scene. They caused the crash, and they killed Alejandra, but they didn't kill you. Why not?"

Tom waits, lets his words do their work. "Did they have bigger plans for you? What, torture? They wanted to make an example?"

Anthony chews his lip.

"And then, while you're in hospital, you're still at risk. So much so that someone has to sneak into the commune, leave a phone so they can get in touch with Dad, tell him that you need to be moved. The commune wasn't as heavily guarded then as it is now, but it was still guarded. You know what these people are like, how seriously they take all this. Hell, we were raised by one of them. But whoever this anonymous caller was, they were able to get in and out without being seen. And the way Dad tells it, they rang that burner phone the moment he opened the box and found it.

"So that tells me whatever is going on, whoever got in touch with you has funding, technology, and the skills to get into places where others ordinarily can't." Tom leans forward, counts off the points on his fingers. "And it sounds like they had a vested interest in keeping you alive. Or else they felt guilty." He watches Anthony's face closer now, watching for any reaction, no matter how small, as he prepares to show his card. "Were you undercover?"

There is a twitch, a small one, in Anthony's bruised cheek.

"Who were you undercover with?" Tom says. "Who for? Who was your handler?"

Anthony looks pissed. Won't answer.

"I imagine he's the one who left the phone, made the

call. What happened, Anthony? Speak to me. How did you get yourself into that situation? What was your objective?"

"Stop," Anthony says. He stares at him, hard. "Leave it alone. I don't want you to do this for me. This is for me, Tom. *Me*. I will deal with this. When I can. I *have* to."

Tom gets to his feet.

"Tom," Anthony says.

Tom promises nothing. He leaves the room.

Anthony calls after him, shouts his name, demands that he come back.

Jeffrey and Sylvia wait for him outside the room. They have been listening in, as he thought. Sylvia's face is ashen. Jeffrey's is hard. "What are you going to do?" he says after Tom has closed the door.

Anthony is shouting, still trapped in his bed. "Tom! Tom, get back here, damn it!"

Jeffrey speaks to Sylvia. "Go make sure he doesn't hurt himself."

She nods, slides past Tom into the room, goes to Anthony, tries to calm him.

Tom and Jeffrey walk away from the door, from the shouting. "I'm going to find the people responsible," Tom says, "and I'm going to kill them."

"How you going to do that?" Jeffrey says. "He wouldn't tell you anything."

"He told me enough." He pulls the phone Jeffrey gave him out of his pocket, holds it up. "As for the rest, I'll find a way."

Jeffrey looks at the phone, raises a doubtful eyebrow. "I hope you do. When are you leaving?"

"Now. But I'm gonna need some things first. Equipment. Weaponry."

Jeffrey nods. "You know I can supply."

17

T om is back on the road in an hour. He drives to the nearest town, still adhering to the speed limit, but wanting to go faster. He pulls over at the first pay phone he spots, gets out of the car and goes to it. The area is clear, no one to overhear. It's still early enough in the morning that the sidewalks and the road are quiet. Some of the stores haven't yet opened.

He slides in some coins, calls Zeke Greene.

Zeke is at home. "Hello?" He sounds confused, no doubt wondering whose number this is, possibly recognizing the area code.

Tom doesn't waste any time. "It's Rollins."

"Tom? Holy shit, man," Zeke says. "We shouldn't be talking. You're a wanted man."

"I'll make it quick." In the past, Zeke has told Tom about his cousin. His cousin spends all his time locked away in his room, designing websites, or wasting time on message boards, in chatrooms. And he hacks. "I need to know if your cousin has any contacts in either New Mexico or Texas. They'll have to be on a similar skill level as himself, or better."

"I can ask him," Zeke says, not asking him why or what for. Zeke trusts him, his judgement in whatever he is doing, and he knows Tom trusts him, too. If he didn't, he wouldn't have called.

"Call me back on this number," Tom says. "I'll wait by this phone for twenty minutes; then I'm gone."

"I wouldn't do you like that, Tom," Zeke says.

"I know you wouldn't. You're not the problem."

He hangs up. He checks the time, then gets back in his car. Sits with the window down so he can hear all the better. He watches the street before him, this main stretch of road as it slowly comes to life. As people go into the diner for breakfast, as people cross over to get from one store to another. Cars begin to roll by. A worker comes out of the hardware store, goes two buildings down into the bank.

Tom keeps one eye on his watch. It's closing in on twenty minutes. His fingers are on the ignition as it hits exactly twenty, but before he can turn it, the pay phone begins to ring.

"I'm here," Tom says.

"Sorry it took so long," Zeke says. "He was searching."

"He get anyone?"

"Only one good enough, like you asked for. They're in Texas. I got a number here. You ready for it?"

Tom has one of the burner phones from his bag at the ready. "Go." Zeke reads it out. Tom punches it into the contacts.

"When you call, he says to tell them you're a friend of Dark Claw 89." His cousin, he meant. "You got that? They won't talk about whatever it is you wanna talk about if you don't. So maybe open with that."

"Got it. Thank you, Zeke."

"Don't mention it, man. Good luck."

Tom hangs up, gets back in the car, and leaves the small town.

He's going to Texas.

18

Ben sleeps. Carly isn't surprised. He was tossing and turning all night, struggling to settle. She leans over from her side of the bed, checks he's out. "Ben?" He doesn't stir. He breathes softly. His eyes are closed tight, his brow furrowed.

Carly leaves the bedroom on light feet, creeps down the stairs. Her jacket hangs from a hook by the door. She goes into the pockets, pulls out her cigarettes and her phone. Heading for the back door, she pauses at the foot of the stairs, listens again. Ben is not moving around, is still asleep. Carly goes out back, lights a cigarette. The early morning air is cool against her bare legs. She ignores it.

Phone in hand, she dials a number. The door is closed behind her, but she glances back through the glass, watching the foot of the stairs.

The cigarette is an excuse. She came out here to make a call. A man answers. He doesn't bother with pleasantries, gets straight to business. Knows that Carly cannot talk for long. "What do you have?"

"He was on the phone last night, just after midnight," she says. "He was talking to one of the analysts."

"Which one?"

"I don't know. If he said the name, I didn't hear it."

"What *did* you hear?"

"That whoever it is, he doesn't have anything. Can't find a thing."

"Anything in the house?"

She blows smoke. "Nothing. I've looked around. He's not getting close, nowhere near."

"Let's keep it that way."

Carly grunts. She watches the stairs, antsy.

"What about the survivor?"

"Anthony?" she says.

"He was the only survivor."

"He was off the books. Ben got him on drug dealing. He got a notification from a station in Harrow, strong-armed him into going undercover, or else he was facing a lengthy prison sentence. It wasn't his first strike, and he had a pregnant girlfriend. So he took the offer. Didn't exactly have a choice."

"The dead Mexican?"

"That's her."

"Did Anthony find anything?"

"It doesn't look like it."

"Be sure."

"I will."

"We're too close now for this to get fucked up, is that clear?"

"I've got it."

"We're nearly done here. One last thing."

"Shoot. Fast. I gotta go. He could wake up."

"Eric has a task for you."

"Oh?" Carly takes a draw to disguise the shake in her voice. This is unexpected.

"He's in Fort Worth. He wants you to go to him."

"Send me the details. I've gotta go now. I've been out here too long."

She hangs up. The cigarette is barely smoked, still more than half left, but she stubs it out, flicks it to one side, then goes back inside. Her phone buzzes in her hand. It is the details, how to reach Eric. She hits 'Mark As Read' so it doesn't show up on her screen, slips her phone and her pack of cigarettes back into her jacket pockets, then tiptoes back upstairs.

Ben is still sleeping. Carly is relieved to see this. She brushes her teeth, gargles mouthwash, then goes to wake him up.

19

Michael calls Harry around, to his home. Harry comes to the back door. "Let me take a guess what this is about," he says.

"You'd probably be right," Michael says.

They're in the kitchen, take a seat at the table. Linda is already there. "You all right, Harry?"

"I'm good," he says, leaning down, an arm around her, to kiss her on the cheek.

"How's your girlfriend?" Linda says as he straightens back up.

Harry rolls his eyes, takes a seat. "Jesus Christ, I guess that depends on the day of the week."

"We can talk personal lives later," Michael says. "I didn't call you here for pleasantries. We gotta talk business."

Harry nods, serious. "The phone calls."

Michael nods back, solemn. "The calls that saved that motherfucker's life."

"You should've taken his phone," Linda says.

"Could've looked for yourselves."

"Didn't foresee this as being the situation," Michael says. "Thought we were gonna torture and waste the son of a bitch on the night. How we supposed to know someone was gonna tip him off?"

"All we know for certain," Harry says, "is it wasn't anyone present." He circles his finger in the air, indicating the three of them sitting at the table.

Michael and Harry are lifelong friends. They trust each other, perhaps more than Michael trusts Linda. They love each other. They're like brothers. They each know how the other thinks. Michael cannot conceive of Harry betraying him, and he knows that Harry feels the same.

"Ronald was with us when we found out about Anthony," Michael says. "Plus, he's old school as all hell. He wouldn't do it."

Harry nods along with this. "Peter wasn't with us when the call came through."

"Peter ain't said where he was. You ask at the bar?"

"Yeah," Harry says. "And I was subtle about it. He wasn't there."

"Unless he was with a girl, only other place he would be is with his brother."

"Bingo," Harry says.

"You think it was his brother?" Linda says.

"It's looking that way," Michael says. He turns back to Harry, "Only thing is, you saw the look on Peter's face. You know as soon as he left here after the last time, he went straight to see Steve. He would've questioned him."

"I'm sure, but would he give him up?" Harry says.

"If Peter knew for certain? Yeah, I think he would, for sure. Peter's loyalty is to us, it's to our cause. It ain't to his blood, especially not if his kin is a goddamn traitor."

"You think that was his real name?" Harry says suddenly. "*Anthony*?"

"That's what the chick told us it was," Michael says. "But who the hell knows? Maybe she just said it that way 'cause she knew that's what we'd be familiar with."

"Yeah, well, whatever his name was, Anthony spent most of his time with Steve."

"Dealing?" Linda says.

"Yeah," Michael says. "Someone joins our ranks, they don't just shoot straight to the top. They work their way up."

"He seemed awful eager to climb fast, though," Harry says.

"Mm." Michael grunts, nods, remembering. "Didn't think anything of it at the time. He was always asking questions. Just thought he was passionate about it all."

"Me too, man," Harry says, "me too. Son of a bitch fooled us all."

Michael puts his elbows on the table. "But did he fool Steve? Did Steve know – that's the damn question. The two of them spent a hell of a lot of time together. They got friendly. Maybe Steve already knew Anthony was a rat, and he was keeping his secret. Hell, he could've known he was involved with a spic, too, for all we know."

"Steve's heart ain't ever been in this life," Harry says, "not really. Never has been. He only sticks around 'cause his brother makes him. Could've been he was helping Anthony out, feeding him information, on the promise that Anthony would help him get out, get him a new life with his buddies in the FBI, get him into the program. We hadn't got Anthony when we did, we could be looking at a court date sometime in our near future, and who's that in the witness box? Skinny Steve Reid."

The three are silent then, considering this.

Michael is the one to break it, saying what they all know to be true. "If Steve's responsible – if he knew, if he made those calls, however far his complicity in it might go – then we're gonna have to do somethin' about it. Somethin' about him."

"It's gonna break Peter's heart," Harry says.

"Peter's gonna have to walk away from it," Michael says. "Ain't like we'd ask him to do it his own self. No, I wouldn't ask him to get his brother's blood on his hands like that, even if he is the race traitor who got us into this mess."

A silence falls again, each of them contemplating their next move and the circumstances that brought them to this instance.

It is Linda who breaks the silence this time. "One thing that I keep wondering about," she says, "is why he was undercover with y'all in the first place. Like, what was it he was hoping to find out?"

"Drugs," Michael says.

"It's always the drugs," Harry agrees.

"Where they came from, how much we're selling," Michael says. "That's all they care about. And all those other undercovers they got that night, I can guarantee it was the same for all of them."

"Goddamn," Linda says. "Trynna take money outta our pockets."

Michael and Harry both nod along. "They wanna see us starve," Michael says. "But that's just how it is for good, hardworking white Christian men in this country." Linda and Harry mumble their agreement. "It's always been the goddamn same."

20

'S hriek' did not give Tom her real name. However, she did give him her address in Lubbock.

They spoke only briefly on the phone. "I understand you're a friend of Dark Claw 89."

She chuckled. "*Friend* is a strong word. We only know each other from chatrooms. I'm not sure I'd call someone I've never met face to face before a *friend*."

"Do you know who I am?"

"I'm guessing you're the friend of his cousin," she said. "I was told you might call."

"Here I am."

"Here you are."

"What are your rates?"

"It's not exactly by the hour. It'll depend on what you're bringing me, and I only accept cash."

"I've got cash."

"So what is it you need?"

"I'm not gonna discuss it over the phone. It's an in-person deal."

"Fine," she said. She gave the address. "Call me when you're outside the building, I want to get a good look at you first. I like what I see, you can come up. I don't – well, you'd better start running, 'cause I'll be calling the cops to report a prowler."

"I'll keep that in mind."

Now, Tom sits outside the building. He's circled it a couple of times already, checked it out, made sure it's clear. He calls her. "I'm here."

There's a pause; then she says, "Which one are you?"

"I'm in my car." He tells her which one it is.

"Then get out so I can get a good look at you."

Tom has already picked out her window. He gets out of the car, but leaves the door open. If she hangs up without another word, he's straight back inside, he's driving off. He waves.

She doesn't say anything for a while. Tom has to check she's still on the line.

"All right," she says, finally. "I'll buzz the door. Come on up."

Tom makes his way inside the building, takes the stairs up to her floor, wondering what about his appearance has made her let him in. He knocks on her door. He sees her spy hole darken momentarily; then he hears bolts slide, a key turn. The door opens, but it remains on a chain.

"Mr. Rollins," she says. He can only see one blue eye, can't get a good look at her through the narrow gap.

"That's right," Tom says.

She looks him over again, up close now. "All right, then," she says, reaching a decision. The door closes, the chain is slid off, and the door opens again. "Step inside."

"Just out of curiosity," Tom says, getting over the

threshold before he speaks, the door closing behind him. "What do the people look like that you turn away?"

She brushes past him, through into the front room. "It's more of a feeling," she says. "It's never failed me yet."

She takes a seat at her setup. There are three computers. A lot of wiring. A lot of components that Tom does not understand. He gets a good look at her while she's turned away. Her hair is cut short, shaved around the sides and back, bleached blonde and spiky on top. She's wearing a band T-shirt and ripped black jeans, with Doc Marten boots polished to a shine. "Mostly I look out for cops," she says. "I can always tell a cop. Spot them from a mile away."

"They gonna be so bothered if you threaten to report a prowler?"

"You'd be surprised," she says. She looks him over again. "You're military. Ex-military."

Tom doesn't answer, though he's impressed. Instead he looks around for a place to sit. She does not have sofas. There is a folding chair leaning against the wall. He takes it, sets it up, sits.

"Well?" she says when he looks back. "Am I right?"

"I think you already know the answer to that."

She grins to herself, satisfied.

Save for the light coming from the monitors, the room is in darkness. The curtains are all drawn. There are empty Chinese cartons pushed to one side on her desk, an empty pizza box forgotten on the floor. Behind her setup are band posters – Nine Inch Nails, Godflesh, Skinny Puppy, Ministry – and she wears a Fear Factory T-shirt.

"You're getting a good look," she says.

"I've never been in a hacker's home before," Tom says.

"Maybe you have, and you just didn't realize it. They

ain't all the same. You don't know Dark Claw 89 personally?"

"Never met him. What's your real name? I'm not gonna call you 'Shriek' to your face."

She laughs. "Fair enough. It's Cindy."

"Cindy what? You know both of mine."

"Vaughan."

Despite the remnants of junk food lying around, Cindy does not look like this is her sole diet. She's thinner than he expected, a little thinner than she perhaps ought to be. Her skin is pale, porcelain, from the lack of sunlight. He wonders if she ever leaves her apartment, or if she only goes out at night.

"So what have you got for me, Tom Rollins?" she says.

Tom reaches into his pocket, pulls out the burner phone sent to his father. "I have a long shot," he says. "There has been one call made to this phone. I want to know where it came from."

She raises an eyebrow. "On a burner phone?"

"I said it was a long shot."

"And you weren't lying." She reaches out, takes the phone from him. She whistles low. "All right. Sure. Hell, it's a challenge. A new one."

"Ain't something you've had to do before?"

She swivels around, phone in hand. "Not quite. Let's see how this goes, huh?"

"You got an idea of time?"

"Nope." She starts plugging things in, typing.

Tom sits back, folds his arms, doesn't bother watching her work, try to figure out what she's doing. None of it makes any sense to him.

"So who called you?" she says without turning.

"It wasn't to me."

"No? Then why do you care?"

"It concerns me."

She leaves the computer doing something, turns back to him. She studies him again. "Are you AWOL?"

"You *are* good."

"I told you as much. You've got the look – though I'll admit, you don't look as shifty as some of the fugitives I've dealt with."

"You deal with many fugitives?"

"You'd be surprised."

"What do they need from a hacker?"

"Well, I also forge documents." She winks at him.

Tom stores this information away, keeps it in mind.

"What are you running from?"

Tom shrugs. "I saw a lot of things I didn't agree with, and I was the only one who ever seemed to care. Well, me and Dark Claw 89's cousin. I guess he could stomach it more than I could, though. What are you doing there?"

"Tracing the call," she says without looking back. "Searching for pingbacks from cell phone towers. It's gonna take a while. I might have to decipher some noise yet." She looks around the room. "You hungry?"

"I could eat."

"Then go down the block to the deli on the corner and get us a couple of sandwiches. I'll take ham and swiss on rye. Your treat, right?" Her eyes sparkle.

"How could I say no to that smile?" Tom says, getting to his feet.

When he gets back, Cindy is leaning back in her chair, looking very satisfied with herself, victorious. "Found it," she says, holding out her hands.

Tom reaches into the bag, pulls out her wrapped sandwich. He hands it over. "Where is it?"

She tears open the paper, bites into it. "Narrowed it down to a street in Dallas," she says, chewing. "But I can't get a specific house."

"Have you written it down?"

She holds out a piece of paper. "Everything you need."

Tom pays her, then goes to leave.

"You're not gonna eat?" she says as he reaches the door.

"I'll have it in the car," he says.

"Gotta jet, huh?"

He nods.

"I'm sure I'll see you again some time, Tom Rollins." There's a playful tone in her voice, and her eyes are sparkling again.

Tom looks back at her. She swivels side to side in her chair. He winks. "I reckon you just might."

21

The team still need a few items to go with all the fertilizer they currently have. Chuck puts Dix on the case. Sends him out to make some enquiries. Dix is gone a full day and night. When he returns the next morning, he has a seller.

"Russian," he says, talking with Chuck in the back office of the former warehouse they have commandeered. "Goes by the name of Vladimir."

"And he has what we need?" Chuck says, leaning back in an old chair that looks like it might fall apart at any moment, a leftover from when the warehouse was still operational.

"Says he does," Dix says.

The others are killing time throughout the building. Waiting for some action. Al is taking a nap. Jimmy and Pat are playing cards, gambling with bullets.

"You get anything else on him?" Chuck says.

"He asked a lot of questions. Who we were, why we

needed it, but I think he was just busting balls for the most part."

"What'd you tell him?"

"That he didn't need to know. He just laughed at that. He didn't give a shit, not really. Like I say, busting balls."

"You arrange for a buy?"

Dix nods. "Tonight."

Chuck smiles. "Good. The boys will be happy. Give us something to do."

Chuck and Dix will approach the meeting. They'll have the cash. Al, Jimmy, and Pat will be nearby, geared up, ready in case anything goes down.

The meet happens downtown, not far from the warehouse district where they got the fertilizer. Chuck and Dix wear jeans, leather jackets over their T-shirts. Vladimir is dressed in a suit. He hasn't come alone. Flanked by three goons, each one a carbon copy of the others. Big, hooded-brow guys with shaved heads and mean eyes, tattoos on their knuckles, the backs of their hands, and their necks. Vladimir is the only one of them smiling. He's the only one with hair, slicked back. Chuck recognizes his type. An arms dealer, splashing his cash on leather jackets, fancy shirts, rings and necklaces.

"Mr. Dix," he says as they approach, "so good to see you again."

Dix nods. "Vlad."

"You brought a friend," Vlad says, looking Chuck over.

"You brought three," Dix says.

The three men bristle, as if they're supposed to be unseen.

"This is the man you work for, I assume," Vlad says. He holds out his hand.

Chuck takes it, gives his name.

"Chuck," Vlad says, trying it out, grinning at how it feels in his mouth. "Mr. Chuck, you would like to see the goods now, yes?"

"Sooner the better," Chuck says.

Vlad clicks his fingers, says something in Russian. One of his men goes into the car behind them, takes out a bag. Brings it forward, open.

"Feel free to look with your hands as well as your eyes," Vlad says.

Chuck does just that, reaching in and rummaging through. There is a detonator on top. Underneath, there is everything else they need.

The heavy snatches the bag back, steps behind Vlad again.

"To your liking?" Vlad says.

"It's all there," Chuck says.

"Excellent! Now, the cash?"

Dix has their bag. He opens it up, holds it out.

"I will, of course, need to count it," Vlad says.

"Count away," Chuck says.

Vlad motions to another of his goons. He comes forward, takes the bag, steps back. He places it on the ground to count the money. While he does so, Vlad rocks back and forth on his heels, smiling at Chuck all the while.

Finally, the counter stands, bag in hand. He nods at Vlad, then takes another step back.

"Very good, my friends," Vlad says. "It is all there."

Chuck holds out his hand for their bag.

"Not so fast, Mr. Chuck," Vlad says. "It's very clear to me that you are planning on making a bomb. A big one, by the looks of things. Now, call it professional curiosity if you will, but I must ask – why?"

Chuck raises an eyebrow. "You'll have to remain professionally curious."

Vlad's smile never falters. "I hear rumblings, Mr. Chuck. A man in my profession, I have to keep my ear to the ground. And I hear talk of something being planned. An attack, on American soil."

Chuck stays loose, but inside he's on springs, ready to react at a moment's notice. "Oh?"

"Yes, that's correct. I believe the term is *domestic terrorism*. I heard the name Oklahoma City. I think to myself, an attack in Oklahoma, this does not concern me. But again, this professional curiosity, it gets the better of me. So I look up Oklahoma City. And I find out what happened there. I assume you know what happened in Oklahoma City, Mr. Chuck, Mr. Dix?"

Dix nods.

"Of course," Chuck says.

"Mm, yes, I'm sure," Vlad says. "It sounds as if it was a big event. Of course, I was not in America at that time." He shrugs. "How am I to know? I did not concern myself with world affairs, not back then."

"If you have a point to make," Chuck says, "I hope you're gonna get to it soon."

"My point is this – can I allow myself to run the risk of being associated with something as big as Oklahoma City? I don't believe I can."

"What makes you think this new thing has anything to do with us?"

Vlad gives him a look, silently asking him who he thinks he's kidding.

Chuck runs his tongue around the inside of his mouth. "So who was it told you about this prospective attack?"

Vlad waves his hand around in the air. "Oh, you know

how it is. Word gets out in our community; it gets around.
If you're the men who have been hired to carry it out, do
you really believe you would have been the first ones
asked? I doubt it, and I'm sure you do, too. You are simply
the first ones who said yes. The first ones to accept the
money and believe you can get away with it."

Dix is looking at Chuck. He has an eyebrow raised. He,
like Chuck, has worked out how this is going down.

"So you keep the goods, and you're stealing our
money," Chuck says.

"I believe it's best for all involved," Vlad says.

His three men reach inside their leather jackets, pull out
handguns.

"And clean up after yourselves," Chuck says, eyeing
the guns.

"Of course," Vlad says, holding out his hands. "It
wouldn't be very wise of me to not."

Chuck and Dix remain calm. Chuck spots a flicker of
doubt cross Vlad's face at this. His smile falters. He was
expecting fear, panic.

"You should've just taken the money," Chuck says.

A shot, silenced and fired from a distance, cuts through
the air, hits one of the goons. The one who did not carry the
bag of goods, the one who did not count the money. It hits
him in the eye, drops him. The others flinch, look around,
frantic.

"I wouldn't move if I were you," Chuck says.

Vlad's smile is gone completely. He looks at Chuck,
shocked.

The distant shooter was Al. Jimmy and Pat appear now,
behind the goons. They grab the one with the bag and the
one with the money, respectively, and cut their throats.
Vlad is all alone. He looks very aware of this fact.

He chuckles nervously. "Take them," he says, pushing the bag of goods toward Chuck with his foot. "Keep the money! Have them on the house. Let's just not do anything hasty, eh? Anything that might be regretted later."

Chuck steps forward. He pulls his own knife, clipped to his belt at the back, concealed by his jacket. He grabs Vlad by the throat. "This isn't hasty," he says. "I've given it some thought."

He sticks the knife in Vlad's belly, twists it, drags it to the side and pulls it loose. He drops Vlad to the ground. Ordinarily, he'd like to leave him to bleed out, to think about what he's done. In this instance, he can't take a risk of someone finding him, saving his life. He leans down, cuts his throat.

Dix grabs the two bags.

"Are they real?" Chuck says.

Dix checks the goods. "They're real," he says. "Looks like they were going for authenticity with their con."

"In case we got a good look," Chuck says. "All right, we got what we came for and an extra payday to boot. Let's go."

22

Tom reaches the neighborhood Cindy pinpointed for him. There aren't many houses. He's aware that it's the kind of affluent area cops will regularly drive through. He can't stay parked on the road, or else one of the neighbors is likely to report him for loitering, suspecting him of scoping the houses out for a prospective burglary.

He goes to the end of the road, parks under a tree. It gives him a view of the whole street. All the front doors, all the driveways. It's currently midday, and he doesn't see many people coming or going. The few he does, they don't fit the idea he has in his mind of the caller, though he inspects them nonetheless. They look retired, old and fat and bored, nothing to do but go to the store and tend to their gardens.

Tom is watching out for an FBI type. If Anthony was undercover, it was more than likely for the FBI.

Hours go by. The day passes. Tom sits low in his seat, but he remains vigilant. As he suspected, a couple of cop cars have cruised through. Tom sank lower down each time, hidden behind the steering wheel and the dashboard. It gets to after six, and most of the houses are occupied by now, most of the people home.

One house remains empty. He hasn't seen anyone go into or out of it all day. It is the only home that has remained as such. Tom keeps one eye on it now while his other continues to monitor the street.

It's eight before a car pulls onto the driveway. It's still light enough for Tom to make out the driver. Spots his short hair, his cleanly shaven face. Looks the part.

He parks the car, gets out. Tom sees how he carries himself, the way he is dressed. The black trousers, jacket, white shirt, thin black tie.

Then the wind catches him just the right way. Pulls the jacket tight. Tom sees the outline of his gun, the bulge of his holster.

Now he's convinced. It all goes together. The look, the gun.

He's found his man.

23

———————

P eter's shift comes to an end. It's been a quiet night save for one incident. Some antifa agitator-type asshole, looking to cause some trouble. This happens every couple of months or so. Some liberal in town gets themselves all worked up, comes out with the intent of causing chaos, a fight, spraying some graffiti. The guy tonight was trying to sneak inside. Peter made him, was familiar with him from the past. Had caught him red-handed, spray cans at the ready, a stencil that read NAZI PUNKS FUCK OFF.

Tonight, his head was down; he avoided eye contact. He wore a cap that covered his face and hid how long his hair was. Very few people with hair visit the bar unless they're women, and not many women come here. Peter reached down, took him by the scruff of the neck like he was a small animal, and pulled him to one side. Got a good look at him. Confirmed it was his man. Dragged him around the back of the building, gave him a beating, then sent him on his way.

After the bar closes, Peter hangs around, has a couple of beers with some of the boys. The staff and a couple of his close friends who get to stay behind after the doors lock. It's a tradition. They do this most nights, get a buzz on and shoot the shit. Peter doesn't hang around long enough for a buzz, not this time. He has two bottles, then says he has to go.

"What's the rush, man?" one of his friends says. "We're just getting started here."

Peter doesn't tell him the truth. Doesn't tell him that he's got something on his mind and a bad feeling in his gut, and try as he might, he can't shake either of them. "I got somewhere to be," he says, winking, implying that he's off to get some action.

The friend nods in understanding. "I get you, man." He raises his drink in a salute. "Have the time of your fuckin' life."

"I intend to," Peter says, then leaves the bar. His smile fades as soon as his back is turned.

Peter doesn't go straight home. He doesn't go to see any girl. He goes to Steve's.

Steve lets him in. "Wasn't expecting to see you tonight," he says. "You should really start calling ahead. I was about to go to bed."

Peter notices, as they go through to Steve's room and his brother takes his usual seat at his computer, that the monitor is still on, still blaring, and he has his doubts that Steve was planning on sleeping any time soon.

"What can I do for you?" Steve says.

"I've been thinking," Peter begins, and already Steve is rolling his eyes, can guess what this is about.

Anthony.

But despite Steve's prior belligerence the last time Peter

came around to ask these questions, something still feels off to him.

Put simply, he doesn't trust his brother.

"All I'm saying is," Peter says, "I was right here, like we are right now, sitting like this, when I got the call from Michael saying Anthony was a rat. I was with you. I told you that. I told you exactly what Michael had told me."

"Yeah, you did. Looked like you were gonna have a hard time keeping it to yourself. You were about to blow."

"Uh-huh. And I told you exactly what we were gonna do to him."

"Yeah. So?"

"So you knew."

Steve raises his eyebrows. "We ain't getting anywhere like this, Peter."

"I ain't accusing you, Steve –"

"It sure as hell sounds like you are."

"I just gotta be sure, that's all. If it was you – I ain't saying it was – but *if* it was, I can help. I can keep you safe. If you don't tell me, though, I can't help you. If the others find out for themselves, there's nothing I can do for you."

Steve looks back at him, still defiant, still adamant, and says nothing.

"You know what they'll do," Peter says. "They'll cook you, man. They'll put a blowtorch to your balls."

"Do I look worried?" Steve says.

Peter has to admit that his brother does not. "No."

"So what's that tell you?"

"That either you had nothing to do with it, or else you're a great damn actor."

"I ain't taken any lessons."

Peter folds his arms, grits his teeth. It hurts him to doubt his brother, yet he continues to do so. He can't think of anyone else it could have been. Anyone else who would have known, anyone else who would have been able to contact Anthony, to warn him.

"Who do *you* think it was warned him?" Peter says.

Steve blinks. "How should I know? But how about this." He leans forward in his seat, hands clasped, brows narrowed. "Whoever it was, you got a more likely chance of finding them than you do Anthony, right? So you get hold of them, you bring them to me instead of him."

"We find them, there's no reason to ever think it was you."

"Exactly, but at the same time, the motherfucker's got you doubting me in the first place, and I'd say they've gotta pay for that, right? So bring them to me. I'll show you on them what I'll do to Anthony if we ever get him back."

Peter looks at his brother for a long time, almost like he's waiting for him to falter. He doesn't, though. Remains steadfast.

Finally, Peter stands. He doesn't feel any better now than he did before he came. "I'll see you later, Steve."

"Sure," Steve says. "And I hope to hell that the next time you come around, it's to talk about something else."

en is alone. No company. He sits on his sofa,
buttons of his shirt undone, tie discarded, a glass of
scotch in hand. His eyes go to the window, staring
out at nothing. It's getting dark. Soon there'll be nothing to
see but black.

Gerry has had to give up the search of his laptop.
There's nothing to find. No spyware, no signs, no trail,
nothing. Almost as if it hasn't been hacked at all.

Ben is frustrated. He's beyond frustrated. Trying to find
a mole or a leak or a hacker, and he has no leads. All he has
are questions, and they keep piling up. No end in sight.
Keeps wondering if he'll ever be able to find anything at
all, or if this incident will go unpunished.

Something cold and hard is pressed to the back of his
head, at the base of his skull. Ben knows it is a gun.

"No sudden movements, Agent." The voice is unfamiliar to him. "I see you've taken off your tie, but you've
still got your gun. Take it out, nice and slow."

Ben does as he's told. He has to sit forward to comply.

Puts his drink down first. He tries to see the reflection of the man behind him in the window, but can't. Whoever he is, he's positioned himself out of view. "Who are you?"

"Not yet," the voice says.

Ben doesn't understand this. He pulls out his gun, goes to place it on the coffee table next to his drink.

"Not quite. Take the clip out first. Don't forget the one in the chamber. That's good. Now throw it over to the other sofa."

Ben does so.

"You packing anything else you think I ought to know about? An ankle holster?"

Ben puts his feet up on the table, pulls up the cuffs of his trousers to show his bare ankles. "What do you want?"

The gun is removed from his head, though Ben has no doubt it's still pointed at him. He doesn't turn. There's movement behind him. It comes around his side, slowly. It goes to the sofa opposite, to where Ben threw his gun. Ben sees the man for the first time as he takes a seat, gun still raised. There's something familiar about him.

"I believe you know my brother," the man says. "Anthony."

Ben feels the color drain from his face.

"You know who I am?"

"Your name came up in Anthony's file," Ben says. "Tom, isn't it?"

"Well remembered. Now tell me yours."

"Ben Fitzgerald. Agent Ben Fitzgerald."

"Good for you."

"I've been, I've been thinking about him a lot lately – your brother. You here to kill me?"

"I'm not sure yet. Maybe, maybe not. Let's see how this goes, shall we? This here" – he wriggles his gun – "is just

in case you don't feel like answering any of the questions I
have for you."

"Questions?"

"Oh, I have a few. First and foremost, why was
Anthony undercover, and with whom?"

"Do you know where he is? Is he safe?"

"I'm asking the questions, Agent Fitzgerald. Tell you
what, I'll call you Ben, shall I? It's a lot less formal."

Ben doesn't like this situation. He can feel his heartbeat
rising. He bites down on the inside of his cheek, tastes the
familiar tang of blood. All he can do right now is comply.
"He was with the Right Arm Of The Republic."

Tom considers this name. "Can't say I've heard of
them."

"They're niche. Neo-Nazis, white supremacists. Up
until recently, I didn't think they were into anything more
serious than casual hate crimes and selling drugs. But, from
what I've heard, they're looking to get bigger. Make a real
name for themselves."

"And they're the ones who attacked Anthony? Who
killed Alejandra?"

Ben thinks he sees something in Tom's face as he asks
this last part, about Alejandra, but he doesn't question it.
He's not in any position to do so. "Yes," he says.

Tom doesn't dwell on that. He's quick with his follow-
up question. "All right. Now tell me the why."

"Have you seen your brother?"

"Yes."

"How is he?"

"He's alive. I told you, I'll be the one asking
questions."

"Well, how much has he told you already?"

"Nothing."

Ben frowns. "Two of you ain't close?"

Tom looks like he's getting annoyed. "Tell me *why*, Agent Fitzgerald."

Ben takes a deep breath. He tells Tom how they got Anthony for drug dealing. The way Anthony told it, it was because the only job he could get was in a grocery store stocking shelves, he wasn't qualified for anything else, and with a child on the way, this wasn't enough to support his coming family. Apparently, Alejandra had been unaware of his dealings. He kept her in the dark, told her each night that he was going to work, to stock shelves after hours.

Due to prior convictions, Anthony was facing a long prison sentence. He'd miss the birth of his child, miss most of the kid's life. Enter Ben Fitzgerald, who saw an opportunity to recruit him into going undercover in exchange for making it look like this most recent arrest had never happened. Anthony accepted the offer. He didn't have a choice.

"You blackmailed him," Tom says.

"I did what I had to do," Ben says. "You haven't heard the *why* yet."

Ben had to get him undercover fast. It was unofficial, off the books. He'd heard from various contacts that something was being planned, something big, and it would happen on American soil. In Texas. Kept hearing a reference to Oklahoma City. One of his informants had said, "Way I hear it, it's gonna make OK City look like a bonfire."

Ben started pressing on contacts. The consensus was it was being planned by Nazis, though no one knew the target. Ben got a list of all the white supremacist groups in Texas, no matter how big- or small-time they may have been. He tried to narrow it down, get as many undercovers, informants, and contacts into them as possible.

Then he got some more news that helped him narrow it down. It came right before he met Anthony. The timing was serendipitous. FBI analysts were bringing up online search histories. The servers used had been scrambled, but they'd narrowed it down to a town called Harrow. Whoever it was, they were looking up how to build a bomb. Searching through pages and pages of stuff on the dark web. Querying in message boards.

Ben checked for active groups in Harrow. There was one. The Right Arm Of The Republic.

Then Anthony got himself arrested. In Harrow.

"He was dealing drugs," Ben says. "Chances were some of them were *their* drugs. To my mind, he could've known some of them already. He maybe already had an in."

"And did he?" Tom says.

"No," Ben says. "But that didn't stop him from quickly ingratiating himself. He worked fast. I was impressed."

"He had a prison sentence breathing down the back of his neck," Tom says. "You really so surprised?"

"I didn't have time to wait around. Whatever they were planning, I needed to know about it. I needed to know as soon as possible. They had to be stopped. I didn't have time to do things the right way. I still don't."

"And did Anthony find out what you needed to know?"

Ben shakes his head. "Not unless he heard anything on his final night. I haven't spoken to him since then. I doubt it, though."

"And have you heard anything more about the Right Arm Of The Republic? Any more leads?"

Ben thinks that Tom looks curious. His interest has gotten the better of him. He was in the army – perhaps his patriotism is coming to the fore. "One thing," Ben says. "It's recent. Whatever they're going to do, it seems the ball is moving on it now. Couple of days ago, there was a robbery of a warehouse. You know what was stolen? A whole hell of a lot of fertilizer. The men who raided the place were all wearing masks, so we didn't get any positive IDs, but one of them was in short sleeves. The security camera picked out a swastika tattoo."

"You think it's them?"

"They're the only lead I've got."

"What does the rest of your department think?"

"They don't know about the Right Arm."

Tom cocks his head.

"Do you know your brother wasn't the only person attacked that night?"

"I've heard about it. I've looked into things recently."

"I'm not surprised. You strike me as thorough. I reckon you're probably smart enough to guess now why I haven't told them yet."

"There's a mole."

"There's a *potential* mole," Ben says. "There's a leak, or there's a hacker. I'm not sure. But I can't take a risk on what I know getting out. Not unless it can stop them, and I don't believe spooking either the mole or the Right Arm at this point will stop them in their tracks – if anything, it's more likely to speed them up, to rush things forward. They do that, there's a chance more people are going to get hurt."

Tom thinks about this. His next question is unrelated. "Did you get the phone to my father?"

Ben nods.

"How'd you manage that? The commune is off-grid."

Ben smirks. "You really think we don't know where they all are?"

Tom returns the smirk. "You really don't. There are more than you can imagine."

Ben doesn't know what to say to this, so he doesn't respond.

Tom lowers the gun.

Ben raises an eyebrow. "This mean you trust me?"

"I don't trust you," Tom says. "I think you're a piece of shit. But I think we can be mutually beneficial to one another."

Ben had been considering the same thing.

"I'm going to Harrow," Tom says.

"I'd figured as much. Riding off to avenge your brother, huh?"

"It's not just for him."

Ben thinks of Alejandra.

"How much do you know about the Right Arm?"

"I don't know who was directly responsible," Ben says.

"That doesn't matter. As far as I'm concerned, they're all responsible."

"If I had to take a guess, I'd say it was the council. The guys who run the thing."

"I want the names. All the names you have."

"And you can have them. But I want something in return."

Tom looks at him.

"I want any information you can find. If there's a mole, I want to know who it is. I'm sure that's information you'd like to know, too."

"Fine," Tom says.

"Then okay," Ben says. "It sounds like we have a deal."

The two men look at each other in silence, each waiting for the other to either say something more or to make a move.

Ben is first. "What're you going to do when you reach Harrow, when you find them?" He already has a suspicion.

"I'm going to kill them all."

Ben mulls this over. The deaths of the Right Arm are no skin off his nose. The more of them Tom kills, the less likely they are to carry out whatever it is they have planned. It's not an ideal way of doing things, and again, it's not the *right* way of doing things, but that has never stopped Ben before.

Right now, his priority is stopping them from carrying out their attack, by any means necessary.

And finding the mole.

And right now, his best chance of doing either of those things seems to be Tom Rollins.

Ben doesn't say any of this aloud. He just nods his head, a silent blessing.

25

Tom drives through the night, straight to Harrow. He knows the way. It's not his first time.

In his bag, stuffed into the passenger footwell, is all the information Ben gave him. The names of the Right Arm. Where they live. Where they meet. Their haunts. This information, Tom knows, would have been gathered by Anthony.

He wonders how much Alejandra knew, in the end. Was she aware Anthony was undercover, or did she meet her end in confusion, unaware of what he had been getting up to, the trouble he had gotten them in?

It's better not to think about such things.

It's still dark by the time Tom arrives. He goes straight to a motel, checks in. The girl on the desk looks like she's been here all night. She looks tired, but she forces a smile. Her auburn hair is tied back, and she wears makeup to hide the tired darkness under her eyes. She's pretty, though, and her smile lights up her face. Her name tag reads BETH.

Tom pulls the car down to his room. He unlocks the

door, leaves it wide. Checks there's no one around, then goes to the trunk. He has another bag here. It's full of gifts from his father.

He gets the bag inside, locks the car, locks the door to his room. He gives the room a quick look over, checking escape routes. Other than the front door and the window next to it, there is only one. At the back, in the bathroom, out the window. He opens the window up and leans out, gets a good look. It leads out onto a patch of dead land. In the dark, he can make out the shape of an abandoned, rusting tricycle.

Tom empties the bag from his father onto the bed, laying out the contents. There are night-vision goggles, binoculars, flash-bang grenades, a gas mask, an M4 Carbine and the ammunition to go with it, as well as his Beretta and KA-BAR still in his regular travelling bag. Tom examines each item, making sure everything is in working order. He checked them before he left his father's, but he has since driven for a long time.

Satisfied, he packs them back up into the bag, hides it under the bed. He leaves out the binoculars. From his regular pack, he takes the folded piece of paper with the names and locations of the higher-ranking members of the Right Arm that Ben gave him. He goes to the desk in the corner of the room, next to the television. On the map, he marks down where each member lives, as well as known haunts.

Peter Reid, aka 'Terminator', is closest to him. His workplace is a bar known as a regular hangout for other Nazis, and it's theorized that the Right Arm launders their money through it. There is a note next to Peter's name that his younger brother, Steve, is also a member of the Right Arm and is the one Anthony spent most of his time with.

Tom doesn't let this knowledge affect him. He's here to do what needs to be done. He's treating it like a job. He's a professional. Stays cool, stays calm, thinks things through.

The map is marked. He folds it back up, puts it in his pocket. He takes his Beretta and KA-BAR, grabs the binoculars from the bed, and he heads out into the night, back to his car.

He's going to get to know his enemy. He's going to do some recon.

26

A nthony wakes from another fitful sleep. Heavily drugged, it takes him a moment to work out where he is.

The same place he keeps finding himself every time he opens his eyes. His father's home. Anthony remembers that Tom was here. In the chair next to the bed, talking to him. He talked to him for a long time. Anthony blinks, trying to remember. The painkillers fog his brain, make him forgetful.

Either that, or the fracture.

No matter how many pills they give him, the pain never leaves. It barely numbs. It's in his arm, in his skull, and in his heart. Even when he's confused, not fully aware, he knows that something is wrong. That he has suffered a great loss.

And then it all comes back, the same way it always does. A tidal wave of remembrance, an ocean of loss, grief, of despair. It brings nausea, too, roiling within him. He grits his teeth. With his good hand, he grabs the edge of the bed, squeezes it, closes his eyes tight until a tear runs from one corner.

He calls for his father.

Jeffrey is quick to arrive. Anthony doesn't give him a chance to say anything. "Where's Tom?"

"He's gone," Jeffrey says.

"*Where?*"

"I don't know."

Anthony can tell he's lying. "He's gone to Harrow, hasn't he? He's gone after them."

Jeffrey holds out his hands, hesitates before he speaks. "Someone has to."

Anthony is annoyed. "That someone is *me*! Damn it, I told him not to do this! And I told *you* –" he jabs a finger at Jeffrey "– that I didn't want him called! I didn't want him to know. I knew this is what he'd do, *exactly* what he'd do."

"We didn't know if you were going to survive, Anthony," Jeffrey says. "Your brother deserved to know."

"Bullshit," Anthony says, glaring. "You knew someone was responsible, and you wanted them to pay. Tom's a bullet – you got him here, you pointed him in the right direction, and you fired. This isn't Tom's fight."

"You're his brother, Anthony. Of course it's his fight. He cares about you. He loves you."

Anthony laughs, though it's without humor. "Sure, it's for me. That's exactly who he's doing this for." Anthony shakes his head, but it gives him a splitting pain, feels like he's taken an axe to the skull. "It's my fight," he says. "What happened was for me to resolve, not Tom. It was for me to deal with, and I don't care how long it takes me to recover, you don't have the right to take that decision away."

Anthony tries to get up, to swing his legs over the side of the bed and get to his feet, to make a point, but he can't. The room starts spinning as soon as he's sitting up. It feels like his skin is tearing under the bandages, like his bones are going to break through the surface. He has to lie back down, defeated, impotent.

"Calm down, Anthony," Jeffrey says. "You're just gonna hurt yourself more. You need to rest."

"I've done nothing but rest," Anthony says. "And I don't feel any better."

"It'll take time. These are severe injuries you've got. You've broken bones. You fractured your skull, for Christ's sake. That's not gonna just heal overnight."

Anthony stares up at the ceiling, angry. "Just go," he says. He puts his good arm over his eyes, obscures his vision, blocks everything out.

His father doesn't leave, though. He hears him take a seat. Hears it creak as he leans forward.

Anthony raises his arm a little, peers out at him.

"Tell me about Alejandra," Jeffrey says.

27

The last time Ben read anything about Tom Rollins, it was only in passing. Now, in his office, he looks him up, reads the file properly. The first thing that catches his eye, catches him off guard, is the fact he's wanted. He went AWOL from the CIA, though the details are sketchy.

Ben peers over the top of his computer, makes sure no one is approaching. If anyone finds him reading this, they'll have a lot of questions, and he doesn't want to answer any of them. He chews the inside of his cheek, peeling at the strips of already ragged flesh from the last time he was biting on it. Lately, his cheeks aren't getting a chance to heal.

Ben goes to the beginning. Tom joined the army at twenty-one, served three tours of Afghanistan. He never rose above infantry, but it's noted that he never strove to. However, during his third tour, he was commended for bravery when he rescued two fellow soldiers, one of whom was wounded, from behind enemy lines – their unit was attacked; they got separated. Tom kept them alive out in the desert for five days and nights, returned them to camp. This feat caught the attention of the CIA, who recruited him, though it's not clear what they had him doing.

Ben is able to infer what this means. He was off the books. Doing the dirty work. Black ops. All the stuff they won't keep a record of.

He worked for the CIA for five years before abruptly going AWOL. His current age is thirty, though Ben can't help thinking to himself how he looked older. Wonders at the kind of things he has seen, that he has done.

Ben closes the report on his computer, deletes it from his history. As he finishes, there's a knock at his door. It's Carly. "How you doing?" she says.

"I'm good," he says.

"Hope you didn't miss me too much last night," she says.

"No, I … I kept myself busy." He thinks of Tom Rollins.

"That's good to hear. Anything interesting?"

"Not particularly. TV, read a book, y'know."

She tilts her head toward his computer, as if she knows exactly what he's just been looking at. "How's the investigation going?"

"Not great," Ben says. He sighs. "I've got Jake breathing down my neck. He wants results on it yesterday."

"But you've got nothing?"

"Nothing worthwhile."

She nods once, looking solemn. "I'm afraid I'm going to have to bail on you again tonight."

"Something up?"

"I have to go out of town. It's my dad's birthday, so I'm off to see the folks."

"Oh, really? Where do they live?"

"Fort Worth."

"Planned for a while?"

"No, it's a last-minute thing. I was talking to them last night, called to say happy birthday in advance, and we thought, what the hell? Why don't I go visit? I've got the time."

"Well, have a good one." Ben smiles at her. "I'd say tell them happy birthday from me, but I'm pretty sure they don't know who I am."

She laughs. "No, not yet. I'll be sure to tell him a friend passed on his regards."

"A friend, huh? I feel so special."

She winks at him. "I'll make up for it when I get back. *Then* you'll feel special."

28

S enior Special Agent Eric Thompson has checked into a motel room under a different name. He messaged the room number to Carly, told her to come straight to the door, and to make sure she's dressed casual.

She knocks, and when he answers, she says, "Is this casual enough for you?" She wears jeans, a plain white blouse tucked into them.

Eric is in jeans too, and a black T-shirt, which throws her a little. She's never seen him in anything other than a suit, even in his free time. He notices how she looks at him. "Suits me, don't you think?"

"Going for the blue-collar look?"

"You trying to tell me I don't pass?"

"Maybe I just know you too well."

"Maybe. And yes, you look acceptable. Come on in."

Carly steps into the room. She notices the bed is still made, unrumpled, like it hasn't so much as been sat on.

There is no sign of bags – Eric isn't staying here long; he isn't staying here at all. It's just a meeting place for them, away from potentially prying eyes.

He goes to a seat in the corner of the room, next to the top of the bed. There is another chair in the opposite corner, next to the closet. He motions for Carly to take it. She pulls it out of the corner, brings it closer to him. Eric waits for her. He sits with one leg crossed over the other, his hands resting on his thigh.

Eric Thompson comes from money. He's a native Texan, as is his whole family, going back generations. They come from oil money. Some of that money no doubt influenced Eric's speedy rise through the ranks of the FBI. He's in Fort Worth ostensibly investigating the murder of one of the killed informants from the Night of the Long Knives Part Two.

In reality, being here keeps him out of Dallas. It's important he stays out of Dallas for a little while longer. Keeps him away from the scene of the coming crime, and gives him the space and distance to organize and coordinate things more freely.

"How are things going back home?" he says.

"They're coming along," Carly says.

Eric nods; then he seems to get bored all of a sudden. He looks around the room. He's a tall man, lithe, looks like he does a lot of running, or swimming perhaps. His neck is long; his skin is smooth and pale. He begins to tap perfectly manicured fingers on the top of his knee. "I don't like these places," he says.

Carly blinks. "Fort Worth?"

"No, motels."

"Occupational hazard," she says. "I've lost count of the number I've had to stay in over the years."

Eric nods at this. "Seedy little places," he says. "Every time I step foot in one, I can't help but wonder, what did the last occupant get up to? Or the one before? And the one before that, all the way back to the day it opened. What is that stain on the ceiling, this one on the floor, this on the bed sheets? Why is there a handprint on the wall, above the headboard? Of course, I can usually guess what caused these things. Sometimes I'll lie awake at night, and I'll focus on one of these questionable things, and I'll wonder how many junkies have been in here, shooting up in this very bed, on this chair, in the bathroom, in the corner. I'll wonder how many fugitives have hidden out here under assumed names. How many people have breathed this same air, walked through this same space?"

Carly doesn't understand why he's saying this. She sits, listens, nods along politely.

"But mostly, I'll know that most of the people who come to these places have come in twos. They've come together. A secret place for their illicit gathering. And then the question turns to, just how much fucking has gone on in this room? It makes you see every stain, every handprint, in a new way. How well do they clean these sheets? I wonder. Something is always left behind."

"It's crossed my mind too, I have to admit – on occasion," Carly says, just to say something, to prove that she hears what he's saying, despite its seeming irrelevance. "I just try not to think about it too much."

"It's a dirty little business, isn't it?" Eric says. "*Sex.*"

"I … I suppose it is, if it's, y'know, extramarital, as you suspect."

"You've never been married, have you, Carly?"

"No."

"Ever come close?"

"Once. Back in college. I'm glad I got out before it was too late." She laughs.

"That's when it was for me, too," Eric says, holding up his left hand, tapping the wedding band. "Just after, anyway. Arranged by my father and her father. It was far more mutually beneficial to them than it ever has been for us, really."

"How, er, how is your wife?" Carly says, again to be polite.

Eric waves the mention of her off, dismisses her. "Fine," he says. "My point is this – marriage complicates, but sex complicates further. Wouldn't you agree?"

"I suppose I do."

He looks at her, looks deep into her eyes. Carly feels herself begin to fidget. "I don't believe you do," Eric says. "Do you understand what I am saying to you?"

"I, uh … I thought I did."

"What has Ben found?"

"Nothing," she says quickly, grateful for a question she knows the answer to. "Not that I know of, and I've been keeping a close eye on him. I'm with him most nights."

"But not *every* night."

"Some nights I'm busy," she says, defensive. "With the operation. Following *your* orders."

Eric leans back, taps his fingers again. "This has been ongoing for a long time now," he says. "And I'll admit, the discovery of his undercover within the Right Arm may well have saved this entire mission, but I can't help but feel things have stalled somewhat since then."

"How do you mean?"

"We need further answers, Carly, and you're not delivering them."

"I told you, he doesn't have anything."

"Are you so sure? A man like Ben Fitzgerald, a man who will insert an undercover operative off his own back, damn the consequences, you really believe he doesn't have anything going on?"

"He plays his cards close to his chest. He always has," Carly says. "But he'll slip up. He'll leave a trail eventually. He did last time."

"We don't have until *eventually*. We need to know now – everything he's thinking, everything he's doing, we need to know right now. Do you think he suspects you?"

"No," Carly says. She's adamant about this.

Eric strokes his hairless chin. He's so smooth she doubts he could grow a beard. "Sex complicates, Agent Hogan," he says. "For people with no control, it complicates further. They begin to believe in a thing called *love*."

"Are you asking me if I love Ben?"

"Perhaps he loves you."

"Perhaps he does, but that's not a concern. If anything, it helps us."

"Only so long as it remains a one-way street."

"I don't love him," she says firmly. "I don't have any feelings for him. I'm a professional. This is my job. This is for our country. I'm doing what I have to do."

Eric says nothing. She can't tell if she's convinced him or not.

"Is this all you called me out here for?" she says. "We couldn't have discussed this nonsense in a phone call?"

"I wanted to see you," Eric says, "face to face. To gauge for myself."

"And am I *gauged* to your satisfaction?" Carly can't hide her annoyance.

Eric grins. "Close enough."

Carly bristles.

"But no, this isn't the only reason I called you here." Eric glances down at his nails, inspects them, doesn't say another word until he's done. "I have a task for you."

"Oh?"

"I need you to go and check in with our friends," he says. "They should almost be ready to go by now, but with the radio silence between us and them, it's impossible to know where they're at. I'll admit, this lack of knowledge is making me irritable. The time is almost upon us. I need to know they're prepared."

"You haven't been watching the news?"

"Of course I've been watching the news. I've seen what they've done in that regard, but that doesn't mean anything. Go and see them. I'd do it myself, but I can't go back to Dallas yet, can't risk being seen."

Carly nods. She understands.

"Then report back to me."

Carly nods again, buoyed up by this responsibility.

"They can be an uncouth bunch," Eric says, almost as a warning. "Don't let them intimidate you."

"I've faced down worse."

"I'm not so sure you have."

They sit in silence for a moment; then Eric abruptly says, "We're done here."

Carly blinks. "Oh." She gets to her feet. "I'll be on my way, then."

"Put the chair back," Eric says. He doesn't stand.

Carly does as she's told. She goes to the door. Before she can leave, Eric speaks again.

"Remember, Carly, sex complicates. We can't have any complications, not now, not when we're so close."

She nods.

"Do you want to know the key to any lasting and successful relationship?" Eric says. "A successful marriage?" He taps his wedding band again.

"Okay," she says.

"Keep sex out of it. Goodbye, Agent Hogan."

29

Tom is parked across the road from the bar where Peter Reid works.

Peter's nickname, so Tom has been told, is 'Terminator'. It didn't take Tom long to see why. Peter is built like a tank. He's all muscle. There isn't a pound of fat on him. He looks like Schwarzenegger in his youth. It is a fitting nickname.

He waits for it to get later. To get dark. For the bar to close.

Tom has been in Harrow for two days now. This is the end of his second day. He has spent all of his time on recon. He has not left the car. He has eaten food bought from the drive-thru. He has pissed into a bottle. To prevent cramps, he has flexed and relaxed his muscles, particularly in his legs and lower back. Kept himself from seizing up.

He has been by every house. Has watched them for hours at a time. At Steve's, there wasn't much to see. Tom was able to catch glimpses of him as he passed by windows, but that was it. He stayed indoors. People came to see him. These people all looked the same. They were going to him to buy drugs.

Ronald Smith lives by himself. His house is at the end of a neighborhood, away from the other homes in the area. Like he is an outcast, a loner. Like the other people here don't want anything to do with him, nor he them. His home is surrounded by dead grass. There is a rusted old car with a cracked windscreen under a tree. The tyres are flat. The car's original color is unclear. The tree looks as though it once had a tire swing hanging from it, but the tire is gone, so that all that remains is an ominous rope. Ronald is clearly the oldest member of the Right Arm, in middle age. Earlier today, he left town for a few hours. Tom followed him only to the town's limits, then turned and went back to his house. Resumed his parked position down the road, waited for him to come back, wondering if it would be today. He was gone for a few hours. When he returned, he unlocked his house, then went straight to the trunk of his car. He looked around. Convinced it was clear, he brought out packages from the trunk, carried them inside his house.

Shortly thereafter, Harry Turnbull came by. He took some of the packages away. It didn't take a genius to work out that Ronald had picked up their fresh supply of drugs. Harry had taken them for distribution around town.

Harry also lives alone, but seems to have a girlfriend who comes and goes. Tom recognized her. The woman from the motel, the one who checked him in. Beth. He's stored this information away. It may prove useful. He made particular note of the look on her face, too. She didn't look happy to be going there. Even when Harry answered the door for her, she still struggled to force a smile.

Michael Wright, founder and leader of the Right Arm, lives on the other side of town, with his wife. They have an old farmhouse. It's big. Harder to get close to than the others. Tom had to park back as far as he could. He watches through binoculars. There are trees at the back of the house. If Tom wants to get closer, he will have to park further away, continue through the woodland on foot. These are all details he commits to memory. He wonders how much of Michael's activities his wife is aware of. Assumes it will be a lot, as she is always present, always with him. Harry is often there, too, though without Beth. Tom wonders how much she knows. How close she and Harry are.

Tom will take out Peter first. After hours at the bar. With his size, he is clearly their enforcer. The biggest threat. Killing Peter first will send a message. He can't take out all of the Right Arm in one night, not on his own, and they're going to become aware of something happening as he picks them off one by one. Therefore, he wants to give them something to be worried about. Something to be scared of. Something that will make them sloppy, prone to mistakes.

There may be others in the bar with Peter when Tom has to go in, but he has gotten a good look at the clientele. More than likely, they too are members of the Right Arm. He isn't too concerned at having to prospectively hurt them. He is not going to let anyone get in his way.

Being in Harrow is hard. Closer to where Alejandra was, the ground where she walked, the town where she lived. The air she breathed. Tom remembers when she broke his heart. She didn't do it on purpose, but that didn't make it hurt any less. Tom was back off his tour, eager to return to Harrow, to find the girl he hadn't stopped thinking about all the while he was gone. He'd reached out to Anthony, asking if he could stay over again. Anthony said, of course, no problem, "You'll get to meet my new girlfriend."

Tom wasn't interested in Anthony's new girlfriend. He'd be polite, of course, exchange pleasantries, but in reality, all he'd be thinking of would be Alejandra and how quickly he could disengage himself and go searching for her, back to the bar where she worked.

And then he met Anthony's new girlfriend, and she was Alejandra. "Hello, Tom," she said, Anthony introducing them both. Tom thought she looked sheepish.

It was a couple of hours before they had any time alone, pretending that they didn't know each other already, that this was their first meeting. Anthony went to get pizza. Tom and Alejandra stepped out onto the porch.

"So Anthony doesn't know we're already familiar," Tom says.

"Not yet," Alejandra says. "I didn't think it was the best time to tell him, not with you coming to visit. But I will. I'm going to."

"How come you haven't already?"

"It took me some time to realize that he was your brother. He doesn't talk about you, and it's not like there are any pictures here of the two of you together."

"You didn't notice any similarities?"

"Yes, actually, I did. I thought that was why I was attracted to him, because he looked like you."

"Should I be flattered?"

"I don't know how you should feel."

"What about when you found out his last name?"

"At first, I thought it was a coincidence. But it niggled at me. So I started to ask about his family. *Then* he finally told me about you. About his older brother, in the army. I was going to tell him then, but I couldn't. By then, I was in

love with him. I didn't know how he would take it. I was
scared of how he would take it."

Tom couldn't respond to this, not right away. She loved
his brother. This cut him deep.

"I'm sorry, Tom," she said.

"You don't need to be sorry," Tom said, taking a deep
breath. "I didn't expect you to put your life on hold. Part of
me knew you might move on, I just hoped you wouldn't,
but that's out of my hands. I'm happy for you, Alejandra.
Really. For both of you."

Soon after that, Anthony returned with the pizza. That
night, when Tom was in the guest room, Alejandra told
Anthony the truth. That she and Tom knew each other
already, and how. Tom heard them discuss it. They
discussed it loudly, particularly his brother. Tom lay awake,
expecting his brother to come bursting into the room at any
moment. He kept making out like he was going to.
Alejandra kept stopping him, calming him.

The next morning, at the breakfast table, Anthony was
cool toward his brother. He looked at him. "Alejandra told
me how you know each other already," he said.

He got over it. It didn't take long. Anthony was in love
with Alejandra. He wasn't going to jeopardize his relationship with her just because of his petty jealousies regarding
his older brother. The feeling he would never be able to
escape his shadow.

Tom thinks about another time. Just he and Alejandra,
out on the porch again, though under happier circumstances
this time. Tom never stopped loving her, though he knew it
would always go unrequited. She was telling him about
Mexico, about Guaymas. "It sounds like a very beautiful
place," Tom said.

"Maybe I'm just remembering it through rose-tinted

glasses," Alejandra said. "But it shines very brightly in my mind."

Tom nodded along. "Well, you make it sound very special. I'll have to visit it someday."

"Maybe I'll take you," she said. "I'll go back, one day. I'll have to. I miss it too much. Every day, I miss it more."

In the car, around the car, it has gotten dark. It's late; it's after one in the morning. Tom sees activity at the front door of the bar. People are leaving. It's clearing out. Peter is there, seeing them off. He doesn't leave with them, though. He goes back inside. The door is locked. The outside lights are turned off. The bar is closed.

Tom doesn't go right away. He waits. Lets them get comfortable. But it's getting close. It's almost time for him to make his first move.

30

Peter sees off the last few stragglers, escorts them to the door, sends them on their drunken way. He watches for a moment as they weave and stumble off down the road, heading home. A couple of them get into cars. They've had a couple of beers, sure, but they aren't so drunk that they can't be trusted behind the wheel. Peter waves them off, then goes back inside.

It's been a quiet night. Ordinarily, Peter would be annoyed at this, bored out of his mind. He likes when it's busy, when he's had a chance to get his hands dirty, to put someone on their ass or throw them out the door. Now, though, he's grateful. He's got too much else on his mind. Too much to think about, worry about.

He goes behind the bar, gets himself a drink. "You've been awful quiet tonight, Peter," says one of his buddies, leaning over to speak to him. "Ain't like you. You all right?"

"I'm fine," Peter says. "Just tired is all, I guess."

His friend nods along. "I get that, man," he says.

There are seven men still in the bar, not including Peter. Some are members of the Right Arm; some are merely affiliates. They're all friends. They have beers in hand; they're setting up a table in the middle of the room, getting out the cards. They'll play poker for a few hours; then they'll head home for the night. Tomorrow, they'll do it all over again.

Peter takes a seat as the cards are being shuffled, dealt. He takes another long swig of his beer. It's taking the edge off, but only a little. He can't relax, not totally, as he usually would. He's thinking about his brother, still. Hasn't been able to concentrate on anything else lately.

He's deliberated for a long time, but he knows what he has to do. Has to tell the rest of the council of his suspicions regarding his brother. That he believes Steve was the one to call Anthony, warn him that they were on the way. That he's also sure Steve called the police, sent them out looking for a potential altercation.

It won't be easy to come clean about this. If Steve had only told him the truth, Peter perhaps would have been able to help him. But he's lied to him, right to his face, twice now. Like he thinks he's an idiot. Like there's anyone else could have helped Anthony. Like Steve truly is loyal to the cause.

Peter knows what they will do to Steve. They'll get the truth. He won't lie to them, not when they're doing to him what they didn't get to do to Anthony. When they're setting upon him with blowtorches, when they're prying off his kneecaps with a claw hammer, when they have his balls in a vice. Peter won't take part in it, but he can't deny what his brother has done any longer. Steve has betrayed them all. Peter is loyal to the Right Arm, loyal to the cause of white supremacy. To keep his suspicions to himself is just another form of betrayal.

"You gonna play," the man to his left says, "or are you gonna daydream the night away?"

Peter forces a grin, looks at his cards for the first time. "Let's play," he says. "I hope y'all brought enough cash, boys, 'cause I'm feeling lucky tonight."

Before he can play his first hand, the lights go off.

"God damn it," someone says.

"The hell's going on?" someone else says.

"You gonna go deal with that, Peter?" the man to Peter's left says. "Could be the fuse box."

Peter doesn't think it's the fuse box. He's on high alert. He opens his mouth, about to bark orders, to get the others prepared, to let them know something is about to go down, when a window breaks. The sound of shattering glass fills the room. Something rolls across the ground. Peter jumps to his feet. He turns to it, sees it moving. Small and round. Like a grenade. He turns just as it goes off. It's not a grenade, not exactly. It's a flash-bang.

The others cry out, blinded. Their chairs scrape back as they either get to their feet or fall to the ground.

Peter is on the ground. He managed to close his eyes, avoid the worst of the flash, but not all of it. He's perhaps not as badly blinded as the others, but he *is* momentarily sightless, the flash still going off behind his eyes. He can't see anything.

But he can hear.

He hears just fine as the shooting starts.

31

Tom wears the night-vision goggles loaned from his father, is armed with the M4 Carbine. He enters through the back door, runs around after he throws in the grenade, kicks it down. There should be eight men inside, including Peter. He kept track of the men coming and going as he waited in his car. Is prepared to allow for one or two extras that may have slipped by. A quick glance of the room, he sees eight.

He starts firing. Headshots, takes them out. The men panic, scream, run blindly, trying to feel their way out and to avoid the gunfire. Tom picks them off, one by one. He sees their swastika tattoos. Their 88s. Their Norse gods and their crossed grenades, their eagles. He focuses on the ones who have guns, who reach for them. Puts them down before they can cause trouble.

One of them dives over the bar, takes cover behind it. He re-emerges with a shotgun in hand. He fires carelessly into the darkness. Tom kicks over the table the men were gathered around, scatters their cards and their cash, takes cover behind it.

The shotgun blasts are wild. He hears another of the Nazis cry out, wounded by his own friend. None of the shots come anywhere near Tom or the table. Tom turns, aims over the top of it. He shoots the shotgun-wielder through the mouth. He drops the gun, goes down.

It's quiet now.

Tom looks around, through the goggles, counts up the bodies. Seven. One is missing.

Peter. There is no sign of Peter.

Tom turns in time to see him charge. Tom is tackled to the ground by the immense bulk of the man. Peter was more prepared than his friends. He got out of the way, took cover while Tom was shooting. Spotted him in the dark, waiting for the shots.

Tom uses his momentum against him. Rolls through with the attack. They hit the ground. Tom holds onto the front of Peter's shirt, pulls him in close, is able to flip him over the top of his head. Peter rolls with it, is quick to his feet, attacks again as Tom reaches for the M4. He swings a punch, but Tom is able to block it. He hits hard and fast, tags Peter with a couple of shots to the ribs, another to the solar plexus to drive the wind from him, then raises a leg and kicks him away, creates some separation.

Peter spits out the side of his mouth, catches his breath. Tom can see him clearly through the goggles. He wonders what he looks like to Peter. Just a dark shadow, faster and stronger than expected.

"Who are you?" Peter says, keeping his eye on the shadow, circling.

Tom doesn't answer. Peter attacks again. He manages to land a glancing blow to the side of Tom's head, but Tom travels with it, is able to quickly shake it off. He lands an uppercut right under Peter's jaw, shatters his teeth. He doesn't go down, but he does stumble back, spitting blood and broken teeth.

"*Fuck!*"

Peter's getting frustrated. He's never had this happen to him before, especially not with someone smaller than him. He's used to having his way, throwing his weight around. He's never been in a fight he hasn't won. This has made him careless, made him think he's invincible. He cannot conceive of an opponent he may not be able to defeat.

He attacks once again, determined not to be undone. He's careless now, though. He comes in swinging wildly, desperate to land a punch, sure that at least one heavy punch will put this interloper down, allow him to have his way.

Tom doesn't give him the chance. He ducks, blocks, does not allow him to land his one desperate blow. Peter tires himself out. Tom strikes, kicks at his knee, blows it out. Peter cries, goes down onto the knee, the one Tom has just kicked out of joint. Peter cries harder; it turns into a scream.

Tom grabs an arm and twists it around his back, wrenches it up until it breaks. Keeps it held behind Peter's back. He pulls his KA-BAR, presses the blade to his neck. He speaks into Peter's ear. "You're going to answer my questions," he says, "or else I'm going to break all the other bones in your body."

Peter is in pain, but he does his best to remain defiant. "Fuh-fuck you," he says. Blood runs from his mouth. The bones in his arm grind together, his dislocated knee swims around inside his leg, pressed to the hard floor.

"I can make it hurt more," Tom says, slicing the knife a

little across his throat, drawing blood. "Who attacked Anthony Rollins?" he says. "Who's responsible?"

Peter tries to turn his head, to see him, confused. It wouldn't make a difference if he could, even without the night-vision goggles covering most of Tom's face. "Who the hell are you?" he says.

"Answer the question." Tom wrenches his broken arm up a little higher, makes him scream again. Peter gasps for breath, but he doesn't answer anything. "Who attacked Anthony Rollins? Who killed Alejandra?"

Something happens then. There is a change in Peter. It takes a moment for Tom to realize that he is laughing.

"What's so funny?"

Peter continues to laugh, defiant until the end. "You wanna know who killed her, huh? *I* did. I killed that spic bitch. I put a bullet in her pregnant belly, and I put another right through her fucking face!"

Tom does not react. This is supposed to make him react, to make him sloppy. To get him to make a mistake.

Tom turns Peter around, then stands, kicks him onto his back. The broken arm is still twisted behind him; he lands on it. Peter isn't laughing now. Tom stamps on his good hand, feels the knuckles and the fingers shatter beneath the force of his heel. He kneels down, onto Peter, pinning his body. The knife is still in Tom's hand. He presses the tip to Peter's chest, right at his heart. Peter tries to paw at him with his broken hand, to force him off, but he can't get a grip, can't make a fist.

Tom is cool. He's calm. He's never been calmer.

He doesn't need Peter for the answers to his other questions. He can get them elsewhere. Right now, Peter has given him the only answer that really matters.

Tom slides the KA-BAR between Peter's ribs, into his heart.

He does it slow.

T om isn't done yet.

He's left the bar. Set it on fire. As he drives away, he passes the fire engine heading toward it. In the rearview mirror, he can see how the burning bar lights up the night sky behind him, the way the smoke arcs upward, obscuring the stars.

Tom goes to Steve Reid's house. He parks down the block, goes to the back, to the window where he sees lights flickering. Tom is armed with his Beretta and his KA-BAR. He's covered in Peter Reid's blood.

Inside the house, Steve sits at his computer. He rests his face in one hand, taps idly at the keyboard with the other. Looks bored.

Tom goes around the side, to an empty room. He breaks in. Slides his knife under the window frame, breaks the lock. Gets inside in relative silence. He listens to the house. Apart from the room where Steve is, where the only sound is the tapping of the keys, the house is silent. Tom goes to the room, stepping lightly, one foot in front of the other, knife in hand, raised.

Steve does not hear him coming. His ears don't twitch; he doesn't turn. Just goes on staring at the screen. Tom doesn't bother to check whatever it is he's looking at. From behind, he puts the knife to Steve's throat. His other hand is at the top of his head. Steve freezes. Tom turns him around in the chair. Steve gulps; his Adam's apple bobs against the blade. He raises his hands in surrender. He looks up at Tom. His eyes narrow, studying the face. His body goes limp. "You look just like him," he says.

"Who?" Tom says.

"Anthony."

"Then you know why I'm here." Tom keeps the knife at his throat.

Steve nods, just a little, careful not to cut himself. He seems resigned to what is about to happen.

His reaction surprises Tom. He notices how Steve is looking at the blood upon him. "It's your brother's," he says.

Steve acknowledges this with another small nod, but again, he doesn't seem as upset or angered as Tom would have expected. "How's Anthony?" he says.

Tom blinks.

"Is he all right? Everyone has assumed he's survived, but no one knows it for certain. I'm guessing, by your being here, that he did."

Tom's eyes narrow. "He's alive," he says.

"When I messaged him, I had to send it from a number he didn't have, in case … y'know … they got him. In case they checked his phone and saw that I'd warned him."

This part of the story is news to Tom. Anthony did not share any of the details with him. "What did you tell him?"

"I told him to run," Steve says. "That they knew, and they were coming for him. If they *had* managed to keep hold of him, if they'd checked his phone, they probably would have worked out that the message was sent by me."

"What would they have done?"

"Killed me."

"Even your brother?"

Steve snorts. "The Right Arm are his real brothers. I'm just a nuisance he can't shake."

"What happened next?" Tom says.

"When?"

"After you messaged him."

"I called the cops," Steve says. "I called them anonymously, told them I'd seen a couple of cars drive too fast around town, looked like they were heading out of it. I thought they were either racing, or one of them was chasing the other. It was a backup, in case they caught up to Anthony."

"They did catch up to him."

Steve grits his teeth. "I know."

"But so did the cops."

"I'm sorry about the girl," Steve says. His eyes glisten. "I didn't know about her. Anthony never told me about her. I didn't know she was … that they were going to …" He looks like he might be sick.

Tom keeps the knife to his throat, but he's thinking. "Did you know Anthony was undercover?"

"No, but I wasn't surprised. We had to spend a lot of time together. He was put with me, dealing. I could tell he wasn't like the others. He was more like … well, like me. Except, unlike me, he didn't have an older brother forcing him into this life. I couldn't understand why he was doing it."

"Who told the Right Arm about Anthony? Who told them he was undercover?"

"I don't know," Steve says, and Tom believes him. "They don't tell me anything. Nothing important. They just leave me here, and for the most part they leave me alone."

"Then how'd you know they'd found Anthony out?"

"Peter was here when he got the news. Sometimes he'd come by after work, he did that sometimes, just checking in. Not often, but it happened. That was just one of those nights. He was with me when he got the call. That hadn't been the case, I wouldn't have known. And ... and I guess Anthony would be dead."

"So you don't know where the news came from? Not the slightest idea?"

"Nothing. I'm sorry."

"What about the attack being planned? You know anything about that?"

"Attack? What are you talking about?"

"A domestic attack being planned by white suprema-cists. Target unclear, reasons unknown, but right now all arrows are pointing toward the Right Arm."

Steve's eyes go wide. "Jesus, what ... *what*?"

"But you don't know anything about that."

"Like I said, they don't tell me much. But it sounds way outside the ballpark of the Right Arm, they wouldn't ... I mean, I don't think ... it's not something they would do."

"They murdered a pregnant woman."

Steve lowers his eyes at this. "I guess I *thought* it's not something they would do."

"If it's not them, what about another cell, someone they know?"

"I mean, I guess, could be. They just leave me here, out of the way. They don't involve me in anything higher up."

Tom looks at him. He's not much to see. Just a skinny boy, looks like he could still pass for a teenager, dragged along in a lifestyle he doesn't want, all on his brother's say-so. "Why did you warn Anthony? Why didn't you just let your brother and the others take him out?"

Steve considers this, chews on his lip. No one knows what he did, so it's clear no one's asked him this already. He hasn't had to think about it. "Because he was my friend," Steve says. "And a part of me was relieved to know that it was like I suspected, that he *wasn't* like the others. To know that I was right about him. I think that's what I liked about him, why we got along. He could probably see the same in me. And, to be honest, selfishly, I wanted him to get away because that meant maybe the feds would come in, force the disbandment of the Right Arm, and that would be the end of it for me, at least for a while. Hopefully a long while."

Tom needs to decide what to do with Steve. He has two options. Either kill him, or let him live.

Tom looks down at him, the knife still at his throat. His brother's blood is on Tom's hands. Some of it has gotten onto Steve's face. Yet, he doesn't seem too torn up about any of this.

His phone rings. It's on the table next to his computer. It buzzes loudly.

"Answer it," Tom says. "Put it on loudspeaker." He takes the knife away, leans over, checks who is calling. It's Ronald.

Steve picks up the phone.

"Be casual," Tom says.

Steve nods. He answers, puts it on loudspeaker as Tom instructed. "Hey, Ron."

Tom has to commend him, he sounds calm, like he hasn't just had a knife at his neck, a threat upon his life.

"Steve, where are you?" Ronald does not sound calm. He sounds loud, worked up, frantic.

"I'm at home. I was about to get to bed."

"Shit, man, *shit* ..." It sounds like Ronald is doing something else, like he's distracted, maybe driving.

"Ronnie, what's up? Are you all right?" Steve looks up at Tom. He already knows the answer. He already knows what this call is about. The tone in Ronald's voice makes it very clear.

"Shit, Steve, I'm so sorry – it's your brother ..."

Steve raises his voice a little. "What about him? Is he all right?"

"Oh, goddamn, shit, Steve ... there's been a fire at the bar. He's ... he's dead, man. They're all dead, all of them inside ... Harry says they're pulling out bodies, but he saw Peter. He could tell it was him ..." Ronald sounds like he's crying.

Steve puts a crack into his voice. "*What?* Ronnie, what are you saying? What's happened? A fire?"

"A fire, yeah, but Harry's been talking to one of our buddies on the force. He's there; he says something else has happened. Says it looks like the other guys were shot before they caught fire, and it looks like Peter was stabbed. Something else has gone on here, man. There's been an attack or somethin'. Something went down before the fire happened."

"Shit ..."

"Yeah, shit, exactly. Keep your head down, man. Be careful."

"Yeah, yeah, you too."

"I'm sorry about your brother, Steve."

Steve doesn't respond.

"He was one of the best."

"I need to … I'm gonna have to go, Ronnie." Steve puts some more cracks in his voice. "I just need to, I mean, I can't …"

"I understand, man. I'll be in touch. I'm sorry, Steve. Call me if you need anything."

Steve hangs up. He puts the phone back down. Looks back up at Tom. His face is impassive. "Are you going to kill me?" he says.

He sounds calm. He's resigned to this.

Tom puts the knife away. "Do you want out of this life? For good?"

"I never wanted any part of it to begin with."

"Tomorrow morning, you're going to find a burner phone at your front door. It'll have one number on it. That number will put you in touch with me. You keep me updated on anything the Right Arm are doing, anything they have planned, and I will get you out of here."

"You trust me?"

"I don't trust many people, and I haven't known you anywhere near long enough for you to make the list. But you saved my brother, and you tried to save Alejandra, whether you knew it or not, and that counts for something."

"I'll try my best," Steve says. "But like I already told you, they don't exactly keep me up to date. I'm not their first port of call when they have news to share."

"Your brother's just died. There's an opening on the council. Show some initiative, some will. It might impress them."

Steve nods, understanding.

"I'll be in touch," Tom says; then he leaves.

33

B en keeps an eye on the news out of Harrow. He's set up alerts on his personal laptop. It's a new laptop. Recently purchased. He hasn't used the other one since it was hacked. He's put it to the back of his closet, handles it like a poisonous snake.

He gets a notification about the fire at the bar and the eight men killed inside. Names haven't been released, but Ben can guess at least one of them. He knows which bar it was without even checking. He's the one who told Tom about it.

Shortly after he reads about this incident, he receives a call from Tom. "I assume the fire is your handiwork?" he says.

"You're asking something you already know the answer to," Tom says. "And one you're complicit in."

"I'm aware."

"Then don't waste my time with stupid questions. I haven't been able to get any information yet. Nothing about the mole, nothing about the attack."

"Then why are you calling?"

"Because I have a man on the inside now."

Ben is surprised to hear this. "Really? Who?"

"Steve Reid."

"Peter's brother?"

"Yes. They weren't close."

"You trust him?"

"He saved my brother. I trust him as much as I need to. And if I can't, I'll kill him. He's not a great threat."

"You asked him about the mole, the attack?"

"Yes. He didn't know anything, but I've pressed him to dig deeper. He was surprised to hear about the attack. Said he couldn't imagine the Right Arm plotting something like it."

"Yeah, well, all the evidence we've got suggests otherwise. Anything else?"

"No."

"Keep me updated."

Tom hangs up. Ben looks at the phone in his hand. He puts it away, thinks to himself how Anthony must be the more talkative of the two. He at least got a goodbye out of him at the end of their conversations.

34

Michael can feel himself reeling from the death of Peter, and looking at Harry and Ronald, he knows they feel it too. The news was unexpected. It shakes them to their core.

More than that, they lost four other members of the Arm and three men they considered friends and allies. Three men they knew they could call upon if they needed them. Close friends of Peter, and so by proxy, friends of theirs.

"The cops are keeping it quiet," Harry says, "'cause they don't wanna tip off the killer, but those burned bodies were already dead. Bullet holes and knife wounds." He shakes his head. "Someone took them out, then burned down the bar."

"They think the killer was trying to cover up what he did?" Michael says. They're sitting in his basement, around their table. Michael is trying to avoid looking at the empty seat where Peter should be. They all are.

"Could be," Harry says. "They didn't find any discharged

casings from the bullets, so they must've been picked up before the fire was started. At the same time, maybe whoever it was just wanted to burn the bar down, too."

"Sending a message," Ronald says.

"What do you mean by that?" Michael says.

"Killing off eight of our men and friends," Ronald says, "killing *Peter*, that don't sound like retaliation to y'all? We just gonna rule out that maybe this don't have something to do with Anthony Rollins?"

Michael and Harry exchange glances. The thought had crossed Michael's mind, and he's pretty sure it will have crossed Harry's, too.

"It can't be Anthony directly," Michael says. "There's no way he's healed yet. He's still laid up somewhere. He's not going anywhere for a while yet, and he's sure as hell not coming back here. He ain't the one who did this."

"But he could still be responsible for it," Ronald says.

"It would be fitting for an undercover pussy to send someone else to fight his battle for him," Harry says.

Michael nods. "True."

"Only question, really," Harry says, "is how many of them are there? How many has he sent? This is the work of a team. In one fell swoop, we've lost a lot of men – a lot of our heaviest hitters – they didn't go down without a fight."

"Knowing Peter," Ronald says, "he got his pound of flesh. You can guarantee that. Whoever it was got lucky and took him out, but they know they were in a fight. He'd have hurt them."

"True, true," Michael says. "You spoke to Steve?"

"Yeah," Ronald says.

"How was he?"

"He sounded pretty cut up. He was in tears."

"Spoke to him since?"

"No."

"Anyone seen him? Heard anything from him since?"

Neither responds.

"So nothing?"

"I'll go check in on him," Harry says. "See how things are going."

"I wanna know how he is," Michael says. "How he's acting. How he's handling this."

"You're still suspicious."

"Of course I am."

"I'm not saying you shouldn't be."

"Yeah. Watch him closely."

Ronald looks like he has his doubts about this. "His brother just died," he says.

"All the more reason to see how he's handling it," Michael says. "We already had our suspicions about him. This could confirm it."

Ronald still looks doubtful, but he doesn't protest.

"When you gonna give him a visit?" Michael says to Harry.

"Soon as we finish up here."

"All right. Put out the word; tell everyone to be extra vigilant. We may have some more trouble coming our way here. Tell 'em to be careful and to bring us anything they think we oughtta be worried about."

Harry and Ronald say they will; then they take their leave. Michael remains in the basement, at the table. He wants to be alone for a while. Alone to mourn. He feels a chasm opening within himself, widening. It is his grief. He turns, finally, to the chair where Peter would sit. He sees him there. Flashbacks. Sitting listening. Nodding along.

Laughing. Looking worked up when something has pissed him off, when he's desperate to crack some skulls.

Remembers the last time he saw him. How he looked thoughtful and concerned. How Michael knew he'd been thinking about his brother.

Then he's gone. The chair is empty again. It will always be empty, in Michael's eyes. Going forward, no matter who gets to take the seat, they will never take Peter's place. They will never fill the spot he has left behind.

35

Tom's bloodied clothes are soaking in the bathtub. He's rinsed them through already. The water instantly darkened with the blood. Now the water is a light pink.

Tom lies on the bed. In his hand is the Santa Muerte pendant. He has pulled it from his pocket. He holds it tight while he stares up at the ceiling.

It was a gift from Alejandra. She gave it to him the night before he was due to ship out on his third tour. The end of the time he'd come back only to find she was with Anthony, that they'd met and fallen in love in his absence.

She caught him alone out on the porch, gave it to him there. "I wanted to give you this," she said. She held it out. A small pendant with some black string looped through to make it a necklace. She waited until Tom held his hand out; she placed it into it. Tom studied it. He recognized the figure. He'd seen her before. He'd seen her in Mexico, and he'd seen her in other places, on murals and tattoos.

"Santa Muerte," Alejandra said. "Saint Death. She will keep you safe while you are away."

Tom knew why she was giving him this. The night before, as the time crept up for him to be going off to war again, she'd asked him about death, if he was scared. "A bit, yeah," Tom said. "Of course. I just try not to think about it."

"If you died over there, what would happen to your body?"

"So long as they could find it, they'd bring it home."

"And then? Where would it be buried?"

"It'd go to my dad." Tom shrugged. "It'd be up to him, then. I wouldn't care much either way, not by then."

"But America is your home, so they'd bring you back here."

Tom nodded.

Alejandra looked thoughtful at this. "No matter how long I am in America, Mexico will always have my heart. When I die, that's where I will be buried. In Guaymas."

"Have you told Anthony?"

"I've told him. I've tried to, anyway. I don't think he likes to think about such things. He's always quick to change the subject."

Tom thought it probably went back to their mother. It had taken Anthony a long time to get over it, and he'd acted out for a long while after, too. It was debatable whether or not he truly ever had reconciled himself with her death.

"Do you believe in God, Tom?" Alejandra said suddenly.

"Never really given it much thought before. I'm not so sure I do."

"Who do you believe keeps you safe when you are over there, fighting?"

"Me. And the men I fight beside."

Alejandra looked troubled by this. "You don't believe in something greater than yourself, watching over you, keeping you safe?"

"I guess not."

The next night, she gave him the pendant. Tom remembers her words. *She will keep you safe.* He remembers those words every time he touches it.

Alejandra should have had it. Alejandra was the one who needed to be kept safe.

Tom slips it back into his pocket. He checks the time, then leaves the room. He goes to the motel's reception. Beth is there. She's alone behind the counter. There's no one else in the lobby. She leans back in her chair, is playing on her phone. Tom steps in. He clears his throat to get her attention, smiles when she looks up. "Hi," he says.

She smiles back. "Hello there." She sits forward, puts her phone down. "You need help with anything?"

"I could do." Tom strolls to the front of the desk. He makes a show of reading her name tag. "Beth. That's real pretty. You mind if I call you Beth?"

"That's fine. It's my name. I don't know what else I'd expect you to call me."

"You hear about that fire, Beth? At that bar?"

She raises her eyebrows. "Oh yeah, I heard about it," she says. "Think it's all anyone's talking about at the minute."

"Anyone know what caused it?"

She shrugs. "I heard it could've been from a gas pipe, but no one's sure."

The gas pipe is an excessive theory. Had it been a gas

explosion, there'd have been a fireball, nothing left of the building. All he'd done was spread the more flammable bottles of alcohol upon the counter, the tables, the floor, then set them on fire. "Sure sounds like an awful accident. Was anyone inside?"

"Oh yeah, people were killed. One of them was a buddy of my, uh, of a friend of mine."

He notices she doesn't use the word 'boyfriend'. She comes close, but she doesn't say it. "That's terrible," Tom says. "I sure hope your friend is coping all right."

"He'll get over it the same way he always does," she says, rolling her eyes. "He'll probably hit something."

"I'm not sure if I should laugh at that or be concerned."

She waves her hands. "It's fine, it's fine. It's just a joke."

He isn't so sure. "Anyway, say, I was wondering, is there anywhere good to eat in this town?"

"You've been here long enough. You haven't found anywhere yourself yet?" She's grinning.

Tom laughs. He's being charming; they're both being flirtatious. He scuffs his boots on the floor. "I've found some places, but nowhere I'd really consider *good*."

"I can give you some names," Beth says. "There's a diner I usually go to."

"That sounds promising. But I guess what I'm really trying to say is, I'm wondering if maybe I could get some company when I go out to eat. I've been flying solo the last few nights. I was thinking it would be good to have some company."

"You asking if I'd like to join you?" She smiles coquettishly.

"Y'know, if you want to."

"Sure," she says. "I get off in an hour. How about then? Can you hold out that long?"

"For the company of a pretty lady? Of course. I could hold out longer if I had to."

"An hour will be just fine. Meet me back here?"

Tom starts backing out of the lobby, raises his watch high so she sees him check the time. "I'll see you then," he says, winking. Then he leaves, turns his back; his smile is gone. He returns to his room.

36

Harry goes to Steve's house. Ostensibly, this checkup is to see how he's doing after his brother's death, but really he, Michael, and Ronald know that he is going to gauge how he is acting, how he's taking it.

They didn't trust Steve before this happened. How he behaves today dictates how much they can trust him going forward.

Harry doesn't think it'll be much of an improvement.

"Took the wrong fuckin' brother," he mumbles to himself as he gets out of the car. He goes up the walkway to the front door, knocks, rings the doorbell.

It takes Steve a while to answer. The door opens just a crack, the chain still on. The inside of the house is in darkness, but this isn't exactly anything new. Harry can't make Steve out, though. His features are hidden by the shadows.

"Oh, Harry, hi," Steve says, his voice sounding muffled. "Just give me a second." The door closes again. There's another moment before he hears the chain slide off the lock. The door opens fully. "You wanna come on in?"

Harry does so. They go through into the front room. Steve collapses into a chair. There's a lamp on in the corner, the only light. It offers Harry his first good look at Steve. He looks like he's been crying, but Harry can't be so sure. His eyes, and the skin around them, are red. Harry knows this effect could easily have been created by his rubbing at them.

Steve sniffs. "What can I do for you?"

"I'm just checking in, Steve," Harry says. "See how you're holding up."

"That's real thoughtful of you," Steve says. His voice is low, hard to hear. He sniffs again, clears his throat. If the crying was faked, he's committing to it with these sounds.

"When's the funeral?" Harry knows from conversation with Peter that their father is dead, and their mother left when they were both young. Left Peter to raise his younger brother, who now has to organize his burial.

"I don't know," Steve says. "Not until they release the body. I can't do anything until then, and I don't know when that's going to be. I'm thinking I'll just get him cremated. It's cheaper, and from what I hear, he's already halfway there."

"Who'd you hear that from?"

"The cops."

"They been by to see you?"

Steve nods.

"They didn't see anything they shouldn't have?"

"No, of course not. Why do you think the place looks so tidy? This ain't how I usually live."

Harry watches Steve while he talks. Judges his tone, his

mannerisms, his reactions. "They say anything to you about how he died?"

"No, they didn't," Steve says. "Just that he died in a fire. But Ronald already told me the truth."

"And what d'you think of that?"

Steve stares at the ground. "What am I supposed to think? Someone killed my brother, then tried to burn the place down to hide the fact they did it."

Steve answers well, he acts well, but there remains something off about him. Something Harry can't put his finger on. Perhaps it's his own doubt, clouding what he sees, swaying his perceptions. "Whoever they are, they could be coming for the rest of us next," Harry says. "We think it has somethin' to do with Anthony Rollins. Some friends of his."

"Could be," Steve says, looking up.

"What you think of that?"

"What d'you mean?"

"You spent a lot of time with Anthony, and now he's responsible for your brother being dead."

"Well, I'm thinking if we get hold of one of his buddies who's come to town, then we can make them talk, find out where it is he's gotten himself to."

"That ain't a bad idea."

"Yeah, well, that happens, you know where to find me. Be sure to send me an invite. I'll be straight over."

"Mm." Harry taps his fingers on the arm of the sofa he sits on. "Why don't you go get the takings for the week? I might as well take them now, seen as how I'm already here."

"Sure," Steve says. He gets to his feet, leaves the room. Harry glances around, like there's going to be some clue left out in the open that will answer all his questions. but if Steve knows who's responsible, he's doing a good job hiding it.

Steve returns with the cash, hands it over. While Harry is counting it, Steve says, "Listen, I wanna make a request."

Harry doesn't respond until he's finished counting. He pockets the money, says, "Shoot."

"With Peter dead, with his killers still out there, I wanna step up."

"How so?"

"On the council. I wanna take his place. It's what Peter would've wanted. He would've wanted me to be more proactive, to take his place, to know he left his seat in good hands."

Harry is surprised by this request. It wasn't what he expected. Steve has never shown any interest in going beyond his position. "That ain't up to me," he eventually manages to say. "I'll have to run it by the rest of the council. It'll be put to a vote."

Steve nods along.

"But once we reach a decision, I'll let you know."

"Okay. Great. Thanks. Like I say, it's what Peter would've wanted, and right now all I can do is try to honor his memory and find whoever it is who's responsible for killing him."

Harry leaves, goes back to his car, still thrown.

It feels off. It all feels off. It doesn't sit right with him. Steve's mourning feels fake, forced, as does his sudden ambition.

Harry doesn't leave straight away. Puts the keys in the ignition but doesn't move, just sits in his car, mulling over the conversation they have just had, how Steve was acting.

He glances up at the house one more time as he goes to start the engine. He sees a curtain twitch, drawn back into place.

Steve was watching him.

37

Carly is in her apartment. In the kitchen. She makes coffee, though she knows she shouldn't have another mug. She's already on edge. Her hands are shaking. It's a nervous time. She chews her lip.

Her phone rings, and she almost drops what she's holding. She puts the filter down. It leans to the side, and some of the grains spill out over her counter. She glances at the screen. It's an unlisted number. There are two people it could be. One of them is Eric. She doesn't think it's going to be Eric, not so soon after seeing him.

The first thing the voice says is, "How was your trip?" It sounds smug, condescending, as if it knows exactly how her trip was, exactly what Eric said to her.

"It was fine," she says, matching the tone. "Thanks for asking. I appreciate your concern."

There's a chuckle, then, "I understand you have a new assignment."

"Yes. Soon."

"What about the current one?"

He's referring to Ben. "What about him?"

"What do you *think*? I'm not interested in his thoughts and feelings, his deepest desires. I want to know how it's going."

"Not great. He's secretive. I'm spending as much time with him as I can, but I'm not getting anything. It's turning into a waste of time."

"It's not a waste. It keeps him distracted."

"Eric tells me I'm *too* distracting. In the wrong way."

The voice chuckles again.

"I think Ben's running his own private investigation again," she says, refusing to be patronized in such a manner, determined to have something to show for her efforts.

"How so?"

"I've seen him make some private phone calls – not just at home, at the office, too. He leaves the building a lot, goes to his car. Always looks around, makes sure no one's near."

"Being furtive is in the job description, Agent Hogan."

"You know exactly what I mean, so don't try to piss me off. This is more than that. He's always distracted."

"He has a lot on his plate."

"I get the impression, like last time, that he's not being totally honest with what he's doing. He's going off the books again. I was right the last time around. I don't see any reason why I should be dismissed now."

"Have you considered the possibility he's maybe talking to another woman?"

She can hear the mockery in the voice's tone. She doesn't appreciate the quip. "I don't care if that's what he's doing. The only reason I've gotten close to him is because that's what you and Eric told me to do. I'm doing it because it's my job, and nothing else. You don't sound like you care he's potentially running another operation off the books."

"Of course I care, and of course he is. Tell me something I don't know. In fact, you know what I don't know? Who it is he's got working for him, and how many there are. Tell me *that*. That's something that would interest me, interest all of us. Did you hear what happened in Harrow?"

"Of course I did."

"And I'm sure you suspect he has a hand in it."

"I'd be a fool not to."

"Have you mentioned it to him?"

"I'd be a fool to do that, too. We're not supposed to know about Harrow, remember?"

"We can't just let him send operatives to run around unchecked in Harrow, Carly. Not now."

"I understand that, but I don't know what you expect me to do, damn it. Listen to me, he's paranoid, he doesn't trust anyone in the department, and I think his trust in me is starting to slip, too. With this new unofficial investigation he's running, he could find out about me."

The voice is silent for a moment.

"You hear me?"

"If that happens, Carly, then you know what to do. We can't let him ruin this. We're too close."

She sighs. "Are we done here?"

"For now. I'll check in again soon."

"I can hardly wait." Carly hangs up the phone. Her hands are shaking worse now. She finishes making the coffee. She knows drinking so many cups of it isn't good for her, but it's the only thing that calms her down.

38

Tom goes to the reception to meet Beth when she finishes her shift. They stroll back to his car; then she directs him to the diner. They take a booth in the back, away from the windows, and Tom wonders if it's so she avoids being seen with him. By Harry, or someone who would report back to Harry. They order their food – a burger and fries for him, a tuna melt for her – and while they wait, Tom leads the conversation into questions about the town, just a curious tourist passing through.

"So, I heard something about the bar that burned down," he says.

Beth sips on her soda. "Oh yeah? You sure hear a lot, don't you?" She winks at him.

"I like to talk to people. It comes with the job."

"What is it you *do*? I don't think you've said."

"You haven't asked. I'm a salesman."

"A travelling salesman, huh? You go door to door?"

He laughs. "No, no, nothing so archaic. I sell to businesses. Office supplies, mostly. Paper, pens, all that basic kind of stuff."

"You don't look like the idea I have in my head of a travelling salesman."

"No? What should I look like?"

"Well, I mean, you're just more in shape than I would've guessed. I'd expect someone who travels so much to be overweight from eating junk from fast-food restaurants."

"I work out in my room."

"That's commendable. But also, don't take this the wrong way, but with the shaved head and the stubble, you don't look like you're making an effort to impress anyone."

"I scrub up well. When I have to."

"I'm sure. I mean, don't get me wrong, I think you look really –" she cringes, backing herself up into a corner "– nice." She looks like she wants to kick herself.

"Nice, huh? Well, thank you; I appreciate that. You look very nice yourself."

"Anyway," Beth says, eager to move the conversation along, "you like it? Sales, I mean."

"It's all right. It gets me out. I see the country. And I get to meet a lot of interesting new people." He smiles at her, like he's talking about her and only her.

She smiles back, then realizes something. "Oh, we were talking about something else, weren't we? You said you'd heard something about the bar that burned down?"

"Yeah. Kinda troubling, I've gotta admit."

"Oh?"

"I heard it was a Nazi bar?"

Beth sucks air through her teeth, stretches her arms out in front of her. "Well, I ain't gonna sugarcoat it. That's *exactly* what it was."

While she talks, Tom checks the few tattoos he can see on her. Checks for Nazi imagery, symbols. He doesn't spot any. There's a small bird, a swallow, on the inside of her left wrist. A black rose on her upper right arm, poking out under her sleeve.

He goes on: "And people were ..." He leans closer, glances around, acting conspiratorial, like he's being careful not to upset anyone nearby who might overhear. "People were okay with that? It didn't bother them?"

"Honestly, there's people I went to school with have grown up and joined Nazi cells, or run off with white militias. Y'know, like living on those communes out in the woods, that sort of thing. Doomsday preppers, that kind of shit."

"I don't think all those kinds of communities are solely for whites." He knows for a fact they're not. The one his father lives in, for instance.

"Yeah, but the ones I'm talking about are."

"You still in touch with any of those people?" He thinks about Harry. Seeing her going in and out of his house.

"Yeah, sure, I see them around. It's hard not to. Harrow's a big town, but it ain't *that* big."

Their conversation takes a pause as their food is brought over. After the waitress leaves, Tom says, "I've seen a lot of black people around, though. Seen some Latinos, too." He thinks of Alejandra. "It's not like they're being chased off, right?"

"Not exactly, but they know where they're not supposed to go." She sticks her fork in the melt, raises some to her mouth. "How come you're so interested, anyway?"

Tom shrugs like it's no big deal. "Guess I've just never been to a place like this before where people knew there was a Nazi group, that's all. I'm just wondering what it's like."

He leaves it at that for the moment, starts eating his burger.

"How much longer you in town for?" Beth says.

"I'm not sure yet," Tom says. "Just until I get a call from head office and they tell me to move on, and to where."

"That how it works?"

He has no idea how it works, but he's guessing neither does Beth. "Sometimes," he says. "In this instance, yes. Sometimes I'm waiting around for them to call me for up to two weeks. I don't mind so much, though. It gives me some time to myself, to come to diners and eat with pretty ladies."

"You pick up that charm on the road?"

"No, it comes naturally."

"I guess some cynical people would say it's part of the job."

"They can say that, but for me, it just helps me in what I do. I've always been this way. I find someone interesting, I talk to them. I see a pretty face, I tell them so. I find someone who's a combination of both, well, that's someone I wanna get to know."

Beth chews, grins. She shakes her head at him.

"You got a boyfriend, Beth?"

She doesn't answer straight away. Thinks about what she's going to say. "I wouldn't exactly call him a boyfriend," she says. She hesitates, and Tom picks up on this, feels like there's more to the story than she's willing to tell. "It's one of those things where it's easier to just spend some time together rather than trying to find someone new in a town with such minimal prospects. We've known each other a long, long time – most of our lives, in fact – but to be honest, by now we don't have all that much in common anymore."

"How come?"

"He runs with a crowd that I don't want any part of."

Tom raises his eyebrows. "Nazis?" he says, almost a whisper.

Beth looks like she doesn't want to affirm, but she finally nods. "Try not to hold that against me. Like I said, some of the people I grew up with in this town, that's what they're like now. I know how that makes us sound, but it ain't like that. Harrow ain't all bad. It just takes a few rotten apples to spoil the barrel, right? And some of those apples, I still talk to them, y'know? It's hard not to. Like with – with *him*. I've known him forever. Since … *before*."

"Do they do bad things?"

"I … I don't know. I don't ask. I don't want to know."

"What's he do for a living?"

"He's … he's out of work right now."

Tom figures this is a polite way of saying that however Harry makes his money, it ain't legal, and she's not going to ask him about it.

He believes her when she says she doesn't ask because she doesn't want to know. She may be aware of his affiliations, what he does, what he believes, but that is not her life. She's not one of them. Unlike Linda, Michael's wife, who Tom is fairly certain knows everything going on with her husband, and more than likely is an active participant in parts of it.

"You wanna talk about something else?" Beth says.

"Sure," Tom says, his tone still light, sprightly, his smile still warm, making it look like this hasn't put him off her, like he's still interested. "Of course. Tell you what, so far I've been leading the conversation, asking all the questions. Why don't we talk about something *you* wanna talk about."

"Sure. Great. That sounds good." She swallows some melt. "Where do you come from? Tell me about that. Tell me about your hometown, seeing as how you've already got a good look at mine."

Tom takes a bite of his burger and prepares to tell her the lies he already has invented for just such a question.

39

Harry is at home, pacing the floors, bored. He's tried calling Beth, but there was no answer. She hasn't called him back, either. He's getting annoyed. She always answers. When she misses his calls, she always calls him back soon after. She knows better than to ignore him. It's longer now than she usually takes.

He's getting suspicious now. It's in his nature. He tries calling her one more time, still gets nothing. He takes a seat, though he can't settle. Gives her a chance to phone him back. When she doesn't respond in an acceptable amount of time, he snatches the phone up, puts it in his pocket, leaves the house. He drives over to her place to see if she's there.

As he arrives, Beth is just getting back. She gets out of her car, is on her way up to the front door. Harry cuts across the grass to intercept her. "Where the hell have you been?" he says, taking her roughly by the elbow. "Your shift ended hours ago."

Beth snatches her arm back from him. "Jesus Christ,

Harry, that *hurt*." She glares at him. "And so what? I got something to eat. That's none of your business."

Harry doesn't care for the way she looks at him, nor for her belligerent tone. "I tried calling you."

"And I missed it – so what? I'd have called you back once I got in the house. You're too damn impatient, that's your problem."

"Where were you?" Harry says. "Who were you with?"

She doesn't answer him. She unlocks her front door, steps inside. Harry follows after her, pushing his way in. "I don't have to come to your place every night," Beth says. "We were clear on that. That was the agreement we reached. Remember?"

"I remember," Harry says. "Every other night. But I was bored and lonely, and I wanted to call you. You forget that Peter has just fucking died? I wanted to talk to you."

"That doesn't give you the right to come storming over here, demanding to know where I've been. This isn't your night. It's mine. You know it's mine."

"Damn it, Beth!" He's getting annoyed. Getting that feeling in his hands, that itch, like he wants to grab her or hit her, to make her shut up and just *listen*.

She flinches at his rising volume. He's glad to see it.

"If I call you, I expect a damn response," he says. "Where were you?"

"I already told you, I went for something to eat."

"*Where?*"

"I was at the diner. It's no big deal."

"With who?"

"No one. I was alone."

He looks at her, feeling the same way he did when he spoke to Steve. "You sure about that?"

"Of course I'm sure. Who else would I be with? No one

wants to be near me because of you. All my friends, they all stay away. They're all scared of you."

"If I find out you were with someone, and you ain't admitting to it right now –"

"I was *alone*!"

"Hmm." He won't tell her he believes her, because he doesn't, but he leaves it at that.

"Are we done here?" Beth says. "Are you satisfied? Will you leave now?"

"I told you, I want to see you."

"Then you'll have to wait until tomorrow, when it's your night."

"I don't want to wait."

"We have an agreement."

"You're right, we do," Harry says. "And tonight you don't have to stay over at my place. But right now, we're not at my place. We're at yours."

She looks at him, realizes what he's saying. "Please, Harry," she says, begging, pleading. "Just leave me alone."

Harry doesn't budge.

"I'm tired," she says. "I just want to go to sleep."

"Then go," he says. "I'll be right through."

He thinks there are tears in her eyes, though she blinks a lot, trying to get rid of them. Harry smiles at them. This is better. This is how he wants it to be, how it *should* be. She needs to behave herself. She can't speak to him how she did. She should be subservient to him. That's how it's always been, and it's how it'll always be.

She gives up. She turns away from him before the tears can fall from her eyes, and she goes through to the bedroom, her feet dragging.

Harry watches her go. He gives her a moment, and then he follows.

40

Tom heads out into the night. Another round of recon. He wants to see what kind of response, if any, the death of Peter has elicited.

He goes by Harry's first. All the lights are off. His car is gone. It doesn't look like he's home. Tom moves on. He goes to Ronald's next. On the way over, his phone begins to ring. The number is the one he gave to Steve. He pulls over to answer it, into a parking lot from where he can see the diner where he ate with Beth.

"Harry came to see me," Steve says. "To see how I was doing, and to ask about Peter's funeral."

"He say anything of use?" Tom says. He doesn't want daily check-ins. He wants Steve to only call when he has something worth sharing.

"No, not really, but I'm trying to get closer to them, like you asked. I'm trying to get onto the council."

"You offer to take your brother's place?"

"Yeah, yeah, that's exactly what I did."

"They go for it?"

"Harry said they're gonna have to discuss it first."

Tom sucks his teeth.

"I don't know how long that's gonna take. From the sounds of what you were saying, you might not have that kind of time."

"No, I don't think I do."

"But I'm only guessing. Maybe they'll be quick – maybe I'll hear something back tomorrow, right?"

Tom doubts it. "Do what you can, Steve. Keep me updated." Tom puts the phone away, continues on his rounds.

Ronald and Michael are both at home. They haven't gone to ground. This sets Tom's mind at ease about Harry not being at his place. They're not hiding out from him. They're continuing on as they were. He's glad of this. It'll make them easier to take out.

41

B en has the meeting he dreads. The check-in with Jake Lofton. Where Jake asks him how the investigation is going, and Ben has to admit that, officially, he doesn't have anything.

He can't tell him about Tom. And as far as the FBI is concerned, Harrow isn't even on their map concerning this case. They didn't have anyone undercover there.

Jake leans back in his chair, tents his fingers. "That isn't great, Ben."

"I know," Ben says.

"So what are you going to do about it?"

"I'll think of something."

Jake shakes his head, looking disappointed. "I'm not so sure you will. I need results, Ben, and I need them yesterday. Right now, all you're doing is wasting your time. Your time and *our* time. It doesn't look like you're going to find a thing. I'm going to have to take you off this, put you back to some real work."

Ben can't take a chance on being reassigned. There's

the potential it'll take him out of town. He needs to be here, in Dallas, for whatever is coming. "Another week," he says.

Jake raises an eyebrow.

"Another week to try to find the leak," Ben says. "Just a little more time to devote to it. For what they took away from us, it's got to be worth seven more days, right?"

"What do you think you're going to do any differently in seven days?" Jake says.

"Like I said, I'll think of something."

Jake looks at him for a long time. Ben doesn't think he'll agree. Finally, he surprises him by nodding. "Seven days," he says. "And seven days *only*."

Out of the meeting, Ben hurries out of the building, to his car. Making sure there's no one else around, he calls Tom. "I need something," he says. "And I need it fast. They want to pull me off the leak. I've got seven days."

"I'm doing what I came here to do," Tom says. It sounds like there is no urgency in his voice. Ben doesn't like that.

"Well, I need you to do it faster. I need *names*. I need to know who the mole is, or the hacker, or whatever the fuck they were. I need to know what the plot is, who's planning it, and where it's going to happen. If the Right Arm doesn't know all of that directly, then they know who does."

Tom doesn't say anything.

"Are you there? Are you listening?"

"I'm here."

"Everything leads back to Harrow," Ben says, watching his mirrors. "The night of the purging, it's like they were trying to cover their tracks. You understand? They were making the search area broad, pointing it toward all these potential different cells. They were trying to put us off the scent. But it's Harrow, it's the Right Arm. They had to go out of their way to find out about Anthony. They had to go through *me*. They've left too many clues now. The surveillance footage from the fertilizer factory where the dumb bastard didn't cover up his tattoos, the money trail our analysts picked up on, it all goes back to Harrow, to the Right Arm."

"You need to calm down," Tom says.

"And you need to hurry the fuck up."

There's a pause; then Tom says, "I don't work for you, Ben. You'd do well to remember that."

Ben takes a deep breath. "All right," he says, calming. "You're right. I'm sorry. But our country is in danger. Hundreds, maybe thousands of lives are at risk, and I can't help but feel you're dismissing all of that just to go off on some half-cocked revenge mission."

"I know what I'm doing," Tom says. "Don't question me. I've agreed to help you, but you're right. The attack isn't my primary concern."

Ben is flabbergasted. "How can it not be –"

"But I'll deal with it," Tom says, cutting him off. "If it's like you say, and the Right Arm is behind it, then our two issues are walking hand in hand. I'll deal with it."

They end the call, and Ben sits back, catching his breath. He looks in the mirror and sees a dishevelled stranger looking back. He straightens himself out, combs his hair with his fingers, slaps on a smile, and gets back to work.

42

First, Anthony is able to sit up without feeling sick. Then he's able to stand. He can take a few steps before feeling like he needs to hurry back to the bed, his pills, warmth, and sleep.

Now, he's had enough of the bed, of pills, of warmth, and sleep. He's done enough resting. He gets to his feet, changes out of his rancid, sweat-drenched clothes, and puts on a fresh set that Sylvia has loaned him from his father. Anthony steps out of the house.

"You need someone to go with you?" Jeffrey says. He and Sylvia are in the front room, watching him.

"No," Anthony says. He wants to be alone. "I'm just going for a walk. I ain't gonna get far."

They leave him to it. Leave him alone.

Outside, Anthony tires sooner than he expected he would. He finds a place to sit and rest on a tree stump. He looks through the chain-link fence, out across the fields beyond. The grass is long. It sways to and fro in a breeze that feels cool and good upon his face.

He presses a tentative fingertip to the edge of the bandaging wrapped around his head. He goes higher, probes at the wound in his skull. It stings. He quickly snatches his hand back as a throbbing pain courses through his brain, sending a wave of nausea through his whole body.

His arm itches in its cast. He doesn't feel sorry for himself. He's too angry for that. Angry at his brother, off in Harrow. Angry at his father, for calling him in the first place.

Angry at himself.

Angry at Ben Fitzgerald.

Angry at the Right Arm Of The Republic.

Angry at the world.

When he tries to think about Alejandra, to remember what she looked like, all he sees is Peter standing above her, putting a bullet through her face. That is the face that comes to him. Holed and bloody.

He told her that he was undercover five months ago. Told her how it happened, too. How he'd been selling drugs, trying to provide for them, for the baby. She wasn't happy, not about any of it. She looked like she wanted to hit him, ask him how he could have been so stupid, so careless.

Anthony had asked himself the same questions, so many times.

He'd had to keep her secret from the Right Arm. They never went out together anymore, not for a walk, not even for groceries. She had to attend all her birthing classes by herself; Anthony couldn't run the risk. He told the Right Arm he lived elsewhere, gave them the address of a friend who would let him stay over on the nights that he needed to be there, whenever they needed to pick him up for something. Anthony spent all of his free time trying to comfort

Alejandra, promising her that once it was over, they would flee, start over somewhere new. It would be done before the baby was born.

All he had to do was find out about the attack. What the Right Arm had planned. Once he fed that info to Agent Fitzgerald, that would be it, it would all be over.

He tried. He tried so damn hard. He got as close to the Right Arm council as he could without getting his own seat at the table. Tried to get closer. Even snuck around of his own accord, spied on them, taking his very life in his own hands. There was no hazard pay, but he did it to get it done. And what did he find?

Nothing.

There was nothing to find.

As close as he got, no one knew a thing. He was subtle about it, of course, but he always got his point across. Steve didn't know anything, but then again, Steve wasn't interested in that life. He was doing what he did to keep his brother off his back. As for Peter himself, Anthony reached out to him, too. Told him that if they ever needed him for anything heavy, if they ever had anything planned to go down, that they could rely on him. Peter had given him a sidelong look, raised an eyebrow. "Sure," he'd said, as if overwhelmed by the newbie's zeal. "I'll keep that in mind."

It was taking too long. No matter what he did, what he said, how much willing he showed, they kept him at arm's length. A long vetting process – too long. He was getting frustrated. He was missing out on the pregnancy. If it went on much longer, he was going to miss the birth. He told himself, if he was still undercover when Alejandra went into labor, that was it. He was done. Fuck Agent Fitzgerald, and fuck his conspiracy theory – Anthony was out. Fuck the consequences. They'd flee, and they'd hide out. With the help of his father, they'd likely never be caught.

So he thought.

He thinks about the phone. He knows Agent Fitzgerald would have been the one to bring it. Knows now, too, that Agent Fitzgerald had anticipated his potential escape plan, had found out where Jeffrey was, was keeping tabs on the commune in case he ever needed to come calling.

And then Anthony was found out.

Anthony tries to keep his eyes open. When he blinks, he sees her. Dead. Her due date is coming up. Tears are running down his face.

One of the guards on the other side of the fence, weighed down with weaponry he doesn't look strong enough to carry, stops as he gets near, sees Anthony. He comes up to the fence, looking concerned. "Hey," he says. "Are you all right?"

Anthony wipes his face. "I'm fine."

"You sure?" The guard raises an eyebrow, not believing. He can see the tears still in Anthony's eyes.

Anthony stares at him, doesn't say another word until he backs down, has to lower his face. "I said I'm fine," Anthony says. "Even if I wasn't, I ain't gonna tell you about it, toy soldier. Now get outta here. Leave me alone."

The guard moves on, grumbling to himself as he goes. Anthony hears the word *asshole*. He doesn't care. He's been called worse.

43

Tom goes to Ronald's house. He parks down the road, same place he has every other time he's come here. Soon after he pulls up, Ronald emerges from the house. Tom sinks down in his seat. Ronald goes straight to his own car, gets in, pulls out. He heads the same way he did when Tom followed him. Tom doesn't follow him this time. He wonders if he's off to make another collection.

Tom gets out, goes to the house. He goes around the back, glancing in the windows as he passes. The house is empty. The furnishings and decorations are sparse. It is a home without a woman's touch.

Tom breaks in through the back door, picks the lock. He steps into the kitchen, onto the linoleum, and stops, listens. The house is still. He walks through it, looking into the rooms. He sees pamphlets of white supremacist literature in piles on the coffee table in the front room, looking like they're waiting to be distributed. Tom goes up the stairs. A couple of the steps creak. The house is uncarpeted. Tom is aware of every sound of every footstep he makes.

There are three rooms upstairs. One is the bedroom, the bed unmade. Above the bed is a poster of two blue-eyed and blonde-haired naked women. They give Nazi salutes, their other arms around each other's waists. The other room is a spare, filled with detritus. There are some unused weights gathering dust and cobwebs, more of the pamphlets that Tom spotted downstairs, and piles of clothes, a couple of old pairs of boots. The room between the two is the bath-room. There is a wet towel dumped in the corner, filling the air with a potent smell of dampness. The spaces between the tiles above the bathtub are filled with black mold.

Tom goes into the spare room. He looks out the window. It has a view of the street where Tom has parked his car. The car is beneath a tree, the view through the windshield obscured. Tom goes into the corner of the room. He takes a seat, and he waits.

A few hours pass. Tom watches the sky out the window opposite. He listens to the road outside. Only a couple of cars go by. Finally, Ronald returns. His car pulls onto the driveway. The door opens, the house's front door opens, then the trunk opens. Ronald has been on another run. Tom hears him moving around downstairs, footfalls on the exposed wood.

Ronald doesn't come upstairs. The footfalls stop. He starts talking, but Tom can only hear his voice. He's on the phone. The brief conversation ends. The footfalls do not resume. Tom assumes he has taken a seat.

Twenty minutes later, another car pulls up out front. There's a knock on the door. Ronald lets whoever it is in. Tom listens closely. Their voices are muffled. One of them laughs. Finally, he hears that it's Harry. Ronald says his name.

They make small talk. Harry has come to make the collection. They talk about the drugs and about money. This isn't of interest to Tom, but he continues listening in case they say something he might want to hear.

They talk about Peter. Ronald asks if there's a funeral date yet. Harry tells him no, but he'll let him know as soon as he hears something. Finally, Harry leaves. Ronald moves around downstairs; then finally he falls silent again. The television comes on. He settles in. Tom could likely make his move now, creep down and take him out. He waits. The evening is coming in. The darkness is deepening. The later it gets, the less likely it is Ronald is going to receive any unexpected visitors.

Tom's eyes adjust to the dark. He familiarizes himself with the room. Marks out objects that are a trip risk. It gets late. The television abruptly falls silent. Ronald yawns, then groans as he gets to his feet. Tom hears him cross the floor; then he's coming up the stairs. Tom gets ready.

Ronald reaches the top. He groans again, catches his breath, then goes into the bathroom. Tom gets to his feet. He goes to the wall next to the door, presses himself against it. He can hear Ronald pissing. It goes on for a while. Finally, the toilet flushes. There's the sound of running water, of Ronald splashing it over his face. He leaves the bathroom.

Out on the landing, Tom makes his move. He grabs Ronald from behind, wraps an arm around his neck, pressing down on his carotid. Ronald tries to struggle, tries to swing him around, to force him back. Tom stands firm. Cuts off the oxygen to Ronald's brain. Ronald goes limp.

His body sinks to the floor. Tom lowers him, makes sure he's out; then he scoops him up, puts him over his shoulder, and carries him back down the stairs.

44

C arly goes to a warehouse in downtown Dallas. Ostensibly, the warehouse is abandoned. It went out of business years ago; it should be empty. She knows it's not.

As she approaches, she spots the faint outline of a man on the roof against the night sky, watching her approach. If she didn't know he was there, if she hadn't been looking for him, she's not sure she would have seen him. Her throat feels dry. Her heart is pounding. She grits her teeth, takes a deep breath. She's a professional. She won't be intimidated by them. They work for the same person she does, and, more than that, they're just a bunch of mercenaries. She's an FBI agent. They're nothing.

She pulls the car to a stop, kills the lights and the engine, but she remains inside. She pulls out her phone, dials a number. A gruff voice answers. It's Chuck Benton. "You here?" he says.

"I'm outside. One of your boys on the roof has seen

me." She feels satisfied letting him know she picked out one of his guards.

Chuck grunts, then hangs up. Ahead, she sees a door open at the side of the building. He stands there, lit from behind by weak light, sliding his phone back into his pocket. Carly gets out of the car, goes to him.

"Agent Hogan," he says once she's close enough, looking her over and smiling.

Carly does not like the feel of his eyes running over her skin. "Eric wants to know how things are coming along."

"Inside," Chuck says, stepping aside to let her through. He closes the door, says, "Things are coming along well. He didn't hire some two-bit operation – he hired the best, and he knows that."

Carly glances around the warehouse. Three other men are sitting around. It looks like they've been playing cards, but they've gotten bored of it. They're all looking at her now. She feels the same level of discomfort under their gaze as she did under Chuck's.

Carly keeps her back straight, her jaw set, defiant. She doesn't care that they're undressing her with their eyes, that it's probably been a long time since any of them were with a woman. She doesn't care about the awful thoughts that must be running through their heads. She won't be cowed by them.

"Show me," she says.

"Of course," Chuck says. He walks away and she follows. She knows the eyes of the other three will still be upon her, will be watching her ass.

The warehouse is cold. She notices some of the windows have been smashed. Likely by kids with rocks during its years of emptiness. Chuck leads her to the back of the building. There is a van, and next to it are boxes. They are under a tarp, likely to keep them dry.

"Eric sends you down here to check in on us, huh?" Chuck says. "He don't trust us, that what it is?"

"Eric is cautious. You should know that by now," Carly says. "And he's a control freak. He doesn't like things being out of his hands like this, doesn't like having to rely on other people."

"Man from his background, I'd expect he's used to having other folk do things for him."

"I didn't come here to make conversation about Eric," Carly says. "I came here to see the goods."

Chuck smirks. "Sure thing, sweetheart." He steps over to the corner of the tarp, pulls it back. "What exactly is it you want to check? All the fertilizer? You can probably smell it already."

"I can," Carly says. She's avoided wrinkling her nose so far. In all honesty, she just thought it was the smell of five men in close quarters together. "You know what I came to see."

Chuck smirks again, and she wishes she could slap that look right off his face. He picks up the nearest box, brings it over to her. He opens it up. There is ammonium nitrate inside.

"Plenty more like this," Chuck says, tilting his head back toward the other boxes. "We ain't mixed it in with the fertilizer yet."

"I thought it was already inside the fertilizer," Carly says.

"Not enough for the size explosion y'all are asking for."

Carly's mouth fills up with spit suddenly. She has to swallow it before she can speak again. "You're not nervous, being around all this?"

Chuck puts the lid back down, shrugs. "Ain't the first time," he says. He puts the box back with the others. "You wanna check them all individually?"

"No," she says. "One is enough."

"Well," Chuck says, coming back over to her, "there it is, in all its glory."

Carly feels uncomfortable being so close to so much explosive material. It must show, as Chuck starts to laugh. She asks, "How much damage will this all do?"

"A lot," Chuck says. "Just like you wanted."

"Jesus Christ."

"Oh, He don't have nothin' to do with it. Way I understand it, they don't even believe in Him, ain't that right?"

Carly says nothing to this. Her eyes are fixed on the boxes. Now that she's seen the contents, they make her nervous. The hard surface she was determined to wear while she was in here, with these men, is beginning to crack.

"Everything to your liking?" Chuck says. He's enjoying this, how uncomfortable she looks. It sounds like he's mocking her. "You gonna report back to Eric, tell him how hunky-dory everything is on our end, how we've done it all exactly how he told us, and how we've been worth every dime?"

Carly looks him in the eyes. "I'll tell him just that."

"Great. Satisfied with what you've seen here?"

Carly spares another quick glance at the boxes. Thinks about the damage they are going to cause. How many buildings they are going to destroy. How many people they are going to kill. She thinks about one person in particular. "Very."

45

———————

It takes a moment for Ronald to get his bearings. He knows he's in his kitchen, but this is an angle he hasn't seen it from before. He has to raise his head a little to look around. He's on the kitchen table, flat on his back.

Then he realizes he can't move. He's tied down.

And he's not alone.

Tom watches him wake. In his hands are a towel and a watering can. It's the same damp towel Tom spotted earlier in the bathroom. He found the watering can in the garage. It's perfect. It's old and hasn't been used in a while and looks like the last thing it had in it was oil. Tom has filled it up with water from the tap. It's ready to go.

Ronald's eyes settle on him. They blink, narrow, widen. "Who the fuck are you?"

Tom holds up the items in his hands. "Are you familiar with waterboarding?" he says.

Ronald looks confused. "Huh? What?"

"It's an old practice. It goes back to the 1500s, to the

Spanish Inquisition. It's called an interrogation technique, but let's be realistic here: It's a form of torture. Most recently, you might have heard about its use at Guantanamo Bay. There was a lot of controversy about that, right? I bet you were one of those guys who was all for it. Fuck the A-rabs, right?"

Ronald stares at him, slowly comprehending why he is being told this.

"But you ever seen it done? You ever done it? You ever had it done to you?" Tom raises his eyebrows, cocks his head, like he's waiting for an answer. There is none forthcoming. "Basically, this wet rag here, it goes over the person's mouth and nose. And then, the water in this can here, it gets poured over the rag. The water gets in your mouth, it gets in your throat, and your gag reflex kicks in. You know what it feels like? It feels like there's a fire in your throat and your nostrils. It feels like drowning. And it feels like it ain't ever gonna end."

Ronald looks scared. He tugs at the cords that bind him to the table.

"Oh yeah," Tom says, "you're gonna want to struggle. You're gonna kick and scream and thrash around, try to break free, but you're tied down *real* tight, believe me. I know a thing or two about knots. You'd think I was a Boy Scout or somethin'."

"Who are you?" Ronald says. "What do you want?"

Tom ignores him. "Ideally, the table should be inclined about ten or twenty degrees, just to really get the water in there, but we can make do, right? I don't have the time to be sawing and sanding down table legs, getting them just right. And trust me, it'll work just *fine* on a flat surface. You understand why I'm telling you all this, right?"

"You're trying to scare me," Ronald says.

Tom laughs. "I'm gonna do a lot more than just scare you."

"Fuck you."

"I'm gonna waterboard you, Ronald. And it's gonna hurt like hell. So much so you're gonna wish you were dead."

"Fuck you."

"Yeah, you're acting tough now, but believe me, when it comes down to it, you're gonna cry like a baby. Unless, y'know, you just tell me everything I wanna know right now."

"I'm not telling you anything. I ain't telling you *shit*."

"You don't even know what I'm curious about yet, Ronald." Tom grins.

"It don't matter – you ain't gonna get a damn thing outta me!"

Tom sucks his teeth. "Well, we'll see." He puts the towel over his face. It covers his head. Ronald tries to shake it off. It's damp already and it clings to him. Tom pours the water over his mouth and nose, his other hand holding him tight by the jaw, keeping him still. Ronald's body spasms. He tries to cough and splutter through the towel, but nothing gets through. Tom counts to ten in his head. He stops. Takes the towel away, drops it onto his chest.

Ronald gasps, wheezes. He throws up on himself. The bile is watery. "Told you, didn't I?" Tom says. "Feels just like drowning."

"Who the fuck are you!" Ronald says. "I got nothin' for you!"

"My name is Tom Rollins," Tom says. "My brother is Anthony Rollins. I believe you know him already."

Ronald's eyes go wide. They fill with realisation, with

understanding, with fear. Quickly, he tries to hide it. To be tough. Belligerent. He juts his jaw. "You killed Peter," he says.

"Guilty," Tom says.

"Who's with you?" Ronald says. "How many guys you got? We're gonna waste 'em all, then we're gonna find your brother! We're gonna finish what we started!"

"Guys?" Tom says.

"Who's helping you?"

"I've always worked better alone, Ronnie." Tom winks.

"Bullshit."

Tom shrugs. "Who told you about my brother, Ronald?"

Ronald closes his mouth tight, breathes through his nose.

Tom leans down close to him, rests his elbows on the table. "A mutual acquaintance of my brother thinks it came from within the FBI. That true? They got a mole?"

"Fuck you." Ronald spits the words through gritted teeth.

"Have it your way." Tom puts the towel back in place. He pours the water. Pours it intermittently, gives him a chance to catch his breath. By the time the can is empty, Ronald is screaming.

Tom removes the towel so Ronald can see what he does next. He takes the empty can to the sink, fills it back up from the tap. Fills it all the way to the top. Makes sure Ronald is watching him while he does so.

"All you gotta do is talk, Ronnie," Tom says. "Just tell me what I want to know. It ain't a big ask."

Ronald's eyes dart left and right as Tom approaches with the freshly filled can. There is no way out. There's no one to help him. No one has heard his screams, come running. There's no way out. No help.

Only one thing he can do to make this all stop.

Tom can see he's close to breaking. He doesn't say anything as he picks the sodden towel back up from his chest, prepares to put it back in place.

"Wait!"

Tom looks at him, raises an eyebrow.

Ronald breathes hard, panting. When he doesn't say anything, Tom moves the towel again. "I'll talk!"

"I'm listening."

Ronald grits his teeth. He looks ashamed of himself. "We don't know who she was," he says.

"She?"

"Yeah. She called Michael, direct, but she wouldn't say how she got his number. She told him about Anthony, how he was undercover."

"You were there?"

"Yeah. Me and Harry. We were at Michael's just hanging out, having some beers, watching a game."

"I don't need your life story, Ronnie. Stick to the details that interest me."

Ronald swallows. "Michael asked why he should believe her. He had got her on speakerphone, so we could all hear. All she said was, *Do whatever the hell you want, but there are twelve other cells in four other states taking out their trash tonight. Do y'all wanna be the ones who don't?*"

"And you believed her? Just like that?"

"Harry got on the computer, started checking the news. He saw a report about two other undercovers getting wasted right here in Texas, just minutes before."

"How'd he know they were undercovers?"

"They fit the bill she was telling us. How else would she know about them? It was breaking news."

"You didn't ask who she was?"

"Sure, Michael asked her exactly that. And she says, *You've got friends in places you don't know about.*"

"You heard from her since?"

"No."

"Michael try calling her back?"

"It was an unlisted number. He almost didn't answer it. He's destroyed that phone since, got himself a new one."

Tom grunts. "He really think that's gonna make a difference?"

"Better than doin' nothing."

"That's true. I agree, it's always better to be proactive, in any kind of situation. Now, on that note, tell me about the attack you've all got planned, Ronnie."

Ronald's eyes narrow. "Attack? The fuck you talking about?"

Tom brings up the towel.

"I swear, I swear, I don't know what you're talking about!"

"Hell, I barely know what I'm talking about here, Ronnie. I was asked to ask. But apparently y'all are planning some big kind of attack, a real case of domestic terrorism, something big and dangerous like this country hasn't had for decades."

Ronald is confused. "Who the hell told you that?"

"Money trails, security cameras."

"What?"

"What about Michael and Harry? They gonna do something? Maybe they've left you outta the loop?"

"They wouldn't do that," Ronald says, adamant. "They wouldn't leave me out of anything. There's never been a decision they made they didn't bring me in on first."

"That so?" Tom says. "Then let's forget about the attack

for now, because I believe you when you say you don't know anything about it. Look at that, Ronnie, I *believe* you. We're making real progress here, aren't we?"

Ronald doesn't respond to this.

"Let's go back to the night you found out Anthony was working against you, shall we? Let's go back to when you ran him off the road, and you found he wasn't alone. His girlfriend was with him. You remember all this, right, Ronnie? It wasn't all that long ago. So you find him with his girl – her name was Alejandra, by the way, Alejandra Flores, I want you to remember that – and you see that Alejandra is pregnant. You couldn't miss it. She was real far along. I mean, you must have seen, right? Did you notice, Ronnie?"

Ronald looks scared to answer this.

"Sure you did. So here's a question. If there'd been a child with them, an actual living, breathing, out-of-the-womb child, half-white, half-Latino, what would you have done then? Put a bullet between its eyes?"

Ronald doesn't answer. Doesn't want to answer. But Tom knows. He knows that this is exactly what they would have done. Tom raises the watering can.

"Hey, hey – what're you doing?" Ronald is panicking. "I told you everything you wanted to know! I answered all your stupid questions!"

"You didn't answer the last one," Tom says without turning.

"Fuck you," Ronald says. He chooses to be angry instead. He knows how this night ends for him. "Fuck you! Fuck you! *Fuck you!*" He starts screaming for help.

Tom puts the towel back over his face, shoves it into his mouth. He starts pouring the water. He doesn't stop. Ronald's body spasms; it struggles; it strains at the bonds.

The movements begin to slow, become languid. Tom empties the can. He fills it again, leaves the towel in place. By now, Ronald is still. There are choking, gagging sounds coming from the back of his throat. Tom returns to the top of the table, empties the can into his face once more. Ronald moves a little, but it's not long before he's completely still. Tom watches him choke to death.

46

B en is sleeping.

As far back as he can recall, he's never been able to remember his dreams. He's always put it down to falling into too deep a sleep, tired and weary from the busy events of his daily life. Lately, however, he has been plagued. Nightmares. Visions of death and destruction. He finds himself running through the night, pursued. Eventually, it's like he's running in place; he can't go fast enough. The person chasing him catches up, runs him down.

It's Anthony. It's usually Anthony, out for his blood.

Sometimes, it's Tom.

Ben wakes in a cold sweat from these dreams. He wakes with the inside of his cheek chewed ragged, the taste of blood in his mouth and burning in his throat. Of course, this is only when he's able to sleep at all. Some nights he just tosses and turns. He stares at the ceiling. He goes downstairs and paces the floor, fretting.

Tonight, he wakes to the sound of his buzzing phone.

He reaches for it, but doesn't answer it immediately. He pauses, glances back, then remembers he is alone. Carly only returned from visiting her family in Fort Worth earlier tonight. She said she'll be tired; she'll stay at her own place; she'll see him tomorrow at work.

The caller is Tom Rollins. Ben feels a lump in the center of his chest. He coughs, then answers. "Hello."

"I've spoken to Ronald Smith," Tom says.

Ben clears his throat, breathes through his nose. "Is Ronald still capable of speaking?"

"No."

"Color me surprised."

"Do you want to hear what he had, or not?"

"I'm listening."

Tom tells him. Tells him how Ronald doesn't know anything about a planned domestic terrorist plot, and doubts the others on the council do, either. Tom tells him that he believed Ronald.

"How can you be so sure?" Ben says.

"He wasn't lying," Tom says. "I know."

Ben feels a cold chill run through him.

"I asked him about the mole."

The chill intensifies. Ben's throat is dry. "And?"

"He didn't have a name." Tom tells him how the call came unexpectedly. They didn't have the number. The caller didn't introduce themselves or explain who they were. All they did was tell them the truth of who Anthony was, and they had knowledge of the other undercover murders happening that night.

"He said it was a woman's voice," Tom says. "When they asked who she was, she told them they had friends in places they don't know about. I assume she was referring to the FBI."

Ben isn't sure if his heart is still beating. He turns his head to the side of the bed where Carly usually sleeps. The pillow there is still indented with the shape of her head. His eyes go across the room, to the closet where he has hidden his old laptop, the one that was hacked.

His stomach sinks.

"You still there?" Tom says.

Ben grits his teeth. "I've been so blind," he says.

"What?"

"All along. I've refused to see it, but it was right in front of me. It's *her*. It was her all along."

"You know who the mole is?"

"I ..." Ben doesn't want to jump to conclusions, but at this point, he doesn't think that is what he's doing. "I think so."

The laptop. It was never hacked. Gerry said as much. She watched him. Saw him type in his password. She accessed it for herself, either while he was sleeping or downstairs or out.

"But why?" he says, thinking out loud. "Why would she do this?"

"Who, Ben?" Tom says. "Who are you talking about?"

"Did she get close to me *just* to do this?"

"What's her name, Ben?"

Ben is about to answer; then he clamps his mouth shut. "Tomorrow," he says. "Tomorrow, I'll confront her about it. Tomorrow, one way or another, I'll know."

"Who is she, Ben?" Tom says. "What's her name?"

Ben hangs up. He bites down hard on the inside of his cheek. This is for him, not Tom. He has to ask her. He has to.

He feels like he's going to be sick.

47

nthony called the police in Harrow, asked them about Alejandra's body. They tried to ask him if he knew anything about that night, if he knew who had shot her and why. He lied, said he didn't. Said he was her cousin, and he'd only just heard what had happened.

The cops will be looking for him, since his father snuck him out of the hospital. He's a witness to what happened that night, to the death of Alejandra. He can't tell them who he really is. Luckily, they buy his lie. Believe he's her cousin. They put him through to the coroner's. Her body has been cremated. No one came forward to claim her.

"I'm coming," Anthony said.

"And who are you, sir?" the voice on the other end said. "Are you family?"

"I'm her boyfriend," Anthony said. He didn't lie this time. "I'm the father of her child. The child that was still inside her when you burned her to ash."

He was holding the phone tight against the side of his face. There were tears in his eyes.

"Oh," the voice said, suddenly quiet. "I'm so very sorry for your loss."

Now Anthony is going back. He's returning to the town where it all happened, where it's *still* happening, but he's not thinking about his brother or the Right Arm of the Republic. He's thinking only of Alejandra, of the baby.

Jeffrey is with him. He's driving. Anthony is in no state to do so.

"It's gonna be uncomfortable for you," Jeffrey said before they left, "on the road, in your condition. Don't try to be a hero. If you're in too much pain, if you need to stop, you just say so. You need painkillers, you need to throw up, you need to rest, anything, just say the word."

They've been on the road for two hours now. The journey has been in silence. Anthony is sore, he is uncomfortable, but he will not admit it. He will not do as his father said and tell him so. He doesn't want to stop, doesn't want to rest. He just wants to get Alejandra and their child. He can suffer anything for this.

He looks out the window. They listen to Springsteen on the CD player. Earlier, Jeffrey had asked, "If you ain't gonna talk, you mind if I put on some music? It's gonna be a long trip for me otherwise."

"Please yourself," Anthony said. He'd known his father would put on the Boss. He's not sure he's ever heard him listen to anything else.

With every mile, they get closer to Texas. Back to her. She'll return to him. Anthony keeps telling himself this, his teeth gritted, trying not to make a sound to give away how sore he is. His back hurts, his arm hurts, but it is his head that is the worst. It feels like it's splitting open again, like all the healing his skull has gone through thus far is being undone.

It's hot, too. Even with the air conditioning blowing. Anthony feels sweat drip down his spine.

Jeffrey begins to pull off the road.

"What're you doing?" Anthony says.

"Gas stop," Jeffrey says.

While his father fills the tank, Anthony gets out of the car, takes a walk around the building to stretch his body, try to clear his head. The pains abate, for now. When he gets back to the car, Jeffrey is waiting for him. He's bought snacks, too.

"Hungry?"

"Not right now," Anthony says. The sight of the candy, of the chips, makes him feel sick.

Jeffrey puts it all on the backseat, then pulls out, back onto the road.

Another ten minutes pass. Anthony wants to ask. Wants to know. He can't keep it to himself any longer. "Have you heard anything from Tom?"

"No," Jeffrey says. "But I've been keeping an eye on his progress."

Anthony looks sidelong at his father. "What's that supposed to mean?"

"Means I've been checking the news."

"And?"

"He's killed a few of them already, far as I can tell. But, y'know, he's a pro. He covers it up, makes it so it ain't so obvious. If I didn't know what I was looking for, I wouldn't see it."

Anthony takes a sharp breath through his nose. He shouldn't have asked. "You get any names?"

"I saw names," Jeffrey says. "But they didn't mean anything to me."

"You didn't think I'd wanna know?"

"I didn't think you were gonna ask. You've been real stubborn about this whole thing."

"I've got a right to be stubborn."

"I didn't say you don't."

"You shouldn't have called Tom," Anthony says. "You never needed to call him."

"So you've said."

"And I'll keep saying it, because it's not getting through to you."

Jeffrey doesn't respond. Anthony looks at him, staring straight ahead. The sinews flex and tense in his father's jaw. He's gritting his teeth. Hard, by the looks of it.

"You had no right," Anthony says.

Again, Jeffrey does not say anything.

Anthony turns away from him, back to the window. He tells himself, every minute that passes, they get closer to Texas. Closer to Alejandra.

They continue the rest of the way in silence. It's not comfortable.

48

B eth has left for work. Harry is still in bed, lying back. He's not wearing anything save for his underwear and the blanket tangled in his legs. He's smoking a cigarette and flicking through his phone. Looking at old photos that he hasn't looked at in years. Peter is in them. They're all in them, all the council of the Right Arm and a few other members. He can't remember who took the pictures. There are shots of Peter and Ronald, Peter and Michael, Peter and Harry. Harry is with Michael. They were all hanging out in the bar where Peter was killed. They were having a party. Harry can't remember what for. Celebrating some kind of victory, maybe a big sale. It might've been after a successful hunting trip out at Michael's cabin. They hold up beer bottles. They're all smiling, laughing.

Harry's eyes are burning. He closes the pictures on his phone. He clears his throat, presses his palms into his eyes, then takes another draw on his cigarette.

His phone begins to ring. He looks at it, surprised. It's Michael. "Hey."

"What're you doing?" Michael says.

"Nothing," Harry says, confused, feeling as if Michael can see him, can see his near-teary state, is demanding to know what has gotten him so worked up. "I'm still in bed."

"In bed? You sleeping? I wake you?"

"No, I wasn't sleeping. What's up?"

"I've been trying to call Ronald. He ain't answering. You heard from him?"

"I ain't tried to get in touch today. What d'you need him for?"

"You know what I need him for."

Harry grunts. "You're bringing that forward, huh?"

"I don't see any point in holding out any longer," Michael says. "You saw him yesterday."

"That's right."

"How was he?"

"Fine. He was fine."

"You live closer to him – how long's it gonna take to get dressed, get over there and check in?"

"It'll take two minutes to pull on some jeans and a shirt, about twenty to get over there."

"I don't like not hearing from him. Not with what's going on, what's happened to Peter. Go check on him, make sure he's all right, then get back to me. And if he *is* all right, kick his damn ass and ask him why the hell he's left me hanging."

Harry is already getting out of bed, reaching for his jeans crumpled on the floor. "I'm on my way," he says. "I'll be as fast as I can."

Harry pulls on his clothes, then hurries from the house. He doesn't run, but he's walking faster than he ordinarily would. Drives a little faster than normal, too. When he gets to Ronald's house, he sees his car parked in the driveway. Harry parks behind it, knocks on the door. There's no answer. He tries the handle. It's locked. Harry has a key. Ronald gave him his spare in case anything ever happened to him and Harry needed to get inside to get at their goods. He unlocks the door, enters.

"Ronald," he calls to the house, "it's me. You home?"

Ronald doesn't respond. The house is eerily silent. Harry pulls his gun from his waistband, from under his jacket. He holds it down low, in both hands, feeling on edge. He glances into the front room, but he's not there. Harry sucks his teeth, aware of how loud his footfalls are on the bare floorboards.

He goes upstairs, checks the rooms there. They're empty, too. On the way back down, he picks up on a smell. It's familiar to him. It worries him. It's the smell of death. The smell of a body voiding itself.

Harry goes to the back of the house, to the kitchen. The only room he hasn't investigated. He should have checked it before he went upstairs, but he thought for sure Ronald would just be sleeping. He hoped Ronald was just sleeping. If he was in the kitchen, he would have responded to Harry's calls.

Ronald is in the kitchen. He's tied down on the table, a wet towel over his head, some water still dripping to the floor. His face is covered, but Harry knows it is him.

He makes sure the room is clear, that there's no one else here, or outside the window, before he steps into it, goes to Ronald. He presses two fingers to the side of his wet neck, searching for a pulse. There isn't one. He's dead, but Harry already knew this, really.

He backs out of the room, still clutching the gun. He

leaves the house, hurries back to his car. Drives away from
the house, from the killer who may still be lurking. He
parks down the road, looks around, checks his mirror while
he pulls out his phone and makes a call to Michael.
"Ronald's dead."

"*Shit*," Michael says after a sharp intake of breath.
"What happened?"

"Looks like he was tortured."

"Tortured?"

"Waterboarded."

"What the fuck? Who we dealing with, here?"

"If they're friends of Anthony's, they were probably
asking about us. Trying to find out who was involved,
where we're at."

Michael is silent while he considers this. "You're
right," he says. "Ain't nothing else they could've been
asking him about."

"They're picking us off," Harry says. "First Peter, now
Ronald. What we gonna do? We can't just sit around, let
this happen."

"No. Fuck that. We strike back. Get yourself over here.
We're gonna have to do this alone."

49

Ben goes to Carly's home.

All day, he has had to be near her with the suspected knowledge of who she really is, and what she has done. He's had to force smiles, small talk, to act comfortable. To be himself, how he usually is. And all the while, he's been watching her, searching for some kind of clue that would give away her true nature.

Nothing. She hides it well. She looks the same to him as she always has.

"What's wrong with you?" she said, coming up on him from behind, surprising him.

"What do you mean?"

"You've got that look on your face, when you're thinking about something; you're getting yourself all worked up."

The inside of his mouth tasted like blood. He'd been chewing hard on his cheek, so much so he'd had to move to the other side of his mouth. "Just work stuff," he said.

She nodded, made a face like she understood, because she was living it too. "Are you free tonight?"

"No," he said, almost too fast. "I'm not, sorry. I've got work to do. I'm swamped."

"Sure," she said, like no big deal. "Maybe tomorrow, then."

He nodded.

He hasn't shared his suspicions with anyone. He can't. Can't run the risk of anyone tipping her off, helping her out. Being on the same side as her.

He can't trust anyone.

He's felt sick all day. Carly has not been the only one he's viewed with suspicion. He's looked upon all of his fellow agents with wary eyes.

Now he's pulling up outside Carly's home. He hasn't driven straight over from the office. He's circled a little first, given her a chance to get home. More than that, he was building up his nerve. Preparing himself.

He rings the doorbell, and she's surprised to see him when she answers. "Oh, hey, I thought you were gonna be busy," she says. "You get all that work done?"

"Almost. Can I come in?"

She lets him in. Ben goes straight through to the front room. He waits until she joins him, until she gets in front of him so he's blocking the way out; then he doesn't waste any more time. "Are you the mole?"

Carly blinks at him. "Uh, what?"

Ben runs his tongue around the inside of his mouth, over his ragged cheeks. "Did you leak the details from my laptop?" he says, speaking slowly. "Did you go onto my laptop, find out about Anthony, and tell the Right Arm of the Republic? Did you tell all the other cells about all the other undercovers and informants? Did you cause the purge? Are you the fucking mole?"

Carly takes her time answering. She tries to play it cool. "I don't know what to say to that, Ben."

"Then just answer the question."

"Ben, I shouldn't have to answer. You should already know. Do you really think I could do such a thing?"

Ben chews his cheek, feels a piece of flesh come off in his teeth. He looks into her face, into her eyes. He wants to believe her. Doesn't want to think this could be true. That she has betrayed him. That she was with him *only* to betray him.

Carly looks right back at him. She's not backing down. She's looking into his eyes. She's daring him to doubt her.

"I need you to answer me," Ben says, but his voice is weak, it wavers. It's lost the authority he was earlier able to imbue it with, before she spoke.

"You know I didn't, Ben," she says. "You know it wasn't me. You know I wouldn't do that to you."

Ben bites his lips now. He doesn't know what else to say. He's losing the situation.

Then there's a voice. A new voice. It comes from behind him. It's familiar.

"I don't know that," it says.

Ben turns. It's Tom.

"I don't know that at all. What I *do* know is that my brother's bones were broken, his skull was fractured, and his pregnant girlfriend was murdered in the middle of the road. So now you can look me in the eye, and you can tell me what you're telling him."

Carly doesn't look so calm anymore. "Ben, who is this?" she says. She takes a step back.

Ben is as surprised to see Tom as Carly is. "What're you doing here?"

Tom doesn't answer, just stares straight ahead at Carly. He hadn't liked the sound of Ben on the phone. He came to Dallas. Has followed him since he left the office. Followed his loops around the block, then to here. Had a feeling that if Ben was involved with the woman he suspects might be the mole, that he may not have the nerve to follow through on his accusations. Tom sees that he was right.

"Get out of my house," Carly says. "Both of you. Get out. Now."

"Or what?" Tom says. "Answer the question."

Carly looks between them both. Her eyes silently plead with Ben. Ben can't look back at her. He gives the room to Tom.

Carly sees this. She grits her teeth. Looks back at Tom. Her earlier, cooler demeanor returns. "So who are you?" she says. "His heavy? Running around doing his paranoid wet work?"

She's backing up. Tom notices. He watches her.

"What's he got you doing, huh?" she says. "You said something about your brother, about his girlfriend – what happened to them?"

"I think you know what happened to them," Tom says.

She backs up into the coffee table, knocks the edge of it. The remote control falls, hits the ground. Tom thinks she did it on purpose. Carly looks back to see what has fallen. She raises her hands. "I'm just going to pick that up," she says.

"Leave it where it is," Tom says.

"Just calm down, big boy," Carly says, already lowering herself, lowering her arms, reaching.

"Stand up," Tom says.

She snorts at him. "Relax," she says. "I just hate mess, is all. Ben will tell you it's true. Isn't that right, Ben? I can't leave it lying there. It'll drive my OCD crazy."

As she reaches the ground, the remote control, she moves faster. Her hands lash out. There is a gun strapped to the bottom of the coffee table. She pulls it loose. She stands, spins, but Tom has been watching her, expecting this. Ben sees her pull the gun, too. Tom's own gun is already out. He fires, hits her in the arm, the one holding the gun. She drops it instantly; it hits the floor with a louder clatter than the remote. Ben fires a second after Tom. Carly jerks with the impact of Tom's shot. As Ben's bullet reaches her, it hits her in the chest. Through the heart.

Tom snaps a look at Ben, furious. "I had it," he says.

Carly remains upright for a moment, stunned. She looks down at her chest, where the blood is pumping through her white blouse. She falls back, hits the ground.

Tom goes to her, checks her pulse. She's dead. "We needed her incapacitated, not killed."

"How was I supposed to know you had a gun?" Ben says.

Tom looks at him like he's an idiot for not making such an assumption.

Ben goes to her body, looks down. Carly's eyes are still open. They look back up at him. He has to close them. Tom is checking her pockets. "What're you doing?"

Tom pulls out her phone, holds it up. "Do you think she was working alone?"

"No," Ben says.

"Then we need to find out who she's been in contact with. Do you have someone who can unlock this?"

Ben bites his cheek. Thinks about Gerry. "Maybe. I don't know."

Tom nods. He understands. "Search the house," he says. "Find her laptop. Any clues that might give us an idea who's with her."

"She never admitted to anything," Ben says.

Tom looks at him again. A hard, cold stare. "She pulled a gun."

"You'd broken into her house."

Tom shakes his head. "It's a good thing I came along. I wasn't here, you'd be lying where she is right now."

Ben looks at her body again. There's a pang in his chest.

"Go upstairs," Tom says. "I'll search down here."

"I know where her laptop is," Ben says, going for the stairs. He goes up to her room, goes straight to it, looking only ahead, not to the side of him, not looking at anything in her house that could bring back any memories. He takes the laptop back down. Tom is searching in some drawers in the kitchen. "I've got it."

Tom hands him the phone. "Leave," he says. "Get those unlocked; get back to me with what you find."

"What're you going to do?"

"I'm going to clear up in here," Tom says. "And then I'm going back to Harrow."

50

Anthony has Alejandra's ashes. He sent his father into the morgue to get them. Told him to say he was her uncle. Anthony holds the urn close to his chest with his one good arm. They're going back to New Mexico.

He and his father have not spoken since the argument. It has been a long and uncomfortable journey. Jeffrey turned off Springsteen hours ago, and he hasn't replaced him with anything else. The only sounds have been that of the car. The hum of the engine, the rattle of something indistinct.

As they cross into New Mexico, Jeffrey pulls over suddenly. Anthony looks around. They're at the side of the road. There's nothing here. No gas station, no amenities, nothing.

"What're we doing?" Anthony says.

"We're talking," Jeffrey says, turning off the engine and turning to his son. "You gonna talk to me? No? That's fine, 'cause I'd rather you just listened."

"I'd rather you just drove. It's hot, I'm tired, and I'm sore."

Jeffrey ignores this. "I called Tom, and I don't regret it."

Anthony feels a flash of anger. He especially doesn't want to talk about this, not again. He bites his tongue.

"You're my boy," Jeffrey says. "You're my baby boy, and those Nazi fucks were gonna kill you in the middle of the road like a dog. And they did it to her, and they did it to the baby inside her." He points at the urn. He looks like he's trying not to cry. "They killed my grandchild. They were going to kill you. I want them dead as much as you do, but I'm an old man now, Anthony. I'm old, and you're injured. And Tom is neither of those things. Tom is a *soldier*. He can do what we can't. He can make them pay."

The tears in Jeffrey's eyes are gone now, replaced instead by an indignant glare. "I'm not going to apologize again," he says. "I stand by what I did."

Without another word, he turns the key in the ignition, checks his mirrors, and pulls back onto the road. Anthony watches him. Jeffrey's jaw is set. His hands are tight on the steering wheel. His eyes stare straight ahead.

Anthony turns his attention back to the urn. He holds it tighter to his chest. This is as close as he will ever get to Alejandra again. As close to his child as he will ever be.

"All right," he says.

Jeffrey turns his head, an eyebrow raised.

"All right," Anthony says again. "I don't agree with what you did, but I understand why you did it. I understand." His lip begins to tremble. He presses his forehead to the urn. He's crying.

Jeffrey pulls over again. He reaches over to his son,

takes him in his arms, hugs him. He holds him close. Anthony doesn't feel like he'll ever stop crying, but he does. Eventually. And then they continue the journey home.

51

Harry picks Steve up from his home, drives him to Michael's.

"What's this about?" Steve says.

"It's good news, don't you worry," Harry says, not looking at him, studying the road ahead. "Good for all of us."

"Is this about the council?" Steve says.

Harry tilts his head a little. "Could be," he says.

Steve doesn't say anything else, but Harry can feel excitement emanating from him.

They reach Michael's. Linda answers the door. There is no sign of Michael. "You know where to find him," she says. She smiles at Steve.

Steve follows Harry. This is his first time in Michael's home. He tries not to stare, to look around too much, taking everything in. Harry leads him downstairs, into the basement.

The council.

There's not much of a council anymore. Just Michael and Harry, co-founders.

Of course, Steve doesn't know this. He doesn't know about Ronald's death – or at least, they don't think he's aware. They've wondered how big a role he has played in what is happening to them. Is he responsible for Ronald's murder? For his brother's? It shouldn't seem comprehensible, but he's never been one of them, not really. They don't know what's going through his mind.

"Michael," Steve says, nodding.

Michael returns the nod. "Any plans for that funeral yet?"

"Not yet," Steve says.

"They're taking their time."

"I think it's to do with how he died," Steve says. "They're still looking into it."

Michael grunts.

Steve looks around the room. This is his first time in Michael's basement, too. "Peter would tell me about this place," he says.

"Yeah?" Harry says. "What'd he tell you?"

"He made it sound like some kind of party house," Steve says.

"Used'ta be," Michael says, glancing at Harry. "Not so much of that these days. Ain't really been in the partying mood lately. Not with what's happened to your brother and his buddies. And now Ronald."

This is it. This is the moment they find out. Michael and Harry both watch Steve closely, his reaction to this.

Steve stops looking around, turns his attention back to them both, his eyes narrowed. "Ronald? What's wrong with Ronald?"

"He's dead, Steve," Michael says.

"Dead? What? When?"

"What do you know about it already?"

Steve blinks. "This is the first I'm hearing anything about it."

Michael and Harry exchange looks. "You sure about that?" Harry says.

"What do you mean? Of course I'm sure. I think I'd know if I'd heard that Ronald had died. How'd it happen? When?"

"Same people who killed your brother, we figure," Michael says.

"Ron was killed?" Steve says.

Harry watches him. "Yeah," he says. Steve is playing it good. He looks suitably shocked. But then, he always has. How long was he fooling his brother for? Harry doesn't believe he didn't know anything about Ronald or any of it. About Anthony. He can't believe him, because there's no other explanation. There can't be anyone else responsible from within their own ranks. "Tortured to death."

"Jesus Christ," Steve says.

"You wanna know how?"

"Not particularly."

"Why not? You ain't got the stomach for it? You don't think you oughtta hear about how one of your brothers was murdered on his own kitchen table?"

Steve grits his teeth.

"Tell him how it happened, Harry," Michael says. "You found him. Tell him what you saw. Tell him how long it must've gone on for. Tell him how Ronald must've suffered."

"Waterboarded," Harry says. "You know what that is?"

"I know what it is," Steve says.

"That's what was done to him," Harry says. "They tied

him down to the table, they stuck a wet rag in his mouth
and over his face, and they poured water until he drowned.
You imagine that? Drowning on dry land. Air all around
you, but you can't get a single lungful of it."

Steve grimaces.

"Now, what do you think they were trying to find out
from him that they had to torture him in such an extreme
way?"

Steve looks confused. Holds out his hands. "I don't
know," he says.

Harry grunts. "'Cause, goddamn, that's a hell of a way
to do someone in, ain't it? Shit, makes you wonder how
long it went on for, don't it? Could've been hours. You
imagine that? Like being dragged underwater for hours on
end, you don't know how long it's gonna go on for, you
can't get a breath, and all the while your lungs are burning,
you're panicking, you're all alone in the world, knowing
ain't no one gonna come help you. I don't wanna know
how that must've felt."

Steve nods his head, agreeing.

"Like, whoever did it to him, it was personal to them,"
Harry says. "Y'know? They *wanted* him to hurt. *Wanted*
him to suffer. They had fun with it. They were enjoying
themselves. So what's their vendetta? You got any ideas?"

Steve has to clear his throat to speak. "I'd reckon, uh,
I'd reckon it's probably something to do with Anthony.
Right? That's all it could be."

"Same as with your brother."

"They've got to be connected," Steve says.

"That's right," Harry says. "They *gotta* be. No other
explanation. See, this is the thing. You know how I know
they were doing it for fun?"

"No?"

"'Cause they sure as hell weren't doing it for information."

"How'd you reckon that?"

"Only thing they could ask is where *we* are. Where the rest of the Arm are, where we live, hang out, that kinda thing. They weren't gonna be asking that. They didn't *need* to. Right? 'Cause if they wanted to know that, all they had to do was talk to *you*. Ain't that right, Steve?"

Steve looks like he's been slapped. He looks between them both. At the top of the stairs, the door leading into the kitchen is closed suddenly. It locks.

Michael pops his knuckles.

"What're you, what're you trying to say?" Steve says.

"Ain't trying to say nothin'," Harry says. "We're telling you what we know. Now you're gonna tell us what *you* know. Who are they?"

Steve has gone pale. All the color has drained out of him. He sways a little on his feet, light-headed. "I, uh … I-I don't know what you're talking about."

Michael shakes his head. "Time's up on that excuse, Steve," he says. "We *know*. We fucking *know*. Now just come on out and tell us everything you got before this situation turns real nasty for you."

"I swear to you," Steve says. "I don't know what you're asking me about. I'm loyal. I'm *loyal*. This is my life, always has been."

"It was your *brother's* life," Michael says. "He just dragged you along for the ride, and you never once looked happy to be on it."

"I wouldn't have my brother killed," Steve says. "You gotta understand how ridiculous that sounds. I wouldn't do that. I would *never* do that. I loved Peter. I loved him. I would never do that to him."

"What about Ronald?" Harry says. "You love him? He was your brother, too. Same as all those guys killed with Peter. Same as me and Michael here. We're your brothers. You love us, too?"

"Yes!"

"And you wouldn't ever do anything to hurt us, right?"

"No, no, of course not."

Harry takes a step forward. Steve takes a step back. He's scared. His mask is slipping. Harry can see right through him, now. He knows Michael can, too. He knows they're both feeling the same thing. He knows they're both ready to break this little boy. This traitorous little piece of shit.

"You hurt us by lying, Steve," he says. "You hurt us when you send Anthony's buddies after us. But it don't have to be that way. You can come clean. You can tell us all you know. You do that, we'll go easy on you."

"Just don't keep lying to us," Michael says.

"That's right," Harry says. "Don't lie to us again, boy."

Steve backs up, but he doesn't have far to go. He hits the wall. He looks left and right. The only way out is up the stairs. The door there is locked, and Linda is on the other side. Even if he were somehow able to make it that far, she wouldn't let him leave.

"Just talk to us, Steve," Harry says. "Tell us everything you know."

"Everything," Michael says.

Steve swallows. "I-I –"

Michael looks at Harry. "This kid is gonna try to lie to us again, ain't he? You can see it, right? It ain't hard to tell."

"That stammer sure sounds like he's trying to make up some excuse," Harry says.

"*Oh, I don't know anything, guys, I swear!*" Michael says.

"Please –" Steve says.

"*Please?*" Harry says.

"You believe this fuckin' guy?" Michael says.

Harry makes a grab for Steve. He twists out of it. Michael is at the other side of him. He makes a grab, too. Steve ducks this time; he dives for the council table, rolls over it, tries to scramble to the other side. Harry races to the other end to greet him, slams him with his shoulder, knocks him to the ground. Steve lands hard. He tries to keep moving with the momentum, to keep rolling, but Michael is coming up fast, kicks him in the gut. This knocks him onto his back, makes him cough. It slows him all the way down, but he doesn't stop. He knows what's going to happen if he stops.

"And now he's trying to run," Michael says, reaching down, grabbing for his head.

Steve rolls again, to the side. Harry stomps him on the chest, pins him. Steve squirms beneath his boot.

"He just don't give up, does he?" Michael says.

"And he don't have any fuckin' sense, either," Harry says.

"You should've talked, boy," Michael says. "It would've been a lot easier."

"I'm sorry," Steve says. He's almost in tears. "I'm sorry – please –"

"You're sorry? Little late for that, ain't it? You know how many men, good men, are dead now because of you?"

They get him up. Harry holds him so Michael can soften him up, some shots to his ribs. "Quit your snivelling," he says, then hits him across the face to shut him up.

They swap, then. Michael holds him so Harry can take

a go. Harry doesn't hit him as hard as he can. They want him to hurt, but they still need him to talk after.

They put him into a chair. "That's your brother's chair," Michael says. "It's as close as you're ever gonna get to this fuckin' council."

Steve is bloodied now. He winces with every breath, tries to cover his ribs with his arms in case they go to hit him again.

"Who are they?" Harry says. "Who's coming after us?"

"It's not a they," Steve says. He coughs.

Michael rolls his eyes. "He still don't get it, does he? Hold him down, Harry."

"No, wait, *wait*!"

They ignore his cries. Harry puts an arm around his neck. Michael pulls on two of his fingers. They snap. Steve screams. It's right in Harry's ear, almost deafens him.

"Why don't we start easy, huh?" Michael says, letting go of his arm and straightening up. Harry remains behind the chair, holding him in place. "Nice and easy, right? You don't wanna tell us who's comin' after us just yet, you wanna play it like you're cool, like you're tough, then let's try a different question. What happened with Anthony? Did you know he was undercover?"

Steve shakes his head, tears dripping from his face. "No," he says.

Michael looks pissed off now. He reaches for the hand with the broken fingers again.

"No, wait! I didn't know, I swear – but I called the cops!" Steve says. He's frantic. "I didn't know he was undercover, I found out same time y'all did, but I messaged him, told him to run – that was me. And I called the cops, sent them out looking for you."

Michael and Harry look at each other. "Fuckin' knew it," Harry says, clenching his jaw.

"All right," Michael says, rubbing his hands together. "All right, that's good. Don't that feel good, Steve? To share?"

Steve doesn't answer.

"I'm sure it does. Sure it feels like a weight has been lifted off you. I bet that secret's just been eating you up inside all this time. Now, your other secret. Who are they? Who's comin' after us?"

"I tried to tell you," Steve says, "it ain't a *they*, it's a *him*."

Michael and Harry look at each other again, confused. "What do you mean?" Michael says.

"There's no *them*," Steve says. "It's one guy. It's Anthony's brother."

Michael snorts. "One guy? Bullshit. Bull*shit*. You think we're gonna believe that? Harry, hold out his other hand."

"No, no, I'm telling you – it's one guy! It's one fuckin' guy!"

Harry watches as Michael hesitates. Thinks about this. Wonders if it could be true.

"Anthony's brother?" Michael says. "What's his name?"

"Tom," Steve says. "Tom Rollins."

"You in touch with him?"

"He gave me a phone, but it's just a burner."

"You got it on you?"

"No. It's at home."

"We could get it," Harry says. "Message him, pretending to be Steve. Get him to meet us somewhere, ambush him."

Steve laughs. "You think he'd fall for that?" He laughs

harder, like something has come over him. He doesn't sound like himself. "He ain't some asshole amateur like all of y'all – this guy is hardcore. He knows what he's doing, and he's coming for you all. He's gonna fuckin' kill you."

"That sound like a smart thing you should be saying right now?" Michael says.

"Fuck you!" Steve says. He spits at him. "I'm already dead. You think I'm an idiot? I already know it."

Harry hits him in the back of the head. "We could make him talk," Harry says, to Michael. "Down the phone, to Tom. If he hears the voice, he's more likely to believe it."

"I won't do it," Steve says. He laughs again, but it sounds more like a bark. "There ain't nothin' you can make me do. This is the end. I told you everything you wanna know; this is the end for me. I ain't stupid."

"You sure sound stupid," Michael says, "running off at the mouth like that."

"He's gonna kill you all," Steve says. "I can die happy, knowing that. He's gonna kill you all!"

Michael looks at Harry. They've gotten all they're going to get from Steve, and now he sounds like he's losing his mind. Michael nods. Harry snaps his neck, then lets him fall from the chair.

"Call in whoever we've got left," Michael says. "We're going to ground. If this guy, Anthony's brother, if he's coming for us, we're gonna be ready for him this time."

52

Tom returns to Harrow. It's time to wrap this up. Michael and Harry are all that remain. By now, they're probably aware of what has happened to Ronald. Tom didn't want to leave it this long. He wanted to strike them straight away, but he couldn't. They had to wait. He needed to be sure Ben would be able to carry through on what needed to be done. He couldn't. Tom did the right thing. Now, the person responsible for leaking the information about his brother is dead.

Worryingly, though, there is probably more than just her involved. It could be anyone within the FBI. It could go further.

He goes by Harry's house first. There's no sign of him. He doesn't see Beth there, either, but he assumes she's at work. Next, he goes to Michael's. Watches through his binoculars, but there's no sign of life. He goes around the back, creeps through the woods. Gets close. The house is silent. It's empty. There's no one home. No sign of the wife, either. Tom waits a while, to see if they return, but they don't.

They know about Ronald. It's spooked them.

He tries calling Steve. There's no answer. Tom goes to his house. There's no answer at the door. Tom goes around the side, to the back. Tom can see him through the window. He's in his room, at his computer, his back to the glass. Tom knocks. Steve doesn't turn. Something feels off. Then Tom sees that the computer is not switched on. He checks around the inside of the window, craning his neck. It's wired. A booby-trap. It'll go off if he tries to get in through the window. There's likely one around the door, too. Maybe every window. The whole house is a time bomb, just waiting for someone to try to get inside.

Steve is dead. The Right Arm has killed him and rigged his house. It's more than likely they tortured him first. Got all the information out of him they could.

They'll know about Tom, now. They'll be expecting him, ready for him. Looking for him.

Tom needs to find them.

He goes to the front of the house, leaves a note on the door. *This house is booby-trapped. Call the bomb squad.* By the time it's seen, Tom will likely be done with his business in Harrow.

53

A few people, knowing the relationship between Ben and Carly, have asked him where she is. He's played dumb. All he's given by way of explanation is to say that she's been complaining about feeling ill lately. Has worried she's maybe coming down with the flu. Maybe something she picked up while she was visiting her parents. She hasn't called in? No one else has heard anything?

In reality, he doesn't know where she is. He doesn't know what Tom has done with her body. Taken her away to dispose of her elsewhere? Cut her up into small pieces? Ben chews on his cheek, and he tries not to think about it too hard. It makes his stomach turn.

He has her laptop. It's in a bag under his desk.

Tom asked him, "Who do you trust?" Ben couldn't answer. He thought long and hard – he's still thinking – and there's no one who springs to mind.

He has to take it to Gerry. He has no choice. It's a big risk, but it's one he's going to have to run. Carly's laptop could contain the names of everyone involved, everyone within the FBI secretly working against everything they stand for.

Ben makes his move.

He grabs the bag, slings it over his shoulder, tries to look casual as he travels down the hallway to Gerry's office, nodding at fellow agents, saying hello, wondering all the while how many of them are his enemy.

Gerry looks up as he enters. He raises an eyebrow at the bag Ben carries. "That looks suspiciously like it's carrying a laptop," he says. "I've told you, Ben, I've done all I can already. There was nothing on it."

Ben puts the bag down in front of him. "This one isn't mine."

"No? Whose is it?"

"Agent Carly Hogan's."

"And what's happened to this one? She been hacked, too?"

Ben takes a deep breath. He glances back at the door. He goes to it, locks it. When he turns back, Gerry is alarmed. "She's the one who got into mine," Ben says.

Gerry's jaw drops. "You serious?"

Ben nods.

"What the hell? You're sure? How do you know?"

"I know."

"Well, what have you done about it? This is a big fucking deal, Ben. Have you told Jake?"

Ben is pleased by Gerry's reaction. It looks, it feels, genuine. "I haven't told anyone," Ben says. "Only you."

"Me? What do you expect me to do about it?"

"I expect you to get into her laptop and find out who she's involved with. It wasn't just her. There are more."

Gerry bites his lip. He looks at Ben. "Where *is* Agent

Hogan?"

"She's elsewhere." Ben isn't going to give details. "I can't bring her in until I know who else is involved. You understand? I don't know who I can trust."

Gerry's eyes narrow. He looks fearful of Ben's paranoia concerning the rest of the department. "But you trust me?"

"I had no choice," Ben says. "I need your help. And if I can't trust you, well, I guess I'm royally screwed."

Gerry holds eye contact. "Ben, I swear to you, whatever Carly is involved in, I have no part of it. I promise you."

Ben nods, pushes the bag with the laptop closer. "Can you get inside?"

"I'll try." Gerry pulls the laptop from the bag, opens it up.

"Her phone's in there, too," Ben says. "Can you do anything with that?"

"Maybe. But if she's as deep in this as you think, you really think she's going to have been communicating on her phone?"

"It's worth looking."

Gerry pops his fingers, then gets to work. Ben steps to one side, takes a seat, leaves him to it. Chews his cheek while he waits, keeps one eye on the door, fearful that there should come a knock, that someone will try the handle, try to get inside. Ben is confident he can play it cool, but can Gerry?

"Shit," Gerry says.

Ben looks up. He isn't sure how much time has passed; he hasn't been keeping track. "What is it?"

"Whoever she's been talking to, it's encrypted. And it's *real* sophisticated."

"Can you break it?"

Gerry's fingers have never stopped typing. "I'm trying."

"Can you tell how many people, at least?"

Gerry shakes his head without looking up.

Ben lets him work, knows that the only way he can help him is by remaining silent.

Minutes pass. Gerry never stops working. His eyes never stray from the screen; he barely blinks. He's engrossed in his work, determined to get through.

"I'm in," Gerry says.

Ben jumps to his feet, comes around the desk.

It's there.

It's all there.

They read it together. They read in silence for ten minutes, every piece of communication. Ben feels his stomach sinking. A quick glance at Gerry, and he knows he's feeling the same thing.

"Who is this?" Ben says. "Who's she talking to?"

"I don't know," Gerry says. He starts tapping at the keys again.

"What're you doing?"

"I'm trying to see if I can find where these messages came from, and from who."

Ben waits, watches him work. What he's doing isn't clear to him; it doesn't make sense. Nothing seems to be happening. "Well?"

Gerry shakes his head. "I can't get it. There's a deeper encryption."

"So we don't know who's helping her," Ben says.

Gerry raises his eyebrows, points at the screen. "But we know all *this*."

Ben nods, solemn, thinking. "Get the phone open," he says. "The answers might be there."

Gerry takes the phone from the bag. He plugs it in,

connects it to his laptop. He taps at his keys, taps at the phone's screen. It's open. He hands it to Ben.

Ben looks through, reads the messages, looks at her calls. His own name pops up. He ignores it. Can't find anything out of the ordinary.

"Well?" Gerry says.

"There's nothing here," Ben says. "Like you suspected."

"But there's a lot *here*," Gerry says, pointing at the laptop. "This is huge. We can't let this happen. We have to share this information."

Ben looks down at him. He notices Gerry has started sweating. He's breathing hard. He's gone pale. "We can't," Ben says.

"*What?* Are you insane? How can we not? Do you realize how many lives are on the line here? We can't just allow this to happen."

"We're not going to," Ben says. "I'm not going to."

"What do you mean?"

"I'll stop it," Ben says, his mind made up. "I'll do it. I know it all now. I know their plan, their target; I know what they're going to do. But we don't know who else is involved."

"You can't do this on your own," Gerry says.

"I have no choice. We don't know how high this thing goes – what if we tell the wrong person, or they find out? That won't stop it. It'll just change the plan, or else we get silenced and it still goes ahead."

"Silenced?"

"You know exactly what I mean," Ben says. "We'll be dead. We can't do anything to stop this if we're dead."

"We should tell Jake," Gerry says, a hint of panic in his voice.

"We can't tell anyone."

"You don't trust Jake?"

"I don't trust anyone, not right now. Only you. Do you understand that? Only *you*. And I need to know that I can trust you, and that you'll trust me that I know what I'm doing. That I'll stop this."

Gerry is trembling.

"Gerry, look at me. Calm down. We're the only two who know. No one knows we know. It's happening *tomorrow*. Right now, we have the element of surprise. This works in our favor."

"I'm just a computer analyst, Ben," Gerry says. "I can't, I mean, this is beyond me. I'm not an agent. I don't know what to do. This is the kind of thing, I find out, I pass it on. Someone else deals with it."

"And someone else will," Ben says. "Me. I'm going to deal with it."

"You're just one man. You can't do it alone."

Ben thinks about Tom. "I won't be alone. I'll have help. Someone from outside the bureau."

Gerry narrows his eyes at this. "Who?"

"He's a friend. Let's just leave it at that."

Gerry looks doubtful still.

"Gerry, it's one night. Keep your mouth shut for one night. I'll stop this, you'll see. And after that, we'll find everyone else involved. All right? We'll flush them all out. You'll see. Everything will be all right. Everything will be how it should."

Gerry's lips are pinched tight. He looks like he's going to be sick. "Carly's dead, isn't she?"

"No," Ben says. "She's not." He can't tell him the truth. He needs him on his side. The truth of what happened might scare him too much, more than he already is. It might scare him off, send him running. Send him talking. "She's alive, and after tomorrow, she's going to give us the names of all of her friends, too."

Gerry runs a hand down his face, covers his eyes.

"Gerry, come on, get up." Ben takes him by an elbow, pulls him to his feet. "We're going to leave. Right now, together, understand? We're going to leave, and I'm going to go home and get ready, and I want you to go home and keep your head down. Lock the doors; stay inside. Don't call anyone; don't talk to anyone. Keep the lights off; pretend you're not in. That clear? Look at me, Gerry. I need to know that you understand what I'm saying."

Gerry gives a feeble nod.

Ben packs the laptop back into the bag. He hooks it over Gerry's shoulder. "Keep studying it. See if you can break the encryption. See if you can find out who the others are. You do that, you call me."

Gerry is almost catatonic, in a state of shock.

Ben shakes him. "You need to stay with me, Gerry. Look alive. We're about to leave the building, you and me, together. Come on."

Ben takes him by an arm, leads him out of the office. Stands close to him while they walk, using his body to disguise the fact that he's holding his arm, leading him along.

They reach the parking lot without incident. "Where's your car, Gerry?"

After a moment, Gerry says, "I take the bus."

Ben bites his cheek. "Of course you do. Come on, I'll drop you off."

They go to Ben's car. He shoves Gerry inside, then hurries around to the driver's door. He looks back at the building as he goes. No one is following them. He starts the car, pulls out, and thinks about what he has to do.

Tom goes to the motel, looking for Beth. She's on reception. She smiles at him as he approaches. "Hey," she says. "How you doin'?"

"I'm good." He smiles back at her, takes a seat.

"You looking to make dinner plans again?" She winks.

Tom did not use his real surname to sign into the motel. He wonders if Beth knows who Tom Rollins is. If Harry has told her about him, this name, to be wary of it. If he told her how they got it. "I could eat," he says, playing along. "When do you finish?"

"Pretty soon," she says. "You hold out another hour?"

"Sure," Tom says. "Meet me at my room. I'll wait for you there."

"See you then."

Tom goes to his room. He checks it over before he enters it, looks around. Steve didn't know he was staying here, but it won't hurt to be careful. In the room, he removes the Beretta and KA-BAR from his bag, keeps them on him, then puts the bag in the trunk of his car. He waits for Beth to come. Watches for her. Makes sure she's alone. If there's anyone with her, he'll have the element of surprise. He'll take them out; then he'll get what he needs from her.

When she finally comes, she's alone. She's smiling as she makes her way, in between whistling. Looks like she's in a good mood. Because of him, the prospect of another date?

Or because of something else?

When she knocks, Tom is ready, waiting. He grabs her, pulls her into the room, closes the door, clamps a hand over her mouth. Holds her from behind, keeps her subdued. He can feel the way she shakes, her shock.

Tom speaks into her ear. "I'm not going to hurt you," he says. "I just need to know where your boyfriend is."

He can see the side of her face, the way her eyes widen.

"I know all about Harry," he says. "I know all about the two of you. I'm going to take my hand away from your mouth. Don't scream. I don't want to hurt you. Do you understand?"

She nods.

Tom removes his hand. Beth doesn't scream. "Tell me where he is," Tom says.

"Who are you?" she says.

"Harry and his friends killed someone very important to me," Tom says. He's still holding her tight from behind, close to him, preventing her escape, ready to silence her again. "And they tried to kill my brother. I want to know where he is, 'cause he ain't at home."

"What do you mean? Who did they kill?" She gasps suddenly, realizing. "It wasn't … it wasn't the pregnant girl … was it?" She sounds scared to ask, scared to know the answer.

"Her name was Alejandra."

"He promised me," she says, "he promised me they had nothing to do with that! He played dumb, said he didn't know anything about it, knew as much as I did!"

"Tell me where he is."

"He's not my boyfriend," Beth says. "We just, we have an … an arrangement. It's his arrangement, his idea, his rules. I managed to get a little leeway on some of them, but for the most part, it's whatever he says goes."

"I'm not interested in your setup, Beth. Don't make me ask again."

"No, listen, I'm explaining – I'm not with him every night, just every other night. And when I have to be there, I don't ask about what he's been up to, what the Right Arm is doing – I don't wanna know. I asked about that pregnant girl on the road because I had to. I had to know about that. And he fuckin' *swore* to me –"

"I heard you the first time," Tom says, cutting her short. "You told me already. Don't repeat yourself."

"Okay, okay. The point I was trying to make is, I don't see him every night. I was supposed to be at his place last night, but he wasn't there. I waited, but he didn't come home."

"You call him?"

"Yeah, but his phone was off."

"He tell you where he was going?"

"No, but that isn't uncommon."

"Do you know where he's gone?"

"No."

"I need you to think, Beth," Tom says. "I need you to think long and hard about places Harry might have gone, places he and his buddies might hang out. Anywhere you know about."

She does as he says. She thinks, tries to remember. It doesn't take her long to come up with somewhere. "Michael has a cabin in the woods outside town," she says. "They go hunting there, the council, some of the other guys."

"And you think that's where they've gone?"

"Could be."

"Anywhere else?"

"If they ain't at Michael's place, and they can't go to the bar anymore, I'd reckon that's where they'll be."

"Tell me where it is."

She does so, giving directions as best she is able. "I've never been," she says. "I just know vaguely where it is."

"All right. I need you to take a seat now, Beth."

There's one already pulled out ready, waiting for her. Tom had the room set up before she arrived.

"Why?" Beth says. "What're you going to do to me?"

Tom makes her sit down. He ties her to the chair with electrical cord. "I'm grateful for the information you've given me," he says while he works, "and I believe everything you've told me. I believe you're not overly fond of Harry or how he lives his life. I believe you, Beth, but I can't take a risk that you're not lying to me, that you won't try to warn them I'm coming."

"I won't tell them anything, I promise you, I swear it," Beth says.

"I'm sure you do," Tom says. "But that's not good enough."

"What are you going to do to them?"

"You already know what I'm going to do to them, Beth," he says. "You already know what I've been doing. You shouldn't worry too much, you should feel hopeful, because if you truly dislike being around Harry as much as you say you do, you won't have to suffer that life for much longer."

He finishes tying her up, checks the binds. They're tight enough she can't escape, not so tight they're going to cut off her circulation. "I'm going to have to leave you like this," he says. "But I'll be back. Once I'm done."

"What if they kill you?" Beth says.

"You'd best hope they don't." He puts a gag in her mouth to stop her from screaming, then gives her a reassuring wink. "Housekeeping comes round every morning, don't they? Relax. One way or another, you won't be here longer than a day." He leaves the room, locks the door, pockets the key. With Beth's directions in mind, he goes to his car, sets off.

55

It's late evening when Senator Seth Goldberg gets back to Dallas. He's been in Washington all week, pushing through his bill. Taking calls, meetings, answering questions, enduring verbal assaults. He's tired.

The girls are already in bed by the time he gets home, but Abigail is waiting by the door as he steps through it. She embraces him, holds him tight. "How was it?" she says, the side of her face against his chest.

Seth sighs. "Rough," he says.

"Mm, I saw some of the news reports," Abigail says. "I thought you did well. You handled yourself. You didn't let anyone shoot you down."

They break the hug, move through to the sitting room. "Thanks," Seth says. "I feel like we're getting somewhere. We're moving forward. I guess the more they push back, the more they're scared of us, right? They're scared of what we're doing, all that we've accomplished, and how close we're getting to finishing the job."

Abigail nods along.

"How was your week?" Seth says. "How are the girls?"

"We're ... we're fine," Abigail says. "It's been fine."

Seth knows she's keeping information from him. No doubt they've had a tough time, too. He doesn't press it, though. If Abigail wants to share details with him, then she will do so. He reaches out, strokes her cheek, squeezes her shoulder. "It'll get better," he says. "I promise. It won't be like this forever."

She takes his hand, kisses his knuckles. "I know," she says. "I know. Are you hungry? Do you want to eat?"

"I'm starving," Seth says. "But what I really want is a shower. Then we'll eat. Then we'll sleep. In that order. I know it's still pretty early, but I'm exhausted."

"Are we going to synagogue in the morning?" Abigail says.

"Of course," Seth says. He takes a deep breath. "It'll be good for us. We need it."

56

Tom has found the cabin. He's in the woods, dirt smeared across his face to hide him amongst the underbrush. It was light when he got here. It's getting dark now. He's been watching through his binoculars. He's seen Harry and Michael and Linda. They stay indoors. There are other members of the group here, too. Only four of them. Tom wonders if this is all they have left.

A phone buzzes in the bag next to him. It's the one he gave the number for to Ben. Tom answers. "I can't talk," Tom says. He edges back, away from the tree line, deeper into the woods.

"I need you in Dallas," Ben says. "I know what's planned. I know what's going to happen."

"From the laptop?"

"Yes."

Tom watches the cabin through the branches. It's lit inside, but the lighting is dim, almost like it's with candles. The four men guarding it outside are heavily armed. "When?" he says.

"Tomorrow. Early. But I need you here now."

"I'm wrapping up in Harrow. I have them right where I want them. I'm going to take this chance."

"Are you fucking kidding me? Do you understand how big this is?"

"No, I don't, because you haven't told me yet. Are you going to do that over the phone?"

Ben sighs hard down the line. "I need you here. You're the only one I can trust."

"And I'll be there."

Ben is silent. He knows Tom won't be swayed. He has a mission he needs to carry out, a task that needs to be accomplished. He won't be deterred, no matter what. "Fast," he says. "As soon as possible. I need to brief you."

"Sure," Tom says, still watching the cabin. "How bad is it?"

"It's really fucking bad," Ben says. "The rumors I heard about it, comparing it to Oklahoma City, they're gonna be true. It's gonna be worse than that."

"Shit."

"Shit, yeah, exactly."

"I won't be long," Tom says.

"I'll hold you to that."

Tom hangs up the phone, puts it back into the bag. This accelerates his plans somewhat. He'd planned on waiting at the cabin longer, making sure all the people present are the only ones going to be here. Making sure they haven't set a trap for him. Ben's call cuts down on his time. He won't be able to watch for as long as he would have liked.

Tom crawls forward again, back to the edge of the forest. It's too dark for the binoculars now. His eyes have adjusted. He watches. Just a little longer, then he makes his move.

57

M ichael knows there's a chance that Steve told Tom about this place. About the cabin. He'd have been aware of it, because of his brother. Peter came out here often enough, with the rest of the council.

They're ready for him, though. They're waiting for him. They've got the cabin as fortified as they can get it. They're expecting him.

Linda is getting antsy. She paces the floors, watches out the windows. "How long we gotta be here for?" she says.

"You know exactly how long, Linda," Michael says. "As long as it takes."

"Yeah, but that ain't exactly an answer, is it?"

"I don't have an exact answer. We're here until we kill this son of a bitch, and we ain't gonna get a chance to kill him until he turns up."

Linda stops pacing. Her body is turned toward the door, her arms folded, like she expects Tom Rollins to come bursting through at any second. "He could've been lying, y'know," she says. "Steve. He could've been lying about it just being one guy. You really believe one guy could've done all this?"

Harry reclines in the corner of the room, letting them talk. He's armed, has a rifle resting across his lap. His head turns from the two of them to the window, keeping an eye out. He looks surprisingly relaxed. Michael wishes he felt how Harry looks.

"Frankly, no," Michael says. "I don't. I don't believe that one guy alone could take down Peter Reid and all his buddies. But Steve wasn't lying. If Rollins has friends, he's kept them secret, kept them hidden from Steve. Steve didn't know about them."

"And you're sure about that?" Linda says, looking at him now.

"Oh, we're sure," Harry says from behind her. "We're very, very sure."

She chews her lip, rocks back and forth on her heels.

Michael stands, goes to her, holds her by the elbows. "Try to calm down," he says. "You walking up the walls like this ain't helping anything. It's just putting me on edge. Take a seat."

Linda nods, does as he says. She goes to the table where, in the past, the victorious hunters have eaten their roasted kills. Michael can hear the laughter still, resounding through the room, victorious men celebrating after a successful hunt.

He goes to Harry. "I'd feel better if we had more men here," he says.

Harry grunts agreement.

"Four ain't any kind of number."

"It'll be enough," Harry says. "These are good men.

Plus, there's us. He shows up, the first sign of him, we'll blow his fuckin' head off."

"A lot of guys didn't even respond when I put the message out."

Harry nods. "They were freaked out about their friends being picked off so easily, being killed," he says. "They're scared, I reckon. Rollins knew what he was doing, taking out Peter first. Sent a message, and a lot of our boys heard that message loud and clear. We're here feeling the consequences of that. Well, ain't nothin' we can do about it now."

Michael sucks his teeth. "We'll deal with them later," he says. "The treacherous, cowardly sons of bitches. Right now, we gotta deal with this bastard."

Harry nods along. Together, the two of them look out the window, into the woods, searching for the man they know is coming for them.

58

G erry didn't stay home for long.

Ben dropped him off, stared him long and hard in the eyes, impressed upon him once again the urgency and importance of what they were doing, made him swear to secrecy once more, then went off.

Gerry sat in the dark for ten minutes, thinking, deliberating, sweating and breathing hard.

It was no good. He couldn't just leave it at that. Couldn't leave Ben alone to go off half-cocked on a mission he had no hope of accomplishing alone. He was putting himself in too much danger and, more than that, he was putting the lives of thousands of other people in danger, too. If Ben were to get himself killed, which was very likely, and everything went ahead as it was planned on Carly's laptop, Gerry would be complicit.

He couldn't have all those lives on his conscience.

So now he's back on the bus, heading back to the office, because despite swearing to Ben he will keep silent, support him in this way, Gerry can't simply sit at home and do nothing.

Returned, he goes straight to the office of Supervisory Special Agent Jake Lofton. He tells him everything.

"It's ridiculous," Gerry says, wrapping up, "and it's dangerous, and he's putting more people than just himself at risk. I don't know what he's thinking, going off on a one-man mission. I don't know if he's got visions of glory in his head or what, but he's going to get himself and a lot of other people killed."

Jake listens to the story in silence, one hand cupped around his chin. He watches Gerry unblinkingly, taking it all in. When Gerry finishes, he raises his eyebrows. "That was a lot to take in," he says.

"I understand that, sir," Gerry says. "I apologize for the info dump, but I didn't want to take a risk of forgetting anything."

"I need to clarify a few things," Jake says. "Agent Carly Hogan was the mole? She leaked the information on our informants and our undercovers to the various white supremacist groups?"

"That's right, sir." Gerry nods.

"And where is she now? Have you seen her?"

"No, sir. And, to be quite frank, the way Ben was acting, I have a bad feeling she's either being held captive somewhere, or she's dead."

"And Ben has sworn you to secrecy regarding all of this? He's going to try to deal with it himself?"

Gerry pauses. "He said he had a friend," he says, remembering. "Someone who could help him out, from outside the bureau. Someone he thinks he can trust."

Jake's eyes narrow. "He give a name?"

"No, sir. And to be honest, it all happened in such a

blur, I was so stunned by everything I was hearing, I don't recall if I even asked."

"Okay. Well, Gerry, you did the right thing bringing this to me."

Gerry looks relieved. Like a weight that has been crushing him has finally been removed. He sits up a little straighter.

"For now, go back to your department," Jake says. "Do not say a word to anyone about what you have told me here. I'll deal with this. The situation is well in hand, now. You've done the right thing."

Gerry nods, getting to his feet. "Thank you, sir," he says. "Thank you. Please, I'm sure Ben thinks he's doing the right thing. I just think he's doing it the wrong way."

"I understand," Jake says. "And you're right. And it breaks my heart that he didn't think he could trust me enough to come direct to me himself."

Gerry nods again, smiles with relief, then leaves the office.

Jake watches the door after he has gone. He rests his hands flat on his desk and counts to ten in his head. When he's sure Gerry will be gone, will have strode off to his office with an extra spring in his step, he reaches into his top drawer, pulls out a phone. He dials a number.

It's answered by Senior Special Agent Eric Thompson.

"We have a problem," Jake says.

59

B en is in the basement. His gun cabinet is kept here, under lock and key. He brings out an assault rifle, ammunition, body armor.

Tomorrow, early, he is going to war. As soon as Tom arrives, he will tell him what is happening, and then they will move. From what Ben knows Tom has been doing in Harrow, he assumes he is already prepared for battle.

In the center of the basement there is a small table directly below the one hanging light bulb. There is one chair. Ben places his weapons here. The assault rifle, his handgun. He strips them both down, cleans them, loads them back up.

His mind is empty while he works, distracted. He's glad for the calm. Before this, his thoughts were racing. He doesn't know how he is going to explain what he has found out, the unofficial – and illegal – paths he has taken to get this information. That doesn't matter right now, though. It can be dealt with after. His career pales in significance to what is being planned.

Another part of him believes the FBI will not fire him. They can't. They'll need to get to the bottom of who else within the department is dirty. After this, the only person they'll be able to trust is him. They'll need him. Him and Gerry. They'll have to clean out the ranks.

Prior to cleaning the guns, Ben did his research. The sight of what they found planned on Carly's laptop is burned into his brain. He checked locations, routes. He has it all committed to memory. He knows exactly where he needs to go first. If that fails, he knows where he needs to go next, and so on. He has mapped out every possibility in his head.

What cleaning the guns distracts him from most, however, is Carly herself.

He feels a mix of emotions. Mostly, sadness and betrayal. Occasional flashes of anger.

When he's done, Ben leaves everything on the table. He sits back, looks over the weaponry he has cleaned and prepared. Thinks about holding it tomorrow. About using it.

He realizes he can't taste blood. He's not chewing his cheek.

He takes a deep breath and leaves the basement, goes upstairs. Now he has to wait for Tom. This will be the hardest part. He doesn't know how long he will be. Hours yet. Ben will have to try to pass the time. It will be torturous.

As he reaches the top of the basement steps, the doorbell rings.

Ben freezes. Doesn't move. The basement comes out into his hallway. He's not far from the door. He peers around the corner of the wall, watching.

There's a knock; then the doorbell rings again.

Ben goes to the door, checks through the spy hole. It's

Jake Lofton. He's looking right back at the spy hole. He'll have seen it darken, know that Ben is looking through it.

Ben's heart races. Jake has never come to his home before. His thoughts go immediately to Gerry, wondering if he's said something.

"I know you're there, Ben," Jake says. "You gonna leave me standing out here all night?"

Ben opens the door. "I was just wondering to what I owe this unexpected pleasure," he says, playing it cool.

"Can I come in?" Jake says. He wears an overcoat, both hands plunged deep into the pockets, protection against the cold.

Ben steps aside. Jake strides through, the bottom of his coat flapping. Ben hesitates once he's inside, checks the road for anyone else, for suspicious cars, then closes the door. He turns.

Ben hears something; then he's flung back against the door. He's been hit in the chest. He looks down. He's bleeding. He looks up. Jake is holding a smoking gun.

"We've come too far now," Jake says, "for it to be screwed up by a dirty operative like you."

Ben coughs blood. It tastes thick in his throat. He knows this isn't good. He goes limp, slides down the door. He lands on his backside, then rolls over. He lets his eyes close, lies very still. Holds his breath.

Jake comes closer, crouches down beside him. Shakes him. "Who's your friend, Ben?" he says. "Who are you working with? Where is he?" He shakes Ben harder. Ben keeps his eyes closed, stays as limp as he can. It's not hard to do. Even now, playing dead, he can feel death creeping up on him. He hasn't got much longer left.

"*Shit*," Jake says. He stands. Pulls out his phone, dials a number. "It's done," he says, speaking into the phone. "No,

I didn't get a name. He wouldn't talk. Look, don't worry about it. It's only supposed to be one other guy; we can deal with it. Listen, it's done, there's no point getting worked up over how it happened. We don't have time for this." He hangs up the phone. Ben can feel him looking down at him.

Finally, he leaves the house. The door remains open. Jake isn't done here.

Ben knows he doesn't have much time. He doesn't try to get up. With what little strength he has left, he reaches into his pocket, pulls out his phone. Brings it up to his face. He's able to open one eye. He types a message, hits send, then closes his eye.

60

Tom attacks.

The four on guard duty aren't expecting him. They aren't watching. They've gotten lax as the night has worn on.

It's like in the bar. Tom wears the night-vision goggles. He blinds them first, throwing in a flash grenade. While they stumble, covering their eyes, crying out, he takes them out with the M4 Carbine. One fell swoop, four down. The guards are dead, headshots all.

Tom tears off the goggles, runs in low, ducking beneath the windows. The door to the cabin bursts open. Harry is in the entrance, armed. The gun swings from side to side, searching him out. Tom can hear him cursing. "Come on, motherfucker! Show yourself, you stinking son of a bitch!"

Tom surprises him from the side, slams the butt of the gun into his stomach. Harry keels over; the gun goes off, blasts through his own foot. He screams, stumbles from the steps. His fall ends with him lying flat on his back, looking up. Tom pulls out his Beretta, shoots him twice through the face.

Into the cabin. The lighting in here is dim, but everything is clear.

A banshee shrieks. Tom turns. The wife, Linda, she charges him, eyes wild, hair flying out behind her. There's a knife in her hand, raised, for him.

Behind her, a shout. Michael. "Linda, no –!"

Tom catches her as she reaches him, has to drop the Beretta to do so. She's too close; he needs both hands. Reaches up as the knife is arcing down. He grabs her wrists, twists her arms, steps to the side. Drives the knife into her stomach. Her own hands are still wrapped around it. She falls silent with a gulp, looks down as her blood comes spilling out. She falls to her knees, then drops to her side.

Before she hits the ground, Michael is charging. There is a gun in his hand, but it's forgotten in his fury. He slams into Tom with all of his weight, knocks him off balance, down to the ground. He drops the gun as they land. It skitters across the floor. He punches Tom across the face. The back of Tom's head hits the floorboards, dazes him. He comes around as Michael wraps his hands around his throat. He's spitting words as he does so, cursing him for what he has done to his wife, his friends, his men.

"I'm gonna kill you," Michael says, saliva flecking his teeth and lips. "I'm gonna fuckin' kill you!"

Tom grabs his hands, stops him from setting the choke in fully. Michael battles against him.

"This is for them," Michael says, leaning down, putting all his strength, all his weight into strangling Tom. "This is for all of them – this is for Peter and Ronald and –"

Tom grabs his thumbs. Michael feels something change

and falls suddenly silent. "They were easy," Tom says. "You were all too easy." He snaps his thumbs.

Michael rears back, hands high, thumbs bent back at unnatural angles. Tom gets a boot up, kicks him back, off him. He gets to his feet, pulls out his KA-BAR, spins it in his hand.

Michael shuffles back across the floor, holding up one useless hand. "No," he says, "no, please, no, back off, no!"

Tom grabs him by the front of his shirt, drags him up to his feet. "You're the first one who's begged," he says. "Aren't you supposed to be the leader?"

Michael's mouth clamps shut.

"Did Anthony beg? Did Alejandra? Would it have made a difference?"

Michael closes his eyes.

Tom sticks the knife into his gut. Michael's eyes shoot open. Tom tears the knife upward, spills his guts. Tom drops him onto the floor, in front of his dead wife. Michael isn't dead yet, but it won't take long. He tries reaching out for Linda, but he doesn't have the strength.

Tom gathers up his things. He leaves the cabin. Behind him, as he goes, he can hear Michael crying.

61

Despite the discomfort of the chair she's bound to, and the gag in her mouth, which dries out her throat and her lips, Beth manages to fall asleep.

When she wakes, someone is untying her. "Tom?" she says.

Mary, one of the maids, looks at her, raises an eyebrow.

"Mary!" Beth coughs, clears her throat, swallows down the little spit in her mouth. "Do you have any water?"

Mary finishes untying her, then goes to her trolley. She takes a bottle of water from it, hands it over. She says, while Beth gulps it down, "There was a phone call came for you."

Water spills from Beth's mouth, down the front of her blouse. "What?"

"Told me you were in here. He said to tell you he's sorry he couldn't come back to untie you himself, but he had to leave." Mary gives her a wry look.

"Oh," Beth says. "Did he, um, did he say anything else?"

Mary ignores the question. "You know we're not supposed to do anything with the guests," she says. "And specially not anything like ... well, whatever *this* was."

Beth opens her mouth, but says nothing. Mary has a kinky idea in her mind, and she won't be swayed from it.

"I won't tell Mr. Cooper about it," Mary says. Mr. Cooper is their boss, the owner of the motel. "Just consider yourself lucky I'm the one answered the phone. Don't let nothin' like this happen again, Beth, y'hear me? You ain't gonna get so lucky twice, I'll bet."

Beth nods, thanks her, leaves the room. Stumbles outside into the early morning sunshine. She finishes off the bottle of water, feeling sore and tired still from sleeping all night in the chair. She heads home. She knows by now that Tom will have left town. She knows she will never see him again.

62

I t's Saturday morning. Seth Goldberg gets out of the shower, dries, combs his hair, gets dressed and goes downstairs. His wife and his daughters are in the kitchen, at the table, waiting for him.

The girls are happy to see him. They've missed him while he's been in Washington. Abigail has told him they tried to stay up for his return last night, but tiredness got the better of them. They smile up at him as he enters the kitchen, joins them at the table.

"Morning," he says, then kisses them each on the cheek.

"Morning, Daddy," they each say after their kiss, the younger echoing the older.

The girls wear matching peach-colored dresses. Seth is in his black suit. Abigail wears her sky-blue dress. Seth smiles at it. "My favorite," he says.

She smiles back, tinged with sadness. He knows why. She's worried about him. Worried about them all. "I thought you'd appreciate it," she says.

"I certainly do," Seth says. To the girls, "Doesn't Mommy look like the most beautiful woman in all the world?"

"Always!" Deborah says. Danielle giggles.

They have breakfast. The girls, as ever, lean forward over their plates, are careful not to get crumbs on themselves. Seth notices Danielle is getting better at staying clean. When they finish eating, this time he doesn't have to wipe her face clean, pick the detritus from her hair.

Abigail clears the table, places the dishes in the sink. "Shall we go?" she says.

They gather themselves up and leave the house. The agents assigned to watch them are patiently waiting. They know the routine. They've been expecting this. They speak into their wrists as Seth and Abigail strap their children into their seats.

The reporters parked across the street have been expecting them, too. Seth can hear the snapping of their cameras. They'll follow them, but the bodyguards make sure they keep their distance. At a glance, Seth notices there are more there now than there used to be. The further along his clean energy bill gets, the more everyone wants to take his picture.

They pull away, following the agent car in the lead, boxed in by another behind them. They make their way to synagogue, to Shabbat; No doubt the crowds will be waiting there, too. To take his picture, to congratulate him, to encourage him, or else to call him the devil.

The same routine.

The synagogue.

Every week.

Every Saturday morning.

Senator Seth Goldberg and his family leave their home,

leave their neighborhood, unaware that they are marked for death in less than two hours.

63

Tom is in Dallas. After he'd finished with the Right Arm, he found a message on the burner phone from Ben. It had one word.

Shot.

After that was a sequence of letters and numbers. Tom knew what they were. He had been in the army long enough to recognize a set of coordinates at a glance.

Tom didn't go straight to them. He went to Ben's house first. He wasn't there long. He parked down the road, out of view, looked through binoculars. The house was being watched. The men in the cars, trying to look nondescript, had the obvious bearing of agents, just like Ben the first time Tom saw him. They were waiting for him, for Tom. The house did not look like a crime scene. It looked like it always did.

Ben, Tom knew, was more than likely dead.

He didn't stay in the neighborhood. He's destroyed the burner phone that had Ben's number, disposed of it. He's memorized the coordinates and looked them up.

A warehouse, downtown.
He's on his way.

64

"So Carly's dead, huh?" Chuck says, gearing up.

"We think so," Jake says. "There's no sign of her at home."

"Shame," Chuck says, though he doesn't look particularly perturbed. "She was a fine piece of ass."

"I'll be sure to eulogize her thusly," Jake says.

They're in the warehouse. The mercs are getting ready. Their arms are bare and adorned with fake tattoos, Nazi imagery. There are swastikas and some of the more subtle images and numbers, too.

The van is loaded. Jake has looked into the back of it. Felt himself shudder. Couldn't help it. The mercs are surprisingly cool about the whole situation despite the fact that if this thing were to go boom, it would wipe out the whole district. Of course, they've been living with it, sleeping near it, for the last couple of weeks. Jake knows he couldn't. Jake doesn't want to be near it right now. He shouldn't be. It was never in the plan. The stuff with Ben has changed things. He's here with a couple of other agents, men he can trust, men who have also been recruited by Eric, who know what's going down.

Chuck straps body armor across his chest. "So the Right Arm, you're saying they're dead now?"

"Most of them," Jake says. They've been aware of what was happening in the area, in Harrow, though they didn't understand it. A gang war? Internal strife? They've been waiting for it to calm down. Now, so close to their plan coming to fruition, Jake sent one of their agents around town, to search them out. He came up empty-handed. The ones supposed to still be alive, he couldn't find them.

Jake can't shake the feeling it has something to do with Ben's mysterious friend.

He's done his own research. He looked into the unofficial undercover, into Anthony Rollins. Found out all about his brother, Tom. Ex-army. Ex-CIA. Currently wanted for going AWOL. Whereabouts unknown. It might be nothing, it could be something. Jake has circulated this information, in either case.

"So, you gonna set up some new patsies, or what?" Chuck says.

"No time," Jake says. "But it doesn't matter. This will work in our favor. They were all gonna get wiped out anyway, once the finger of blame settled on them. This way, we've already got the bodies and saved ourselves a firefight to get them."

Chuck grins. "So long as it all works out, huh?"

"We've planned too long and too hard to be derailed now."

"What about Ben's mystery friend? You think he's gonna come find us?"

"Waste anyone approaching you on sight," Jake says. "Old, young, cop – I don't give a shit. If there's a risk of you being exposed, of the alarm going up, of anyone trying to stop you, blast the fuckers."

Chuck's grin broadens. "You ain't gotta tell me twice, boss man." He pats the assault rifle across his chest.

"Well," Jake says, "you certainly look like you're going to enjoy yourself."

"If you ain't happy in your work, you're in the wrong line. Ain't that right, boys?"

Chuck's men, standing nearby, similarly strapped and armored, laugh and grunt their agreement.

Jake is pleased he has men of his own standing nearby. Here, alone, he'd feel outnumbered, uncomfortable. He has three inside the warehouse with him, another two outside, on the roof, keeping guard.

Jake checks his watch. "Then I won't keep you," he says. "It's time to go. This is where we say goodbye. I doubt we'll ever see each other again."

"Sure you don't wanna give us an escort? Make sure we get there nice and safe?" There is a joking tone to Chuck's words, something of a taunt to them. Like he thinks it's a joke they might need babying.

"Can't be seen anywhere near you, not when you're getting close to the target," Jake says, not rising to the mockery, pretending like he hasn't picked up on it.

"Please yourself," Chuck says. "Enjoy the fireworks on the six o'clock news."

"Oh, I'm sure they'll make the midday news flash," Jake says, stepping back, giving Chuck some space.

Chuck turns to his men. "All right, boys, showtime! Al, Jimmy, Pat – in the van. Dix, in the car, with me." He pounds the side of his fist against the van. The van filled with explosives. Jake tries not to flinch, though he can't help the grimace that forces its way onto his face. "Let's go!"

The one called Dix goes to the warehouse door, pulls the chain to roll it up and open. Al, Jimmy, and Pat get in the van, all of them up front. Al drives. Chuck gets into the car behind them. They pull forward. Jake watches them go, a swelling in his chest, an increasing of the butterflies in his stomach. This is it. It's like Christmas. So long planning and preparing, feeling like the day will never arrive, and now it's finally here.

The van is outside. It's on its way. Chuck stops the car so Dix can get in. He leaves the warehouse door wide open. They've left other items scattered around the warehouse, further proof that the Right Arm Of The Republic is responsible for what is about to happen, for the thousands of people about to lose their lives.

Jake turns to his men, ready to tell them to move, it's time to go.

A shot rings out.

Jake spins around, looks to the van. It veers to the side, hits the chain-link fence enclosing the warehouse. Stops. Another shot. Jake hears glass shattering. He pulls out his gun, runs to the open door, remaining in cover. He sees the passenger door of the van open, one of Chuck's men jumping out, pulling up his assault rifle. Before he gets a grip on it, there's another shot. His head snaps to the side; there's a spray of blood. He hits the ground.

"*Shit!*" Jake can't see the shooter, where he's firing from.

Chuck pulls the car to the back of the van, for cover. He and Dix jump out, duck low, get to the back of the car. He shouts to Jake, "Give us cover! We'll get to the van. You make sure we get out of here!"

Jake nods, looks out, still can't see anyone. He starts shooting blindly into the distance.

One of his men, on the other side of the open door, calls over, "Where are we firing, sir?"

"Anywhere!" Jake says. "Just fucking *shoot!*"

Jake's men open fire too, bullets going in all directions. Jake prays one of them is heading the right way, prays harder that it finds its mark. He notices the men he had outside, the ones keeping watch, they're not shooting.

Chuck and Dix make it to the van. They roughly drag out the bodies of their dead comrades, get in. The van jerks, spins its wheels as it twists to the side, getting out of the fence. Jake keeps shooting. The sniper isn't firing back. Wherever he is, someone must be firing in the right direction, pinning him down.

The van is free. It gets away. It's heading down the road. He prepares to pull back, into cover, to tell his men to do the same. They need to get out of here.

Then another shot rings out. The man to Jake's right, on the other side of the door, goes down, then the one beside him. Another is hit in the knee. As he falls, another bullet takes him in the face.

Jake watches it happen in slow-motion. He's never seen shooting like it. His men are dead. No doubt the ones on the roof are, too. He still hasn't seen where the shots are coming from.

Then, as he pulls back, a bullet tears through his eye and out the back of his skull.

65

The van has a head start. Tom is in pursuit.

He doesn't shoot at the van. He doesn't know what's inside, but he has a suspicion it can't be anything good. Explosives are his guess. Why else would they be so determined to get it wherever it's going? Everything hinges on the van, its contents.

He puts his foot down, tries to get alongside. The van swerves across the road, blocking him. This road is quiet, but soon they will reach one far busier.

The passenger leans out, raises an assault rifle. Tom's window is down, the Beretta in his lap. He snatches it up, fires in that direction, knowing he won't make the shot, but hoping to spook the passenger back into cover. It works.

The van reaches a crossroads. Without stopping, without looking, it swerves to the right, forcing the oncoming traffic to brake hard to avoid it. This road leads to Dallas.

Tom knew, when he went AWOL, that he needed to

avoid big cities. CCTV everywhere. A much bigger chance of being seen, reported, caught. He had to stick to back roads, small towns. He knows, now, that if he goes to Dallas, if they make it all the way there, he will be seen. His image will be captured. Stopping them will not be quiet. It will draw attention. It will bring cops.

If he goes left, it's like he was never here.

He doesn't know what's in the van. Doesn't know what they have planned.

There's no other option, not really. He knows this. There's no other choice.

He puts his foot down, goes right, cuts into and through the traffic the same way the van did. Horns blare. He hears curses, sees some birds flipped in his direction. He doesn't lose sight of the van. It's cutting and weaving through the traffic. It nudges one car to the side to make space for itself. It moves fast for a van. Tom struggles to keep up. The van's been worked on, he guesses. It's been modified. Possibly for just such an occasion.

Tom can't keep up, but he stays close enough he doesn't lose sight of it. Follows its trail. He goes between cars, too, his foot flat to the floor, pushing the engine for all it has. He spots a gap and takes it.

Getting too close won't make a difference. He can't stop them, not here, not without causing destruction. At least if he can see them, he can follow them, potentially cut them off if he finds an opening.

The passenger leans out again. He's holding the assault rifle. Cars see it; they slam on their brakes. They skid, go sideways. The passenger starts shooting, aiming for wheels and vehicle bodies. The cars hit each other. The passenger is creating a barricade, stopping Tom from following.

Tom's eyes scan, thinking fast. A verge, to the left. A way around. He mounts it, feels all four wheels momentarily leave the ground. The car kisses asphalt again, on the other side of the crash. It throws him around in his seat. Smoke rises from the tires, burning rubber.

He continues the chase.

66

C huck watches in the mirror, sees how their pursuer gets around the pile-up Dix has caused. "Jesus Christ," he says. "This guy don't fuckin' quit, huh?"

"Shit," Dix says, getting back inside. "How far out are we?"

"Not far. Five more minutes, tops."

Wind whistles through the bullet holes in the windshield. The shots that killed Al, Jimmy, and Pat. The smell of their death is thick in the cab. Their blood is on the steering wheel, sticky on Chuck's gloved hands. Glass crunches beneath them whenever they move on the seats. One of the bullet holes is right in front of Chuck, at eye level. He has to duck down a little to avoid the hard wind blowing through.

"Try it again," Chuck says.

"Get some more cars behind us and I will," Dix says.

Chuck starts nudging through vehicles, forcing them

aside. The front of the van must be a mess of dents and scratches. "How many more do you want?"

"He got around the last one," Dix says. "Give me some more."

The car that Chuck and Dix were originally in was supposed to be the getaway. They park the van, drive off, get a safe distance and hit the detonator. Now, without the car, they're going to have to improvise. No problem – it won't be the first car either of them have stolen.

Chuck is going straight down the middle of the road now. Dallas is in sight. Its buildings loom up before them. He checks the mirror again. The car is gaining. Chuck can't get enough vehicles between them. "Now!" he says. "Do it now! At this range, you can blast *him*. Get it done. We ain't got much longer left!"

Dix reloads the rifle, looking in the mirror. "I see him. Slow down a little. Don't make it obvious."

Chuck understands, does as he says. He eases off the accelerator, doesn't tap the brakes, doesn't want the lights to give away what they're doing.

Dix lets him get a little closer. "I got him," he says. He stands to lean out the window. His legs brace against the door, but he is still dangerously precarious. He brings up the rifle, moving fast.

There's a shot, but it isn't Dix.

He goes limp, falls from the moving van. Chuck feels the back of the van rise as the wheels go over him. "Shit."

He's on his own now.

He looks to Dallas again. So close. He's never failed a mission yet. Today ain't going to be the day.

He stamps hard on the accelerator again. "Come get me, motherfucker," he says through his teeth. "Just you and me now. *Try* and stop me, you son of a bitch."

They're in Dallas. Early Saturday morning, and the streets are busy but not crammed, not yet. Tom sees the way people on the sidewalks look at the van, at how fast it is going, at the damage it has sustained. Some of them start pulling out their phones, dialling numbers, suspicious. Others pull out their phones and start filming. They can sense that something is up, that this van isn't right. Tom stays right on its tail, keeps his head low. The people film him, too. The pursued and the pursuer. They don't know who's of more interest.

Suddenly, the van twists to the side, down a road. Tom is too close behind, he misses it, overshoots the turn. He slams on the brakes, but there are cars behind him, coming up fast, blaring horns. He can't turn around. He goes forward, to the next intersection. He runs a red light, hangs a right, races down to the next turn, trying to find the van. He spots it at the next crossroads.

It's outside a synagogue.

68

A bigail grabs Seth's hand, squeezes it. "What was that?" she says.

Seth looks up. His head was lowered, his eyes closed in contemplative prayer. Now, he realizes, everyone is reacting much like his wife. They're murmuring; they're all asking the same questions. They turn toward the entrance.

"Daddy?" Danielle says, tugging at his jacket.

He knows what the sound is, the first sound. They all do.

It's gunfire.

Then it's screaming. Panic. People are fleeing.

Abigail holds him tight. She looks at him. "This is it," she says. She looks terrified, but she sounds resigned, as if she's been waiting for this moment. Here it is. It's arrived, as she always knew it would. "They've come for you."

The bodyguards move on the van as soon as it comes to a stop. Chuck is ready for them. He sees how they reach inside their jackets, to their holsters.

Chuck is faster. He has the assault rifle. He blasts them, drops them fast. Behind him, on the other side of the street, the gathered reporters scream. They start to run. Chuck has pulled up his face covering, concealing everything but his eyes and his shaved head. He pumps the rifle in the air, screams, "White power!" As instructed. At least one of them will have heard it and gotten a good look at the 'tattoos' adorning his bare arms.

He has the detonator. The van is in place. He starts to move, to get away from it. Get to a car, hot-wire it, get the few blocks away necessary before he hits the button, blows this whole neighborhood to kingdom come.

It's been louder than he would have liked so far. It wasn't supposed to be like this. He's had to park closer than he was supposed to. Still, he's got the head start. He's got

the advantage. Senator Seth Goldberg will never clear the
area in time. With how many explosives they've got packed
into the back of the van, it's gonna be a *broad* radius.

Chuck is crossing the road. A car is coming for him. It's
the one that's been chasing him, the one he thought he'd
finally given the slip.

It's coming right for him.

70

The driver dives out of the way just in time. Tom manages to clip his boot on the windshield. Not as much as he would have liked.

Tom stomps on the brakes, skids to a halt. He jumps out of the car, heads for the man.

He's rolled through, got back to his feet. He reaches for a gun. Tom is faster, kicks it out of his hand. The guy reacts quick. Jabs with his left hand, catches Tom in the mouth, bloodies him.

Tom stumbles back. There was force behind the blow. He gets a good look at his opponent. He sees the tattoos on his arms, the way they have smeared. They're not real. Tom guesses he's ex-armed forces, more than likely a mercenary now. He has the hard-edged look, similar to Tom's own. Tom sees the way the merc is appraising him, too, coming to the same conclusions.

"I ain't got time for you," the merc says.

There are sirens in the distance, coming their way.

"I ain't got the time for you, neither," Tom says. "Yet here I am."

The merc reaches down to his boot, pulls out a knife. A KA-BAR. Tom pulls out his own. The merc sees it. "I ain't surprised."

"Neither am I."

They don't circle, don't feel each other out. No time. Straight down to business. The merc slashes first. Tom is able to avoid it, but the merc is fast. He cuts again, this time catching Tom across the chest, then down the arm.

Tom feels the blood running warm down his body. He's aware, all the while, of the encroaching sirens. Knows the merc is, too.

"What d'you say we pick this up at a later date?" the merc says. "I can't wait here for those cops to arrive, and I don't reckon you can either."

"I ain't letting you leave," Tom says. "What's in the van?"

The merc has a twinkle in his eye. "You'll know soon enough."

The merc stabs, going low. Thought Tom wasn't expecting it, wasn't ready for it. Sloppy. Tom catches his arm. He drives the point of his elbow down into the meat, then twists the arm, does it again near the wrist. It snaps.

The merc drops the knife. Tom hits him in the face with his elbow. The merc stumbles, goes down. The merc pushes himself back, looks down at his broken wrist, at the knife out of reach. At Tom above him. He looks at the van. At the synagogue.

"Shit," he says. He reaches into his pocket, pulls something out. He pulls down his face covering so Tom can see him smile with bloodied teeth. "Fuck it," he says, grinning.

Tom sees what's in his hand. It's a detonator. He was

right. The van is filled with explosives. The merc grins wider, seeing it dawn on Tom what is about to happen. The merc won't be beaten, won't fail his mission, even if it means taking himself out, too.

Tom throws the knife. It sinks into the merc's wrist. He cries out, drops the detonator. Tom is on him before he can recover. He snaps his neck.

He takes back his knife, wipes off the blood on the merc's shirt. He picks up the detonator. Looks around. Realizes there is a crowd filing out of the synagogue. They're all looking at him. They've been watching. They're all tense. They don't know who he is, what side he's on. Some of them have seen the Nazi imagery on the other man's arms, though. They understand.

Tom realizes he recognizes the man at the front of the crowd. He's seen him on the television. He's heard about him, too, on the radio. The senator. The one with the Jewish name. He is one of the few who have seen the merc's arms. He understands.

Tom goes to him. He holds out the detonator. "The van's a bomb," he says. "Don't let anyone else have this."

The senator takes the detonator. He looks down at it, eyes narrowed, understanding. He looks at Tom, and he nods. There is a woman standing close to him, eyes wide. There are two children, two little girls. They all look at Tom.

He leaves, runs back to his car. He's going to have to ditch it as soon as he can. For now, it will get him away from here.

71

On the outside, Eric is cool. He's calm. He's collected. Doesn't look any different to how he usually does.

Inside, he is in recovery mode. He's back in Dallas, cleaning up the mess Jake has left behind.

It's for the best Jake is dead. Eric can fix things easier this way, especially with Senator Seth Goldberg pressing for an investigation into what has happened. The dead bodies of the mercenaries have been recovered, and their tattoos discovered to be rub-on fakes. Yet they have no known identities, no known accomplices, no connections. Goldberg can read between the lines. No doubt he has been told about the fake ink.

Eric is in his office. He sent agents to the warehouse to retrieve the bodies of Jake and the others. It didn't take him long to work out where they were. He already had the story planned out in his head – brave agents attempting to stop these mysterious domestic terrorists, gunned down in the line of duty.

He had them move Ben Fitzgerald's body, too. Took it from his home, cleaned up to eliminate any sign of his dying there, and transferred his body to the warehouse. Made sure to spread his blood around a little. Another dead hero.

Eric can spin this, all of it. He can make it work.

Carly Hogan's whereabouts, however, remain a mystery. No doubt she's dead. It's possible they'll never find her body. They don't have the first idea where to look. Eric won't be able to cover for her disappearance, but he won't have to. He's as in the dark as everyone else as to what has happened to her.

The amount of explosives found in the back of the van has caught a lot of people's attention. The potential destruction it could have caused.

Now everyone is looking for the mystery man who saved the day. His face was caught on multiple cameras, on many phones, yet he still managed to slip away. People want to know who he is, what he was doing there. They want to know his name. Goldberg, in a press conference, was careful not to call the man a hero, but Eric could tell he wanted to. Could tell he wanted to fawn and gush over the man who saved his life and the lives of his family and so many others in the vicinity.

They'll know his name soon enough. Eric already does. Jake knew it, too, before he was killed.

Tom Rollins.

Eric has to try to find him now before anyone else does. He's put the word out among his agents – the ones he can trust, his men – to keep their ears to the ground, to watch out for indications of him. No doubt he's out of the area by now. Has likely left the state, too.

Now, Eric waits for Gerry Davies to arrive at his office.

When he does, he looks sick. Pale. Holds his stomach like it's giving him trouble.

"You don't look well, Mr. Davies," Eric says, holding out a hand and motioning for him to take a seat.

Gerry clears his throat. "Stress, I think," he says.

"Oh my. Well, I certainly hope it passes soon."

"Me too," Gerry says, looking like he's trying not to throw up.

"Let's get down to business, shall we?" Eric clasps his hands on the desk, smiles at Gerry. "I've heard good things about your work, Mr. Davies. Jake spoke very highly of you."

"I'm glad to hear that," Gerry says. "I was sorry to hear of his death. I just, I wish there were something I could have done ..."

"You did all you could, Mr. Davies. Try not to beat yourself up. Without your assistance, Jake would not have known about Ben. He and the others would not have been able to follow him to the warehouse, to try to help him."

"It didn't help anything, though," Gerry says. "They're all dead."

"If anyone's to blame for that, Mr. Davies, it's Agent Ben Fitzgerald. If he'd come to Jake sooner himself, this could have all been averted. Jake and his men had to play catch-up. It put them at a severe disadvantage, and all because of Ben's rampant paranoia."

"Do you know who it was Agent Hogan was talking to yet?"

Eric shakes his head. "Unfortunately we don't, but I'm sure with your assistance, we'll be able to get to the bottom of this mystery soon enough."

"Does anyone know where she is?"

Eric shakes her head. "No. And Ben didn't say anything?"

"No. But I have a bad feeling ..."

"I'm sure we share it."

Gerry purses his lips, nods solemnly.

"Anyway, I haven't called you here today to discuss what has happened. I've brought you here today to talk about the future, and what we're going to do about it."

"How do you mean?"

"Our unknown benefactor is still out there, Mr. Davies," Eric says, raising his eyebrows. "The man who saved the day. The man who Senator Seth Goldberg is so high on, so desperate to shake the hand of. Off the bat, I don't suppose Ben ever told you his name?"

"No, he didn't."

"I thought not. To be honest, I was hopeful he had, and you had chosen to keep it to yourself for the time being, but I can see now, looking at you, talking like this, that you're telling the truth. You don't know."

"I wish I did."

"As do I, and that's why you're here. You're going to find him for me."

Gerry blinks. "I am?"

"Indeed. Like I already told you, Mr. Davies, I've heard good things about your work, your prowess. I want you to get back to your desk, your computer, and find this man for me. Don't worry, I'll accompany you. We're going to find our mysterious stranger together."

"Huh-how can I do that?"

"Everyone agrees, it was as if he just disappeared from the scene of the attempted bombing, but we both know that can't really be what happened, can it? He slipped away, but no

matter where he went, a camera, somewhere, will have picked
him up. And once one had him, then another will have seen
him, and another after that, and another, and so on. Do you
understand? I highly doubt he left Dallas on foot. We find the
vehicle he took; then we find him. Come on, now, on your
feet." Eric stands, waves for him to do the same. "Let's go find
him together, shall we? Two pairs of eyes are better than one!"

T om has not gone straight back to New Mexico, to the commune. He has remained in Texas, staying off the beaten track, making sure he hasn't been trailed. It eats at him, knowing that he was caught on camera. Knowing that his face has been flashed across the news.

They haven't given his name, though. They know it by now, no doubt, but no one's saying it. They're keeping it to themselves. More than likely, it's at the behest of either the CIA or the dirty agents within the FBI – perhaps both. They don't want to give his name away, not just yet. They know to do so will likely speed up the process of finding him, but at the same time they can't take a risk of him exposing what he knows concerning members of both agencies.

For the time being, while his face is everywhere, Tom is growing out his beard. He wears a baseball cap everywhere he goes, pulls it down low. While he drives or walks around, he wears sunglasses, too. He's swapped cars twice already, both taken from small towns with low populations.

He's in a diner now, stopped for something to eat. His bag is on the seat beside him, containing all the few necessities of his life. Soon, he will return to New Mexico. To his father, stepmother, brother. He won't be there long. He'll move on again, keep moving, until all this has blown over and he finds somewhere he can lie low, somewhere he can easily hide himself.

The news is on above the counter. It's talking about Senator Seth Goldberg, as usual. About his bill. It's moving along, getting closer to fruition. This time, there is no mention of Tom, no flashing of his picture. He hopes this means it's nearly over, that the news cycle is moving on to the next big thing.

The diner's phone rings. The waitress behind the counter goes to answer it. Tom chews his burger, looks out the window to his latest car.

The waitress comes back to the counter, looking confused. "Any of y'all named Tom Rollins?" she says. There are only two other people in the diner; both of them look like truckers. No one says anything for a while.

"No?" the waitress says. "No one?"

Tom clears his throat, gets to his feet. Ignorance is not bliss. Whatever this is, he should answer it.

The waitress points the phone out to him, leaves him alone. Tom grits his teeth. "Who is this?"

The voice on the other end chuckles. "I'm more interested in who you are, Mr. Rollins." The speaker doesn't give his name. He talks in a mocking, singsong tone. "Enjoying your meal, are you? I assume it's not easy to just kick back and relax while you eat, not when you're on the run."

Tom is silent. He watches the window. The diner is at

the side of the road, surrounded by nothing. "Where are you?"

"Oh, don't worry. I'm not close. Not yet. Truth be told, by the time I'd be able to get any agents to your location, I'm sure you'd have the time to finish whatever greasy thing you're eating and move on. No, this is just a personal call. I just wanted to hear your voice, Mr. Rollins, and I wanted you to hear mine."

"So you've heard it," Tom says. "And so have I."

"And it was everything I imagined it would be. How is it for you?"

"You're Carly's employer, right? The guy who killed Ben?"

"Oh, I won't deny I had a hand in what happened to Ben, but no, I didn't do it directly. You already killed the man who did that."

"So what makes you think it's wise to try and fuck with me?"

The voice laughs. "Oh, my dear Mr. Rollins, I could ask you the exact same question. I'm going to find you, *Tom*. Enjoy your time on the run, enjoy what brief freedom you have left, as marred as it will be by your constant checking over your shoulder, wondering who's behind you. Be seeing you, Mr. Rollins. Stay safe."

Tom hangs up the phone.

He leaves bills on the counter to pay for his food, then grabs his bag from the booth. He leaves the diner. Doesn't go to the car. Leaves it behind. Heads off on foot. He'll find another car on the way.

And he'll make sure this one isn't on camera. Make sure this one can't be traced.

EPILOGUE

Tom returns to the commune.

It has been a month since he killed the last of the Right Arm Of The Republic, the last of the men responsible for Alejandra's death.

Anthony looks better, mostly healed. He's out on the porch as Tom rolls the car to a stop at the foot of the steps. "You got some new wheels," he says.

"Had to," Tom says, getting out. "How you doing?"

"Fine." Anthony comes down the steps. His hair is growing out. It hides what is no doubt a nasty scar from the fractured skull he suffered. "I've caught up on what you did in Harrow. Sounds like you cut quite the path of chaos."

"What do they attribute it to?" Tom says.

"Rival gang activity," Anthony says. "That what you were going for?"

Tom shrugs. "I didn't care what they made of it." He comes around the car and stands in front of his brother. There's only a couple of paces between them.

Anthony's jaw works. He looks like he has something

he wants to say, but is having trouble getting the words out. He clears his throat, spits to the side. "Thank you for what you did," he says. "I'd rather have done it myself, but I thank you regardless."

Tom nods.

"But you can't fight all my battles for me forever," Anthony says. "You've done that long enough now."

"And I won't," Tom says. "This was as much for Alejandra as it was for you."

"Oh, I know that," Anthony says, a knowing look in his eye, something almost aggressive.

Jeffrey comes out onto the porch with Sylvia. "Well, look who's back," Jeffrey says. He comes down the steps, embraces Tom. "You gonna come on inside?"

"Sure," Tom says. "But I can't stay for long."

"I figured as much," Jeffrey says. "We've seen your pretty face plastered all over the news. Guess that was what took you so long getting back to us, too."

"I like the beard, Tom," Sylvia says.

Inside the house, the first thing Tom notices is the urn on top of the fireplace. The Polaroid picture propped in front of it, almost like a small shrine. In the picture, Alejandra is smiling. It's just her in the shot, no one else. The urn contains her ashes, Tom knows. "You went to get her," he says.

"We did," Anthony says behind him. "Wasn't anyone else could claim her."

Tom turns to him. "What you planning on doing with the ashes?"

"What do you mean?" Anthony says, striding across the room and leaning against the fireplace, almost protective.

"Well, where you gonna spread her?"

"I ain't," Anthony says. "I'm gonna keep her. I'm gonna keep her with me."

"All right," Tom says. He hesitates. "It's just that she told me she always wanted to go back to Mexico. She wanted to be buried there. She wanted to be buried there; I'm pretty sure she'd want her ashes scattered there, too."

Anthony grits his teeth. "She never told me any such thing."

"She told me she tried to. You just didn't wanna hear it."

"I ain't got any memory of that."

"I wouldn't lie to you," Tom says.

"I know," Anthony says, looking annoyed. "And that's what pisses me off. She'd tell you that, but not me."

Tom tries to calm the situation down. "You weren't going off to war, Anthony," he says. "Ain't like talk of death came up in everyday conversation between the two of you, I'm sure."

"She's staying right here," Anthony says.

"Sure, I just think you should honor her wishes, is all."

Jeffrey and Sylvia stand between the two brothers, clearly uncomfortable.

"This urn is all I've got left of her," Anthony says. "It's all I'll ever have of my kid. I ain't throwing them away like that. I ain't parting with them."

"Then compromise," Tom says. "You keep half. I'll take the other half down to Mexico, do as she wanted."

"Oh, you will, will you? Such a hero, ain't you, Tom? Everyone's fuckin' hero. America's fuckin' hero, according to the news. 'Cept they don't even know your name! They don't know what you done in Harrow, neither. They don't know *why* you done it. But I know it, Tom." He jabs a thumb back into his own chest. "I know exactly why you did it. Because you were in love with your own brother's girlfriend. You were in love with the mother of my child."

He's not leaning on the fireplace anymore. He's coming forward, across the room, his eyes filled with menace. Jeffrey holds out an arm to stop him, but Anthony bats it aside, never taking his attention off Tom. "The ashes ain't going anywhere. Not half of them, not a quarter of them, not even a fuckin' *eighth* of them, that clear? They're staying with me. Wherever I go, they go. This is my family. They weren't nothing to you, you get it? You mighta loved her, but she didn't love you! She loved *me*! They were my family, not yours!"

"Calm down, Anthony," Tom says, standing his ground.

"Fuck you, calm down!" Anthony says. "You oughtta leave. You oughtta get the hell out of here right now."

"I'm going to say my goodbyes." Tom's eyes flicker to the urn.

"What, to *her*? Get out! You ain't saying nothing to her! Get outta here!"

Anthony tries to push Tom. Tom shoves his hands aside. Anthony takes a swing. Tom easily blocks it. He ducks the next.

"Anthony, stop it!" Sylvia says.

"That's enough, now," Jeffrey says.

Anthony throws another punch. Tom catches it.

"Well?" Anthony says, unable to extricate his fist from his brother's grip. "What you gonna do? You gonna hit me? Come on, hit me. *Hit me*."

Tom doesn't hit him. He lets go of his fist, pushes it back into his chest.

Anthony looks like he's going to swing again. Jeffrey gets in between them, forces him back. "That's your brother, damn it," he says. "You need to calm your ass down."

"Anthony, please," Sylvia says. "This isn't what she would have wanted. And think of your head. It ain't fully healed."

They back him up, force him through into the next room to calm him.

Tom is alone.

He goes to the fireplace, to the shrine. The door is closed to the kitchen, where they have forced Anthony. Tom can hear him shouting, cursing, demanding to be let out.

Tom looks down at the Polaroid. Alejandra is smiling. She's smiling back at him.

He stares at the picture.

He stares at the urn.

He can hear his brother calming, the shouting subsiding. They will return soon. They'll be back in here, with him, with the urn, with the picture.

Tom pockets the Polaroid, slides it in next to his Santa Muerte pendant. He picks up the urn. He leaves the house.

He will go to Mexico.

He will spread her ashes.

He can deal with the consequences later.

ABOUT THE AUTHOR

Did you enjoy Blood Line? Please consider leaving a review on Amazon to help other readers discover the book.

Paul Heatley left school at sixteen, and since then has held a variety of jobs including mechanic, carpet fitter, and bookshop assistant, but his passion has always been for writing. He writes mostly in the genres of crime fiction and thriller, and links to his other titles can be found on his website. He lives in the north east of England.

Want to connect with Paul? Visit him at his website.

www.PaulHeatley.com

ALSO BY PAUL HEATLEY

The Tom Rollins Thriller Series

Blood Line (Book 1)

Wrong Turn (Book 2)

Hard to Kill (Book 3)

Snow Burn (Book 4)

Road Kill (Book 5)

No Quarter (Book 6)

Hard Target (Book 7)

Last Stand (Book 8)

Blood Feud (Book 9)

Search and Destroy (Book 10)

Ghost Team (Book 11)

Full Throttle (Book 12)

The Tom Rollins Box Set (Books 1 - 4)

Published by Inkubator Books
www.inkubatorbooks.com

Printed in Great Britain
by Amazon

43972889R00189